TREEZZ

TREEZZ

RAY GRAF

PROLOGUE

For 370 million years, trees have successfully propagated the earth, surviving all natural disasters. As with any species living on the earth, evolution is a must to survive. The key to survival is a simple form of communication within the species. From the smallest seedling to the mighty redwoods, interaction is essential.

Nature provided the tools through high-voltage lightning bolts. Powerful strikes of electricity were sent surging through the earth. The current pulsed through the smallest roots, eventually traveling to the heart of the tree. Eons passed, and the trees slowly began associating the electrical pulses with approaching storms. This was the first form of basic communication encompassing all species of trees. As time went on a group of older trees became the supreme voice of the world of the TREEZZ.

Proliferation was achieved at an acceptable rate for planet Earth. The trees' life-giving oxygen was released into the atmosphere in huge quantities through photosynthesis. The world's atmosphere was never purer, never brighter, and never cleaner.

Earth's evolution included many animal and plant life species, with each developing special skills to survive. But the trees were just one of the many species evolving.

One species stood out for many reasons. It was a smelly, apelike creature that laid claim to the earth due to its intelligence and adaptability. This creature was called *Homo habilis* (human). It rapidly became a feared predator and reproduced quickly. In a relatively short time, this meat eater selfishly claimed the world. With the introduction of fire, its appetite for wood was voracious, and its goal was to clear the land to grow food. As the human evolved, their greed for cleared land was limitless. Thus began the systematic destruction of the world's rain forests.

As humans became more efficient at clearing land, the forests were destroyed faster than they could reproduce. Deforestation was happening at an alarming rate. In turn, scientists began to see serious depletion in oxygen levels. Some experts dismissed the reduction in oxygen as the normal atmospheric progression of the planet. But others made doomsday predictions, warning of an apocalypse if the forests continued to be ravaged with slash-and-burn tactics. This action accelerated the greenhouse gas effect.

The TREEZZ, now an intelligent species, was desperate to stop the destruction of the forests. The TREEZZ decided to enlist the help of humans—two very special humans with a profound love of trees and their fellow man. The TREEZZ would empower these humans with unique abilities to help save the forest, thus saving Earth. The chosen ones would champion the cause of the TREEZZ. As their ambassadors, they would travel the world, promoting the preservation of vast reserves of untouched land, limiting deforestation, and putting some species on an endangered list. This undertaking would require total dedication and a wealthy benefactor to promote and financially support the cause. It would be given the motto "Save the TREEZZ."

An extensive search was conducted. The TREEZZ chose a boy living on a small farm in Northern California with his mom and stepdad. Also selected was a girl from Sierra City, living there with her older sister. They were selected for their intelligence, love of nature, and consideration of their fellow humans.

The TREEZZ would gradually educate the young boy and girl in their ways. By the time he was twenty years old, the boy would be an expert in the field of dendrology. The boy's name was Jerimiah Simpson.

The girl, Becca, was eighteen years old and would become proficient in cellar biology. In time she would gain worldwide recognition as an expert in that field.

CHAPTER 1

A tourist looked out the window of his hotel in Brasília, Brazil. He was puzzled by a crimson haze obscuring the early morning sun. Stepping onto his balcony, he noticed tiny particles of ash drifting through the air.

He called down to a local man passing by. "Pardon me, senor. Is there a fire?"

Choking from the smoke, the man replied, "There is always a fire in the rain forest." He lowered his head as he walked away. "Soon there will be no more rain forests."

It was unfortunate but true: the rain forests were dwindling rapidly. Mankind had an insatiable hunger for wood products and land to grow crops. This combination spelled disaster for mankind, the TREEZZ, and wildlife.

———

Jerimiah Simpson was a tall, lanky boy with sparkling blue eyes and dark hair. He was on the shy side, but his smile was warm and friendly, reflecting his honest, trustworthy demeanor. He'd inherited those traits from his mother's ancestors; she was of the Tule River Indian tribe of Northern California. His biological father had passed away in a logging accident years ago.

He was an intelligent lad, one blessed with good common sense. Jerimiah lived on a rural farm with his mother, Mattie, and his stepdad, Todd Bailey. They were a kind and loving family. They were God-fearing and always thankful for what little they had. Jerimiah and his mom tended the farm while his stepfather worked as a forest ranger.

All through high school, Jerimiah excelled in dendrology. His teachers advised him to continue his education and major in plant biology. Graduating from high school with honors, the young man set his sights on going to college. Not just any college—he chose MIT, the Massachusetts Institute of Technology.

Enthusiastically he filled out the application. Suddenly his cheerfulness turned to depression as he looked at the cost of tuition: $20,000. Disillusioned, he put the application in a drawer.

———

Several weeks later he received a letter from MIT accepting his application.

He immediately called the school. "Hello. My name is Jerimiah Simpson. I just received a letter of acceptance to your school." He whispered, "Could that be a mistake?"

The receptionist said, "Please hold for a minute." She came back on the line. "Yes, Mr. Simpson. You are enrolled with all expenses paid. We will expect to see you in the fall."

The young man jumped for joy. He ran into the kitchen, boasting to his mom and dad, "I've been accepted, Mom and Dad! I'm going to MIT!"

Shocked at his revelation, they asked, "Who paid the tuition?"

He paused a moment and then replied, "I have no idea."

He and his mom made several calls inquiring about who had paid the tuition and expenses. They were told the benefactor wished to remain anonymous. Jerimiah was euphoric and went out to the forest to tell his friends the TREEZZ the good news. He entered the forest and encountered a colorful butterfly on a small vine. That vine slowly began to wrap around his wrist. His first urge was to pull away in fear, but somehow he sensed the vine meant no harm.

He felt a subtle change in his relationship with the TREEZZ. Now it was like they were old friends, enjoying a warm, trusting rapport. From that day on, Jerimiah began a magical, mystical connection with the TREEZZ.

———

Standing next to a giant sequoia, he telepathically heard, "We are the TREEZZ, and we have chosen you to be one of our champions. This incredible gift comes with huge responsibilities and a total commitment. It's much to ask, but the future of this planet may very well be decided by you. We will give you time to think over our offer. For now, our relationship must be kept a secret. We will always be here for you. We hope you will accept our offer and work with us to save the TREEZZ."

Jerimiah was dumbfounded. He questioned his sanity, thinking, *Am I hearing things, or is this real?* He was bewildered. He slowly meandered back to the farm, trying to comprehend his supernatural experience.

He walked into the house dazed. Mattie, his mom, looked at her son and noticed his pale, expressionless appearance. Concerned, she asked, "Jerimiah, are you all right? You look as if you've seen a ghost."

"I'm fine, Mom. Just a little tired."

Mattie suggested, "Go lie down, Son. I'll call you when supper is ready."

Exhausted, Jerimiah went to his room and fell into a deep sleep.

Later his stepdad, Todd, stood outside the boy's room. "Knock, knock. Jerimiah, supper's ready." When he didn't receive a response, he rapped on the door again. "Knock, knock," he said, speaking a little louder this time. "Jerimiah, are you awake?"

"Uh, yeah, Dad. I'll be right there."

Mattie was a great cook, and as always, the meal was delicious. After dinner Todd and Jerimiah chatted about the weather while they washed the dishes.

Todd asked, "How was your day, Son?"

Excitedly the boy blurted, "Oh, Dad, it was a—" He quickly caught himself and lowered his voice. "Just a regular day, like all the rest."

Todd replied, "For a minute I thought you had some unbelievable news."

"Unbelievable?" Jerimiah stammered. He continued in a subdued tone, "Naw, nothing exciting. Just a normal day. How was your day, Dad?"

The boy could feel his face flush red. He never had lied to either of his parents, and it upset him.

"Well, the forest service is concerned about the drought we're having and wants us to be on alert for any signs of stress among the trees."

Jerimiah declared, "Oh, you don't have to worry about the trees. Their roots have gone deep and found huge supplies of water. The forests will be fine."

Todd quickly looked at Jerimiah. "Son, that's a brilliant deduction, but where did you get that information?"

He thought for a minute, wondering, *How did I know that information?* Then it hit him—the knowledge had been given to him by the TREEZZ. Hastily he replied, "Oh, I probably read it somewhere. I don't remember exactly."

"Well, think, Jerimiah. Information like this is invaluable. We need to find the source."

"I'll try, Dad."

Later on Todd said to Mattie, "You know something? Our son has a penchant for trees, a real understanding of the forest. The forest service is always looking for arborists."

Groggily she answered, "That's nice to know, Todd." She got into bed, rolled over, and kissed Todd. That always made him smile.

"Thanks, Mattie."

"Thank you, Todd."

The following day Jerimiah told his mom he was going for a walk in the forest. She smiled because she knew he always went for a walk in the forest when he had things on his mind.

She said, "OK, Son. Be careful, and don't be late for dinner."

He walked the paths of the forest for hours, contemplating his decision. He thought, *I love the TREEZZ; they are my friends. I would do anything for the TREEZZ. But the TREEZZ admitted this relationship comes with a huge responsibility.* He began to doubt himself. *Do I have the stamina— the guts—necessary to pursue the quest to save the TREEZZ?*

———

Deborah and Becca Carlsbad were sisters. Deborah was twenty-four years old and a very attractive woman. Becca was sixteen, kind of a plain-Jane, nerdy type.

Sadly their mom and dad had been killed in an automobile accident two years prior. The girls found it difficult dealing with their parents' deaths. Deborah struggled to find a new job, finish college, and comfort a sister grieving for her parents. She was finishing her master's in cellular biology, a field she excelled in.

Becca was never the same after the accident. Now in her junior year, she kept to herself, delving into her studies. She aspired to be just like her sister; Becca idolized Deborah. And just like her big sister, she excelled in cellular biology. On the weekends the girls would go camping in the forest. They loved the forest; they felt safe among the trees.

On one camping trip, Becca awoke to a haunting sound beckoning her. Having no fear of the forest, she followed the sound. Suddenly the sound ceased. The forest was silent. A small vine reached out and took her hand. A second vine took her other hand. She looked at the vines and smiled.

She purred, "Hello, little ones. Did you come to say hi?"

A reassuring voice in her head replied, "Hello, Becca. Welcome to our home."

The voice had come from not just one tree but all the TREEZZ.

Becca quickly looked around and questioned, "Who is this? I'm not afraid of you."

"We know you are not afraid; we are your friends, the TREEZZ."

"Are you for real, or is this a trick?"

"We would never trick you."

"Then what do you want?"

The comforting voice answered, "Becca, because of your absolute love of TREEZZ, we have chosen you to help lead a crusade to save the TREEZZ. The forests of the earth are being decimated at an alarming rate. The sacred rain forests that keep this planet alive are being destroyed. If you choose to join our crusade, you will be given extraordinary abilities that will allow you to assist mankind and preserve our forests. This gift comes with enormous responsibilities and requires a total commitment to the crusade. Please take time to review and consider this offer. And please keep this a secret for now."

Becca was speechless—a rare occurrence for her. She was in awe but felt so comfortable with the TREEZZ in the forest. She didn't want to leave. The TREEZZ said, "You must go your sister is concerned."

She returned to the campsite to find an angry Deborah. "Becca, darn you! Where have you been? You had me worried sick—you know better than to wander off and not tell me."

"I'm sorry, Deb. I shouldn't have walked off. It won't happen again."

The following weekend Becca asked if they could go back to their previous campsite. Deborah, finding it difficult to deny Becca's request, agreed to take them back.

"Gee, thanks, Sis. It's real important I get to go back to see the TRE—I mean, an odd flower. I need it for my collection." Becca had almost slipped and given away the secret.

As soon as they set up their camp, Becca asked, "Sis, can I walk down to the lake and look for the special flower?"

"OK, but don't be long, don't get lost, and don't talk to any strangers."

"Yes, Deborah." Becca moaned.

She approached the spot where she had heard the voice.

"Hello, Becca; have you decided?"

"Yes, I have, and I would be honored to help my friends. Whatever it takes to save the TREEZZ, I'm in."

"We are very pleased with your decision. The TREEZZ will begin to educate you in the ways of the TREEZZ. You will have unlimited knowledge and the special skills required to accomplish lifesaving tasks for humans and TREEZZ. Jerimiah Simpson is your counterpart. You will collaborate with him on projects and missions."

Becca cried out excitedly, "When will I see him? Is he good-looking?"

The TREEZZ answered, "All in due time, Becca. All in due time."

Disappointed, she curled her lip, lowered her head, and frowned.

———

Lucius Lattimore and Jerimiah Simpson had been born and raised near the town of Patrick Creek. They attended Crescent City High School, dated the same girls, and played on the same football team. To say they were friends would be a stretch. Lucius had a dislike for Jerimiah. Jerimiah was well liked by the girls and his classmates. Lucius was athletic and made many touchdowns; Jerimiah had better grades.

Lucius surpassed Jerimiah in wealth. Lucius's father, Clay Lattimore, owned and operated a large chemical plant just outside the city. The business did well, and the family was well-off. After high school graduation, Lucius was the big man in town: he had a fancy car, nice clothes, and a high-paying job working for his father.

When Lucius heard that Jerimiah was going East to attend college, he was overjoyed. He wouldn't see Jerimiah anymore, and that made him happy.

Clay Lattimore's company, L&L Chemicals, was the main supplier of manufactured insulin and syringes to a giant pharmaceutical company. Lucius was smart and questioned his father. "Dad, we need to diversify. If we were to lose that contract, we'd be out of business."

Clay Lattimore asked, "What do you propose, Son?"

"Dad, the hot product is growth hormones. Using engineered growth hormones, we can triple the harvest yield for farmers."

"What hormones are you talking about?"

"Oh, ah, well, the research is ongoing, but they're close to making a synthetic hormone."

"That's very interesting. I hope they're smart enough not to mix any human and animal hormones."

"Oh, I'm sure they are. That's one of the first rules of biology."

CHAPTER 2

In the early 1990s, technology was the name of the game. The world was quickly becoming high tech, and if one wanted to succeed, one had to get aboard the tech train.

One business was especially lucrative—the surveillance business. Savvy investors were becoming new millionaires every day.

A skinny sixteen-year-old boy was walking the streets, collecting aluminum cans from the garbage dumpsters to feed his younger sister and himself. A man approached him and asked, "Hey, kid. Do you want to make a quick twenty?"

The boy didn't hesitate. "Yes, sir, I do."

The man handed him a camera and said, "Take pictures of everyone who enters and leaves that building, and make sure you're not seen." He pointed to a building across the street.

"You got it, mister."

The man returned two hours later, handed the boy a twenty, took his camera, and left. The boy thought,

This is the business I want to be in. The boy's name was Robert McAlister.

Several years before, Robert and his sister, Elaina, had been adopted by a couple who lived on a dairy farm in West Virginia. Their foster parents were wonderful people, kind and caring, and they loved the siblings dearly.

Marg and her husband, Harry McAlister, ran a small farm several miles outside of town, but they struggled to make ends meet. Marg was an amateur herbalist and took care of her family's and some neighbors' ailments. Even as a child, Robert was amazed by how many illnesses Marg successfully treated with herbs, roots, and potions.

One day the siblings went outside to help Harry. As they entered the barn, they saw Harry lying on the ground unconscious. Elaina thought he was dead and began screaming. Robert ran to the house, got Marg, and called 911.

The medics arrived and said that Harry had experienced a low-sugar event. The doctor diagnosed Harry with type 1 diabetes. This meant that Harry would need insulin shots daily. But Marg didn't buy that. She'd heard rumors that a woman in Canada had made an herbal concoction for her son that acted like natural insulin.

Marg began a quest to find the herbal recipe. She hit on the formula a year later, and soon Harry was off the insulin shots and ingesting Marg's herbal remedy. Robert never forgot the power of herbs and became an advocate of herbal medications.

One cold winter night, an ember from the fireplace started a house fire. Initially everyone got out safely, but then Marg ran back into the burning house with urgency. Harry yelled to the sobbing children to stay where they were as he went back inside to get Marg. Elaina was sobbing hysterically, fearing that both their foster parents would die in the flames. Robert felt helpless as he hugged his sister and watched their house collapse. Two figures ran out through the flames; miraculously they emerged with only minor burns. Harry laid Marg on the ground. Both were coughing heavily from smoke inhalation.

Harry, scared to death that he'd almost lost his wife and devastated by the loss of their home, turned to Marg and asked, "Why in God's name did you run back into the burning house?"

Clutching her book, Marg sheepishly admitted, "I couldn't let my book of herb recipes burn. They're priceless."

Hearing the reason, Harry, a religious man, was very upset and let loose some expletives the children had never heard before. That was the first time they had seen Harry angry at Marg.

The four of them huddled beneath a blanket as the last wall collapsed in a shower of burning embers. The local volunteer fire department finally arrived, but nothing was left to save.

Unfortunately, with nowhere for them to live, the county social services took the siblings and put them in an orphanage. The first night was terrifying; the newcomers had all their possessions stolen by several older orphans.

Robert wouldn't tolerate the abuse and told Elaina, "We're getting out of here tonight. I promise that I'll protect you and take care of you."

The teenager had heard from other orphans that Washington was the place to go. The brother and sister hitchhiked from West Virginia to Washington, DC. The homeless shelter they found wouldn't allow the siblings to stay together. Robert wouldn't have that, and they left.

Days later, as Robert and his sister huddled in the same alleyway trying to stay warm, a large, rugged-looking man approached the siblings. "What are you two doing out here? You should be inside."

Robert coughed before he answered, "We have nowhere to go."

The big man questioned, "What about a shelter? They'll take you in."

"Yes, sir, but they won't let us stay together."

The big man growled, "Those pieces of shit. Sorry for my language, but they piss me off. Kid, go to the spy shop on the next block and tell Slim, the owner, that Uncle Hank said, 'Take care of the kids.'"

Robert and Elaina quickly hustled to the spy shop. Cautiously Robert opened the door.

A gruff voice called, "Get in here, and close the door. I'm not heating Washington."

Robert timidly said, "Uncle Hank said you should take care of us."

"He did, did he?"

The spy shop was a dingy storefront; the windows were dull from a grimy film. The floor was covered in cigar ash, and newspapers lay strewn about. The garbage can was overflowing with fast-food wrappers. A heavyset man with a round, red face sat smoking a stinky cigar. He growled, "What did this Uncle Hank look like? Was he kind of short with a beard?"

"No, sir. Uncle Hank is a big man, and he doesn't have a beard."

"OK. I guess you're telling the truth. One can't be too careful these days. What are your names?"

"I'm Robert, and this is my sister, Elaina."

Slim got up and waved for the kids to follow him.

He took them to an empty storeroom and snarled, "Here are two cots and blankets. Now you kids, be quiet and don't cause me any trouble. If you do, you'll be back on the streets."

With his voice quivering, Robert said, "Yes, sir. We'll be good, sir. And thank you."

Elaina was too scared to say a word.

———

The next morning Slim came down to the store from his apartment on the second floor. When he unlocked the door to the spy shop, Slim's eyes popped, his mouth opened, and his unlit cigar hit the ground.

"What the hell happened here? Where's my mess?" Slim bellowed.

The store was as neat as a pin, and the windows were sparkling clean.

Robert and Elaina stood there with big smiles, proud of their accomplishment.

Slim shielded his eyes from the bright light shining in. He hadn't seen the sun shining through those windows in years. He hated it. He was just about to yell at the kids but quickly realized they thought they were doing him a favor. He picked up his cigar and put it back in his mouth.

"Gee, kids, you did a really good job," he said, choking on his words. "Thank you. I love it."

Elaina asked, "Is there anything else we can do for you, sir?"

"Oh, you kids have done more than enough." Slim looked at his workbench and frowned. "I don't suppose you know how to solder?"

"Yes, sir, I do."

Slim straightened up, Robert's answer getting his attention. "Is that so? Well, my boy, step right over here, and start soldering these motherboards."

Robert picked up the soldering gun and began making soldered connections. Slim looked on with a smile as he chewed his unlit cigar. Robert nodded to Elaina, signaling her to start sweeping the rest of the shop. She quickly grabbed the broom and began to sweep. Slim didn't have the heart to stop her.

At the end of the day, Slim moved his unlit cigar back and forth in his mouth as he looked first at the pile of soldered motherboards and then at the clean floor. He removed the cigar and smiled. "You've done good, really good. Are you up for more work tomorrow?"

"Yes, sir, I am."

Slim looked at Elaina and said, "And you did good, too, girly."

Pleased with the siblings' work, he arranged to have a friend lease him an apartment in the spy shop building; Robert and Elaina would stay there.

Slim wouldn't admit it, but he grew fond of the kids and kept a close eye on them.

———

Robert's first goal was to enroll his sister in a prestigious girls' school five blocks away. Unfortunately the tuition was much more than he'd anticipated. Elaina was so looking forward to going to the school that Robert couldn't disappoint her. He approached Slim and told him his predicament.

Slim responded, "How much do you need, Robby?"

Robert didn't like being called Robby, but after all Slim had done for them, he let it slide. "Sir, with housing included, it comes to eleven thousand dollars."

"Eleven thousand dollars, you say? That's a healthy sum." Slim went into his office and returned with a brown paper bag. "Here you go, kid—eleven thousand for the school and another two thousand for clothes and other things."

Robert was stunned by Slim's generosity. "I don't know how I'll pay you back, but I will. Thank you so much."

Robert called to his sister, "Come here, Elaina. I have some great news. You're going to that nice girls' school!"

"Oh, Robert, I'm so happy, but where did you get the money?"

Robert looked at Slim.

Slim interjected, "The business made a loan to your brother. Someday he'll be a wealthy man and will pay it back."

Elaina ran to Slim, hugged him, and then kissed him on the cheek. "Thank you, sir. We will never forget your good deed."

Slim blushed. He could never say no to that pretty little girl.

A few days later, a letter came to the shop. It stated that the school had accepted Elaina's application, with tuition and housing paid in full.

———

As time went on, Slim noticed that Robert had a talent for electronics. Soon the young man was making sophisticated surveillance and eavesdropping devices. Slim's business doubled—and so did his profits.

At fifteen, Elaina was a very attractive girl. She was bubbly and outgoing and made friends easily. She had one very good friend, Alexis Bronson, who liked Elaina and invited her to fashionable parties at her mansion. Alexis's parents grew fond of Elaina and treated her like a daughter. She was invited on exclusive summer vacations. Some included trips to Europe, sailing the Mediterranean and rubbing elbows with royalty.

When Elaina reached her early twenties, her intelligence and beauty would bring lucrative offers for positions in the business world, including modeling and designing fashion.

Robert, on the other hand, had put his nose to the grindstone and worked continuously. Those first years with Slim, he'd managed to save $50,000, a tidy sum for an eighteen-year-old boy. At twenty, he operated the spy store for Slim and did a great job with a pleasant attitude. Slim viewed this as an opportunity to get out of Washington and go back to Texas, where he'd grown up.

Robert noticed that Slim's half-burned, unlit cigar was nervously twitching and shuffling back and forth. That meant he had something on his mind. Finally Slim said, "Robert, come over and sit down. I have a proposition for you."

"Yes, sir. What might that be?"

"Robert, how would you like to be partners in this spy shop?"

"A partner? A full partner?" The young man beamed with joy, but it was soon replaced with disappointment. He hung his head. "I only have fifty thousand dollars saved."

"Did I say anything about money? I've got plenty. Just pay me from the profits the shop will make."

"Gee, Slim, that's the best thing that's ever happened to me."

"You deserve it, kid. You're a hard worker, honest, and considerate, and your personality is a whole lot better than mine. What more could a partner ask for?"

Slim moved to his hometown of Huston, Texas. With his excellent reputation, he opened another spy shop. He retained his trademarks: an unlit half cigar and red, white, and blue suspenders.

Sadly a few years later, his unhealthy lifestyle caught up with him. He passed away in his shop. A heart attack was listed as the cause of death.

Robert celebrated both his twenty-first birthday and his partnership in the shop. He couldn't believe his good fortune. Elaina was so proud of her brother. She had his favorite seven-layer birthday cake delivered to the shop. It read, "Happy birthday to the new partner at the best spy shop in DC."

Just as Elaina cut the first piece of cake, a big, husky young man entered the store. His look and presence were menacing. "I'm Vic Bowden, and I'm in a hurry. Did Slim tell you about me?"

"Yes, sir, he did."

"What did he tell you?"

"He said you were rude and arrogant and always in a hurry. He said you were a tough SOB and—"

"That's enough; did you believe him?

"Yes, sir."

"Good." He handed him a drawing and specifications for a special device. "I'll stop by this evening and pick it up, and it better be ready."

"By the way, how's your sister?"

"She's fine, Mr. Bowden."

He grunted as he left.

At 8:00 p.m. Bowden returned. "Where's my package? I don't have all night."

Robert went into the back room to get his device. Bowden looked at the dessert and said to Elaina, "My favorite cake, seven layer. Do you mind if I have a slice?"

Nervously she whispered, "Sure, Mr. Bowden."

The man cut a huge piece of cake and devoured it in seconds. "That was good; thanks."

Robert brought out Bowden's device in a bag. Then he noticed that the cake was half eaten. Robert looked at Elaina. She nodded, indicating that Bowden had eaten it. Bowden grabbed the bag from Robert, threw a credit card on the counter, turned, and left. He walked out of the shop. Suddenly he poked his head back in. "Thanks again for the cake; it was really good. And happy birthday, kid."

———

The spy shop's new owner saw a big increase in new customers. His curiosity got the best of him, and he asked a customer, "Did someone send you here?"

"Oh yea, Bowden. He said if I didn't buy my items here, he would make me disappear. He told everybody to shop here or else."

Robert replied, "That's terrible; he shouldn't do that."

"It's OK. He always helps us out, and so we don't mind."

It was about 8:00 p.m. when Robert finished his last order of the day. He set down his tools, stretched, and yawned. He began to add up the cost of the components for Bowden's device; it would be expensive. He thought, *What if this guy balks at the price? He could snap me in half if he had a mind to.*

The arrogant customer returned that evening. Robert took great pleasure in handing him the bill. Bowden never looked at the price. He asked, "Did you run the card yet?"

"No. I was waiting for your approval."

"Let me see that bill. Ah, hell, that's the price?"

Robert uneasily offered, "I could give you a discount."

"Discount my butt; put another two hundred on the bill."

Robert hesitated. Bowden barked, "I insist."

He hastily added two hundred dollars to the bill. Bowden smiled for the first time. Little did Robert know, the two men would become good friends. He locked the door and turned in for the night.

The young Robert got up the next morning, knowing that he would have a visit from the unfriendly Bowden. At 9:00 a.m. he saw Mr. Rude enter the shop. He thought, *I'm really not up to greeting this nasty man.*

Mr. Rude walked in with two containers of coffee and acknowledged Robert cheerfully. "Good morning, friend. I thought you might like a fresh cup of coffee." He stuck his hand out and said, "I don't believe we've ever been properly introduced. My name is Vic Bowden."

Robert thought, *Is this the same man from last night?* "Hello, Mr. Bowden. I'm Robert Simpson."

"I've heard a lot of great things about you from Slim. He says you're good people, and if he says that, well, that's good enough for me. Hey, I gotta tell you, that device you built worked great—better than I expected.

It just may have saved my life. I owe you a debt of gratitude. Do you mind if I hang out here for a while? You got the place smelling good."

Robert was totally baffled by the attitude change. "I…guess you can. Sure, make yourself comfortable. Do you prefer Vic or Victor?"

He replied, "Actually it's Victorio."

Robert countered, "Ah, yes, Victorio, the brave Apache warrior—a relative of yours?"

"How perceptive, Robert. Yes, he was my great-great-uncle."

"I'm sure he had the same pleasant, uh, attitude that you have."

Vic grinned. "Oh, that's just a facade I put on to intimidate folks."

"Well, I can tell you it works. By the way, what do you do for a living?"

"I'm an agent for the NSA."

Robert was surprised. "Really? You're an agent for the NSA? That's interesting. Are you, like, a secret agent?"

Robert thought, *We're the same age, but Vic seems older. Maybe it's the stress of his job?*

Vic laughed out loud and answered, "I would tell you, Robert, but then I'd have to kill you." Robert chuckled nervously. Vic laughed again heartily. "Just kidding, my friend. Just kidding."

While Robert went about his work, Vic sat back in the chair, put his feet up, and began reading the newspaper.

Robert took a break around noon. He glanced over at Vic and saw that he was sound asleep. The big man looked so peaceful, so relaxed. He thought, *He's not such a bad guy after all.* Leaning back in the chair, Robert put his feet up, closed his eyes, and pondered his life.

He thought of his foster parents and how kind and loving they'd been to Elaina and him. That awful fire at the farm. The orphanage where all their worldly possessions were stolen. The terrible days and nights that he and his sister spent hiding behind dumpsters, their stomachs growling from lack of food. And he wouldn't forget the man who offered him twenty dollars; he would have done almost anything for that money. Then there was the compassion of Slim and Uncle Hank.

Now he was a partner in a lucrative business. He counted his blessings and made a vow: he would work hard, make intelligent decisions, help the less fortunate, and, if he had the opportunity, make this world a better place to live in.

These were lofty goals for a young fledgling entrepreneur.

CHAPTER 3

Business was brisk at the small spy shop, or as some called it, the spook shop. For the next few weeks, Vic drifted in and out of the storefront. One day he came in and said, "Hey, Robert, I got a hot tip for you. I know this guy, Bill Atwood, and he's launching a private spy satellite system. He's in dire need of a cash infusion. This would be a great investment. Think it over, but don't wait too long; he's going public soon. Here's his number."

Robert asked, "How come you're not in?"

"Oh, I forgot to tell you. I'm getting married, and my bride wants a house."

In a disappointed voice, Robert said, "Vic, I appreciate the tip, but I don't have the money. I wish I did; I'd love to get in on that. And congratulations, I wish you and your bride the best."

"Thanks, buddy. I found the most beautiful, wonderful girl in the world. I love her more than anything."

"Vic, you should get out of the cloak-and-dagger game and get a safe job where you go home every night to your wife. Come be my partner in the spy shop. With all your foreign connections, we could make millions."

Grinning broadly, Vic said, "Thanks, Robert. That's a great offer. I've also been thinking along those same lines. I do believe that I'll take you up on it. My Alisha will be thrilled; she's wanted me to get out of that awful business for a long time."

The two men shook hands and sealed the deal.

As Vic left, another man walked in. He was well dressed and carried a briefcase. He was very official look-ing—the kind of person you would rather not speak to. "Hello, I'm looking for Mr. Robert McAlister."

Robert hesitated. *Should I tell him I'm Robert McAlister? Vic's suspicious nature is beginning to rub off on me.* The young man's trepidation subsided, and he said, "I'm Robert McAlister.

"Mr. McAlister, I am an attorney representing the estate of the late Marg and Harry McAlister. My condolences."

Robert sat down in shock. He put his head in his hands as tears began to roll down his cheeks. He asked, "Do you know how they died?"

The attorney answered, "The story is that they were living in a trailer and were poisoned by a carbon dioxide leak."

Robert, visibly shaken by the news of their deaths, regretted not trying harder to stay in contact with them. After the fire the couple had moved out of state, and they'd both lost contact.

The lawyer handed Robert a legal-size envelope and a check for $100,000. Robert was taken aback and wondered where the money had come from.

The attorney continued. "Marg and Harry McAlister left their estate to you. As per their request, the farm was sold to a neighbor, and the proceeds were to be given to you. The envelope contains all the legal documents. Marg specifically directed that the book be handed to you personally." The attorney gave Robert a book and had him sign a receipt. "This concludes my legal duties. Good day, sir."

After much thought he called his sister with the sad news and explained the windfall. Elaina had always trusted her brother, so she told him, "Do what you think is best."

Robert sat back in his chair and looked at the scorched, tattered binding of the book the attorney had presented to him. He immediately recognized it as Marg's herbal recipe collection. He was thrilled that she'd left it to him. The young man contemplated his next move.

He couldn't get the satellite offer out of his mind; it was a risky gamble. Finally he called Bill Atwood and asked if he still needed cash for his project.

Bill excitedly replied, "One hundred thousand dollars will get us into space, partner."

Robert said, "I guess we're going into space, partner."

Robert tried and tried to contact Vic, but it seemed that the man had vanished into thin air. He tried Alisha, but all he got was her answering machine. In desperation he called the NSA, but they denied having any knowledge of a Victorio Bowden. After a week and many dead ends, Robert gave up. He was hurt and disappointed that his supposed friend and new partner had left him high and dry without a word.

Robert moved on and concentrated on profitable acquisitions. He had a sixth sense when it came to negotiating contracts. Clients marveled at his astuteness to project the future. His acquisitions exceeded financial projections. Everyone wanted in on any new business he started. Everything was going Robert's way. He couldn't have asked for anything more, except maybe for news regarding Vic.

Robert asked some of his NSA customers if they had any information regarding Vic Bowden? Weeks later Robert received a call, "Mr. McAlister, I have some terribly sad news. Vic's wife Alisha died; the doctors say it was an aneurysm. No one has seen or heard from Vic since she passed."

Robert was sick with sadness and wanted to find a way to comfort his friend, but Vic couldn't or didn't want to be found.

Days later he got a text from the NSA contact; Vic had volunteered for a dangerous mission overseas, probably one he wouldn't return from. Robert knew that this was Vic's way of saying goodbye, just the way he wanted it. Time heals all wounds, and Vic becomes a memory and a smile.

———

Years later, out of nowhere, Vic knocked on Robert's door with tears in his eyes.

Robert bellowed, "Vic, my God! Where have you been? Are you all right?" Robert pulled him into the apartment, rejoicing at the sight of his long-lost friend. He quickly hugged him. "It's so good to see you; we were so worried." Then Robert noticed the tears in his eyes. "Are you all right? Can I help you? Vic, thank God you're alive. Why didn't you call me? We were so sorry to hear about Alisha."

At the mention of her name, Vic fell to his knees and began sobbing uncontrollably. "Robert, I lost her.

I lost the most important person in my life, and without her I am nothing. I took on the most dangerous missions, ones that would guarantee my death, but it wasn't in the cards. I guess the Lord has other plans for me."

Seeing his friend's emotional distress, Robert quickly dropped to his knees and wrapped his arms tightly around Vic. "Cry, my friend, and I'll cry with you for your loss." Robert did just that, but some of the tears were tears of happiness for the safe return of his friend.

After some time, Vic composed himself, ashamed that he'd shown his deepest emotion but pleased that Robert was there and understood. Slowly Vic began to open up about the years of grief for Alisha. He just went on about his memories of her. He never detailed his suicide missions. Completely sapped of energy and totally exhausted, he crashed on Robert's couch. He slept for a day and a half. A neighbor's door slammed shut. That noise woke Vic. He jumped up and pulled his gun, a natural reflex for him. It was time to leave - another deadly mission awaited.

When Robert returned home, Vic was gone, but he'd left a note: "Thank you for being there for me. I needed you. I will stay in touch, but right now I have another job to do. Stay well, and hi to Elaina and Slim. I love you all."

Through the years Robert and Vic would touch base at least once a year, but with their busy lives, time quickly slipped away.

———

For the next decade, Robert built an empire, becoming a self-made billionaire. His high-tech inventions brought a fortune in royalties. Half the world subscribed to his surveillance business. Many governments and wealthy individuals waited in line for his security systems and the unrivaled protection they provided.

True to his promise, he and Elaina formed a charitable foundation dedicated to funding deserving organizations. Elaina would become the CEO of the McAlister Foundation. She traveled the world, giving grants to needy institutions. She was respected and well-liked by all her colleagues and by dignitaries of many foreign governments. The McAlister Foundation was renowned for its generosity.

Robert wanted to do something special for Elaina's birthday. Back in the spy shop, he looked through a stack of aviation magazines. He dreamed of what it would be like to have his own private jet. Now he could afford one. That's what he would do; he would buy his sister a jet for her extensive travel. He knew exactly what he wanted: the Gulfstream G-5.

For her birthday, he took Elaina to a five-star restaurant located at an airport. He brought her attention to a beautiful corporate jet that had just landed. Elaina commented, "Look at that beauty. Now that's traveling first class."

The plane taxied right up to the restaurant window. Robert pointed out to his sister, "Look at the call numbers on the fuselage—'EM,' your initials. What a coincidence."

The stairway lowered, and the pilot exited. He walked into the restaurant and over to the McAlisters' table. "I couldn't help but notice your interest in the plane. Would you like to see the inside?" Robert looked at his sister, smiled, and nodded.

The trio left the restaurant and proceeded to the luxury jet. Elaina stepped inside to find a banner that read HAPPY BIRTHDAY, ELAINA! Stunned, she covered her mouth with her hands and started to cry. "This can't be true."

Elaina ran her hands over the fine leather seats and kneeled to touch the lush carpet. She peeked into the cockpit and was amazed by the extensive instrumentation. She looked at her brother and asked, "Oh, Robert, is this true? Is this for me?"

Robert hugged Elaina and said, "This is for my beautiful sister. I love you so much."

"Robert, how can I ever thank you?"

"Every day you thank me; now it's my turn to thank you. Here's to many safe and rewarding miles."

Elaina hugged and kissed her brother. The siblings had a wonderful meal as they gazed at Elaina's $50 million birthday present.

———

A year later the profits from worldwide satellite surveillance system subscriptions had made Robert and his sister even wealthier. Now with some free time, he began looking through Marg's herbal recipe book. He was fascinated by the cures and recalled the herbal concoctions that had helped Harry with his diabetes. The more he read, the more he believed in natural cures. He thought, *This might be a way to give back for all my good fortune.*

He had built a worldwide empire. His holdings included satellite surveillance, the center point of his conglomerate. His current clients were primarily countries and large corporations. Governments were especially interested in ground and air observation. Corporations were concerned with industrial espionage. But Robert's pet project would be his high-tech laboratory. This was his dream, his way to give thanks for all his good fortune, to help his fellow man enjoy a better life through free herbal medication.

Thus began Robert's quest to find herbal remedies for the world's most common ailments. He would need assistance in this endeavor; he would need the brightest minds, biologists specializing in medicinal botany and herbalism.

After months of research, inquiries, and investigations, three names topped the list, including Jerimiah Simpson's. Robert had been following this young man's evolution through his college years with much interest. Anonymously he had financially assisted Jerimiah's education and thought, *This was the best investment I ever made.*

Two other names appeared on the list. Surprisingly they were sisters: Deborah and Becca Carlsbad. Deborah was completing her master's in cellular biology. Becca was graduating high school but had already taken advanced college classes in biology. She was brilliant and had a promising future in cellular biology. Of course she did have help: her friends the TREEZZ were always there for her.

Robert pondered, *I have selected three members for the team, but will they accept my offer?* He believed timing would be an important factor.

ONE YEAR LATER

Robert felt this was the time to approach his top three candidates. Jerimiah had graduated from MIT and begun submitting his résumé to large companies specializing in plant biology. He was excited, and every day at eleven o'clock, he would wait for the mailman.

Nervously he waited for the flood of offers for his talents. Day after day went by without one offer. Disillusioned, he began to question his worth, his abilities, and his chosen career. Now he had another problem: he was broke. He was happy to get a job stacking shelves at the local grocery store. Robert believed this was the time to approach Jerimiah and unveil his astonishing proposal to make this world a better place for mankind.

Robert McAlister seized the moment and called Jerimiah Simpson.

CHAPTER 4

"Hello, Mr. Simpson. My name is Robert McAlister, and I'd like to discuss a business proposition with you."

Jerimiah said sarcastically, "Robert McAlister, the billionaire philanthropist, right? I bet you want me to be your new partner in a million-dollar business venture. Who is this? Is this some sort of joke? Look, buddy, I'm really not in the mood."

And with that, he hung up.

His phone rang again. "Please, Mr. Simpson," implored the caller, "don't hang up. Give me the courtesy to explain. You need money, don't you? I may be able to help you."

Jerimiah said, "I'm sorry, sir. Right now I have no sense of humor."

Robert replied, "Young man, this *is* Robert McAlister. If you don't believe me, ask me a question only you would know the answer to."

Jerimiah asked, "What is my favorite tree?"

"That's an easy one: the sequoia."

Jerimiah said, "That could have been a lucky guess. OK, try this one. Who are my best friends?"

Robert said, "The TREEZZ are your best friends?"

There was dead silence, and the young man began to perspire. *No one knows that secret.*

Robert asked, "Are you all right, Mr. Simpson? I'm sorry if I shocked you, but I needed to get your attention. I am Robert McAlister."

Jerimiah composed himself. "I'm so sorry, Mr. McAlister. I'm dumbfounded that you know my secret."

Robert replied, "I hate to say this—someone may want to lock me up—but it was a voice in my head. It said a friend of the TREEZZ will rise above the rest. I would assume that would be you, Jerimiah Simpson. Would you agree to meet me at a place of your choice? I understand that you can't be too careful in this age of eavesdropping."

The young man suggested, "How about the McDonald's on Thirty-Fourth Street? Say, tomorrow morning at ten?"

Pleased with his cautious approach, Robert agreed to the meeting.

The next day Jerimiah watched a black limousine pull up in front of McDonald's. A tall, slender gentleman in his forties wearing dark sunglasses and a hat exited.

Robert McAlister was a handsome, sophisticated gentleman. His dark hair, graying at the temples, made him look distinguished. He had an aura that the ladies couldn't resist. Robert didn't think all that much of himself and wondered if women wanted him for his money. Either way, he enjoyed the attention and had no intentions of marrying.

The self-made man was escorted to Jerimiah's table. Jerimiah stood up and, with a touch of awkwardness, shook hands with the billionaire.

"Mr. Simpson," he said, "it's a pleasure to meet you. I've waited many years to make your acquaintance, and now here we are, face to face."

Jerimiah said, "Thank you, sir. But first I must apologize for my rudeness yesterday on the phone. I feel just terrible. I hope you can forgive me."

Robert laughed. "I understand, and there's no offense taken. You're forgiven." Robert was uncomfortable sitting in the open, especially having firsthand knowledge of listening devices. "Do you mind if we continue our discussion in the car?"

Jerimiah agreed.

Once inside the limousine, Robert relaxed a bit. "With today's sophisticated listening devices, one can never be too careful. Mr. Simpson, I'll get right to the point. I know your special relationship with the TREEZZ, and I believe that we have the same goal—to save as many TREEZZ as possible. Would I be correct in assuming that?"

Jerimiah looked relieved. "Yes, sir. The TREEZZ are my friends, and I want to protect them."

"Jerimiah, I also have a secret regarding the TREEZZ. They have informed me that we will create a team and start a worldwide crusade to save them. You must be wondering how I know all this."

Jerimiah answered, "You're right, Mr. McAlister."

The philanthropist smiled. "I was sitting on a bench in the park when a large oak tree telepathically informed me that you, I, and one other special person would lead a team to save the TREEZZ and, through herbal processes, make natural medications for mankind's common ills."

Excitedly, Jerimiah questioned, "The TREEZZ spoke to you and told you this?"

"They did."

Jerimiah sighed. "You don't know what a relief it is to realize that someone else knows their secrets."

Robert explained, "Make that two other people. Soon I will contact this person, and the three of us will get together at my place. I've had years to develop this plan. The three of us will organize an elite team of plant biologists concentrating on herbal recipes and medications. I know they exist, and I know our team will discover them. What are your thoughts, Mr. Simpson?"

Jerimiah felt a bit overwhelmed. "I commend you, sir, for your optimism. That's a mighty big order, but with the guidance from the TREEZZ, the right people, and your financial support, I think we have a good chance of succeeding."

"I'm pleased that we're on the same page. I'll have my staff put together a list of the most brilliant biologists and offer them a chance to save humanity and the TREEZZ. I'll call as soon as I get the names. Oh, before I leave, may I call you Jerimiah?"

"Yes, sir, please do."

"And you may call me Robert if you like."

"Yes, sir—I mean, Robert."

———

Robert asked the techs for a report on the Carlsbad sisters.

He noticed Deborah was managing a small science department for a local college. This job was beneath her level of skills, but she needed the money. Robert knew Deborah was very protective of her younger sister, and Becca could do nothing without her sister's permission.

Again Robert thought this was a good time to ask her to join the crusade. He made the call. "Ms. Carlsbad, my name is Robert McAlister. May I speak with you?"

"Robert McAlister, the philanthropist?"

"Yes, that Robert McAlister."

"Oh, yes, sir. What can I do for you, sir?"

"Actually a lot, I hope. I have a proposition for you and your sister. I'd prefer not to discuss it over the phone. Would you and your sister be available to meet me at my residence in New York? I will have my corporate jet fly you there and back. Would next Wednesday work for you and Becca?"

"Yes, sir, it would. Should we bring anything special?"

"Nothing special." He thought, *You two girls are special.*

Robert called Jerimiah. "The meeting is on for Wednesday. Can you make it?"

"Nothing could keep me from it."

A chauffeur-driven limousine picked up the girls at the airport and drove them to the McAlister estate just north of New York City—in Nyack, to be precise.

Deborah and Becca were taken aback at the sight of McAlister's opulent estate. His butler greeted the guests and escorted them through the grand hall and a large study exquisitely decorated in hand-carved mahogany and teakwood. The room had a massive stone fireplace set between two large glass walls, allowing a picturesque river view. The ladies were offered seats to enjoy a picturesque view in the observatory overlooking the historic Hudson River. Jerimiah and Robert were just coming back from a walk around the mansion.

"Excellent timing, my friends. Let me make the introductions. I am Robert McAlister; this young man is Jerimiah Simpson."

Becca cried out, "Jerimiah Simpson! I know that name—you're my counterpart. We're going to work together."

Deborah was shocked. "I never heard that name before. Becca, where did you get this idea you were going to work with Mr. Simpson?"

"Sis, the TREEZZ told me."

"And just who are the TREEZZ?"

"My apologies. I'm afraid you deserve an explanation. If you would allow me to continue with the introductions, I will explain everything. Jerimiah, this is Deborah Carlsbad, and this young lady knows your name. Now she will put a face to the name. Would anyone care for refreshment?" The butler took their orders and promptly returned with the drinks.

Robert explained everything in detail, from the beginning to the end. That cleared up the many questions the guests had. "So with all that information, I hope we can conclude our business and enjoy dinner. I can assure you that it will be delicious."

True to his word, the meal was excellent. The guests sent their compliments to the chef.

Robert asked, "Would you please join me in the study so we can get to know each other a little better? Are you comfortable? Is there anything I can get you?"

Jerimiah replied, "No, thank you. I'm good."

Deborah said she was fine.

Becca asked, "Can I have an ice cream soda?"

"Becca! Where are your manners?"

"Well, he asked."

Robert laughed loudly. "I believe we can accommodate your request, Becca. Chocolate or vanilla?"

"Chocolate, please."

Looking around, Jerimiah stated with envy, "I must compliment you on your study. It's beautiful."

"Thank you. The woodwork is old European. I've always relished its warmth."

Robert and his guests engaged in casual conversations late into the night. The group members had enjoyed one another's company, even Becca.

Robert suggested, "It's been a long but fruitful day. Let's enjoy a good night's sleep. The staff will show you to your rooms. Good night."

———

The next morning, the sun rose in the eastern sky. Its brilliance made the estate glow like a castle in a fairy tale. Deborah and Becca slept together—for Becca's sake, of course.

The girls stretched as they walked out on the balcony to greet the new day.

The view was breathtaking; the majestic Adirondack Mountains loomed in the distance. Below, several sailing vessels dotted the famous Hudson River.

After a sumptuous late breakfast, Robert asked, "Would anyone care for a riding tour of the Hudson Valley?"

Hands and cheers went up. "Great. I'll have the chauffeur get out the touring car."

A few minutes later, the chauffeur drove up in a vintage Mercedes convertible. It was pristine and worth over $1 million. The four guests and Robert climbed into the car for the scenic tour. The trip lasted six hours. It was a lovely ride, and the guide—Robert—drew their attention to all the points of interest.

About twenty minutes from the estate, Becca had a request: "Can I drive the rest of the way?"

Deborah barked, "No, you can't, Becca. This car is worth a fortune."

Robert looked at Deborah and nodded. The chauffeur pointed out safety features and handed her the keys. Her face beamed with joy as she shifted the manual transmission into first gear and slowly released the clutch, and they were off. It was a beautiful, warm, sunny day, and the ride was exhilarating. Arriving back at the estate safe and sound, the passengers complimented Becca's driving skills. Even the chauffeur was impressed.

Robert announced, "We will have a very special guest joining us this evening—my lovely sister, Elaina."

After another superb meal, the group anxiously awaited Elaina's presence. As they waited, Deborah talked with Robert. "Robert, my sister and I will gladly accept your offer."

"Deborah, I'm so pleased. Without you and Becca, we would have no crusade. You girls are an integral part of this team. Thank you so much."

The threesome was escorted to the stone veranda overlooking the Olympic-size heated pool. Refreshments were located on a separate table off to the side.

A short time later, a red Ferrari convertible pulled into the circular driveway. That got everyone's attention. The guests watched a beautiful woman open the door, extending a sexy pair of legs with grace. Robert walked over to greet her, and they hugged and kissed.

Jerimiah whispered, "That's his sister—wow!"

Becca cooed, "I like her car."

Robert took her arm and approached the group. "Ladies and gentlemen, I present my beautiful sister,

Elaina. Elaina, please welcome our new partners, Deborah, Becca, and Jerimiah."

Elaina announced, "Hello, everyone. Robert has told me all about you. I am very pleased to meet you."

"Please, let's go sit down and get acquainted," said Robert.

Jerimiah fumbled with a glass of water, and it spilled all over his pants.

Elaina calmly noted, "Take off your pants; the butler will assist you."

Upset with his clumsiness, the nervous young man began to unbutton his pants.

Elaina giggled. "Please, not here. Go inside with the butler."

Again Jerimiah's face turned crimson with embarrassment, and he quickly ran inside. Deborah and Becca tried to hide their humor as they chuckled at Jerimiah's expense.

Elaina looked at the ladies and Robert, laughing. "I think I'm going to like our new partner."

Robert cautioned, "Now, Elaina, be gentle with the lad."

"Robert, you know I'll take good care of him."

"Yes, that's what I'm afraid of."

She looked at the girls and winked. Deborah knew exactly what Elaina meant; Becca didn't have a clue. Jerimiah returned apprehensively, hoping he wouldn't make a fool of himself again.

The threesome enjoyed cocktails and hors d'oeuvres as Robert explained in detail some of Elaina's responsibilities. "As chairwoman of the McAlister Foundation, Elaina makes the final determination of which organizations are worthy of the grants. Many times an environmental issue will be the deciding factor. Because of the substantial amount of the grant, greed and politics will try to influence the outcome."

Elaina smiled. "You wouldn't believe the bribes I've been offered. Someday I'll tell you." Then she winked at Jerimiah.

Robert continued, "Elaina's good judgment and powerful political connections will prove to be invaluable in achieving the foundation's goals, as well as ours."

"This sounds a lot more complicated than I thought," Jerimiah replied.

"You and I will visit the countries applying for grants. I will introduce you to important political allies with the same goals in mind. With this incentive, potential recipients will be inclined to look favorably on your requests."

"Will you assist me in the final decision?" Jerimiah asked.

"We must strive to keep the two objectives separate. At the hint of any impropriety, the McAlister Foundation will lose its credibility and integrity. In the end, it's your call. I must add that you, too, might be a victim of bribery or blackmail. I will give you some tips on how to avoid potential scams and blackmail."

Robert commented, "All this sounds daunting, and it is, but working as a team, we will succeed. The futures of the TREEZZ and the world are in our hands. Now for the second goal: a team of biologists will concentrate on discovering herbal remedies and medicines to alleviate the common ailments of the world's inhabitants. Elaina will start setting up your itinerary, and in the meantime, I need Deborah's, Becca's, and your assistance with selecting our potential biologists. Are you ready?"

They all agreed. "We're ready. When can we start?"

"We are screening prospective applicants in two weeks." Robert signaled the butler, who immediately pulled out a bottle of vintage champagne from the ice bucket and filled the guests' glasses. He held his up in a toast. "Here's to our success in endeavoring to make the world a better place to live."

"Hear! Hear!" was the boisterous reply.

Jerimiah made the mistake of gazing into Elaina's hypnotic blue eyes. Robert looked at Jerimiah's expression; the young man was smitten. Robert shook his head and whispered to his sister, "You did it again, Elaina. Another man has fallen under your spell."

Elaina said nothing; she just smiled at her brother.

CHAPTER 5

A real estate agent in Northern California called Robert. "Mr. McAlister, I have great news. The owner of the property on which you made the offer has accepted. The closing papers are on their way to your attorney."

Robert had purchased a run-down resort near Patrick Creek, California. This would be the future home of McAlister Laboratories. It was remote enough to be discreet but close enough to the medium-sized municipality of Crescent City, where good food and entertainment were readily available.

Robert wasn't fooled enough to think that the remodeling would go unnoticed. As construction progressed, locals would pack a lunch and watch the ongoing work. Naturally, the news stations began poking around, asking all sorts of questions ranging from "Is this a secret facility to incarcerate aliens?" to "Is it a high-tech nudist resort?" The town gossipers were having a field day. Robert took it all in stride and enjoyed the conjecture and speculation. A reporter for the *Crescent City Post* had placed several calls to the McAlister Foundation, seeking information on the remodeling of the onetime resort.

Robert figured it was time to let the cat out of the bag. He asked Jerimiah, "Would you fly out to the construction site and give the local reporter an interview? You know, things like the projected schedule and estimated cost of the project. Also inform them of the economic impact on the local construction industry, as well as jobs for maintenance and hospitality personnel and the all-important scientists."

"Sure thing, Robert. I'll make my travel reservations."

"Don't bother with plane reservations; take Eliana's jet." Chuckling, he said, "It needs a good run."

Jerimiah called the *Crescent City Post*. "Hello, may I speak to the editor? My name is Jerimiah Simpson, and I represent McAlister Industries."

In a heartbeat the editor, Mr. Harold Brown, replied, "Yes, Mr. Simpson. What can I do for you?"

"I'll be available tomorrow at three p.m. at the construction site for an interview."

Excitedly, Mr. Brown replied, "Yes, sir. Our senior reporter will be on site at three tomorrow. Thank you, Mr. Simpson."

The G-5 touched down at the Crescent City airport. Jerimiah rented a car and drove out to the construction site; it was 2:45 p.m. A few minutes later, the news reporter arrived.

Jerimiah walked over to the man and introduced himself. "Hello, I'm Jerimiah Simpson."

"Hello, Mr. Simpson. I'm Arthur Boeing. It's nice to meet you. I understand you're a local boy, born and raised right here in Patrick Creek."

"Yes, I am, and it's nice to be back for a visit. My parents live just down the road."

The reporter looked at his notes. "That would be Mattie and Todd Bailey?"

"Yes, it would. You did your homework."

"That's my job. It looks like the construction is moving right along."

"It is. We're even one week ahead of schedule. Mr. Boeing, I'm pressed for time. Shall we proceed with the interview?"

Surprised by Jerimiah's eagerness to give the interview, the reporter fumbled for his pen. "Ah, yes, now I'm ready. First, when do you expect to be completely open, and how many people do you plan to hire?"

"We expect the construction to take approximately eighteen months. As far as employees, that depends on whether we hire in house or subcontract."

"I see. And the total cost of this remodel?"

"The estimate came in at eight-point-three million."

The reporter swallowed hard. "Eight-point-three million, just to remodel? I see."

Jerimiah continued, "You might say that we at McAlister Industries like to spread the wealth among the locals."

"May I quote you on that, sir?"

"Be my guest."

"What will be the main function of the complex?"

"The primary purpose is to provide rest and relaxation for our employees worldwide, a quiet retreat away from the hustle and bustle of the big cities."

"That's very benevolent of your company."

"Our biggest asset is our employees. Their health and welfare are our paramount concerns."

The two men began to walk around the complex while avoiding the ongoing construction.

"Mr. Simpson, will Robert McAlister frequent this resort?"

"I can't answer that question. Mr. McAlister is a very busy man."

The reporter quickly changed subjects. "That's a beautiful lake. Do you have plans for it?"

"Yes, we do. We plan to build ten chalets along the shore, in compliance with environmental guidelines."

"Thank you, sir. That was my next question. And that domed building, is that something special?"

"That is a planetarium for the stargazers. It will also house a small botany lab."

"Well, Mr. Simpson, the interview went better than I expected. You answered all my questions to my satisfaction."

As they walked to their vehicles, the reporter asked, "One more question: Are you building a road out in that field?"

"Oh, that will be a private airfield for the corporate jet."

"Corporate jet, huh?" whispered Mr. Boeing with envy.

The two men shook hands. Mr. Boeing thanked Jerimiah for the interview and departed the construction site.

————

Jerimiah drove to his mom and dad's farm, twenty minutes from the site. He was scheduled to stay for two days.

He pulled into his parents' driveway with a big smile on his face, waving his hand vigorously. He jumped out of the car and yelled, "Hi, Mom! Hi, Dad!" When he reached the porch, he hugged and kissed his mother. "Oh, Mom, it's so good to see you both. I love and miss you."

"Good to see you, son. We miss you so much."

Jerimiah looked at Todd, who had tears in his eyes. Their son jokingly said, "Thanks a lot, Dad. Now you have Mom and me crying."

He looked closely at his parents; they seemed a little frail. He thought, *Gee, Mom and Dad seem to be aging quickly. It's probably just my imagination.*

Todd smiled. "Sit down, boy, and tell us all about your job."

He started from the beginning, from when Robert McAlister contacted him, to the building of the resort. His mom and dad listened intently to every word. When he finished, they told him how proud they were of his academic achievements and partnership with Robert. He was happy to tell them that Robert was the anonymous financial donor. His parents were shocked but pleased that they finally had the identity of the benefactor.

The next two days went by like two hours. On the last morning, Jerimiah got up early and went into the forest. He stood in front of the giant sequoia and exchanged greetings with them. Messages flashed through his mind. As he returned to the house, he instinctively picked a few leafy plants and some odd-colored ferns. Once home, he mixed the assortment of plants with honey and aspen sap. He made a quart of the herbal mixture.

Soon afterward his mom entered the kitchen. "Son, do you know what liquid is in the refrigerator?"

"It's just some vitamin juice I thought you and Dad might enjoy."

"Thank you, Jerimiah. That's so thoughtful." She took a sip and said, "Wow, this packs a bit of a punch. I like it."

Just then Todd came into the kitchen. "Todd, dear, you must try this juice Jerimiah made for us."

He took a sip and grinned. "That's good. Can I have more?" Within minutes Mattie and Todd had finished off the juice and begun to feel spunky.

Later that day Jerimiah said his goodbyes and drove to the Crescent City airport, where he boarded the G-500 back to New York.

Robert called him during the flight. "Jerimiah, I loved the interview. Congratulations. A job well done, partner."

————

Lucius Lattimore walked into his father's office and threw the local newspaper on the desk. "Did you see this?"

He pointed to a picture on the front page that featured Jerimiah standing in front of the new resort complex. "That no-good SOB—I hate that guy. Now he's back in my town. I won't have it!"

Clay Lattimore calmly said, "Take it easy, Son. You're getting much too upset. Sit down, and we'll discuss this. Lucius, be careful of what you say. Threats like that will get you in big trouble. It won't do our business any good either."

Lucius composed himself. "You're right, Dad. I'll watch what I say."

In his office Lucius sat back and pondered the next move for the business. *We need to have an alternative source of revenue. If I could find a way to combine a human growth hormone with a crop plant, we could make a fortune. I just need two biologists to assist me.*

Later that day he approached his father. "Dad, I'd like to hire two biologists to research growth hormones and the feasibility of using them on crops."

"I think that's a good idea. We do need to diversify. You'll be in charge of that project."

Lucius was obsessed with discovering what Simpson and the lab were researching, so much so he hired a spook tech to install a listening device in the lobby.

The tech said, "Installing it now, during construction, would be the best time."

Lucius gave him the go-ahead.

———

Months later a piece of specialized equipment was installed in the L&L lab. The project manager commented, "That's a mighty expensive microscope for a small lab."

That remark raised a red flag for Lucius. The spook tech installed a program that would send an alert if certain words were used in conversations. As time went on, bits and pieces of conversations suggested that the lab would research herbal compatibility with other existing medications. The goal was to find a natural drug to replace manufactured insulin.

The tech played back the conversation for Lucius; he became upset. His first thought was *Simpson's trying to put us out of business. He knows insulin is our cash cow.*

He paced the room as he contemplated his options. One option seemed to solve his problem. If he could steal the natural insulin formula and patent it before McAlister, the business would be set for life.

He knew his father would have nothing to do with stealing the formula. He would have to keep this a secret from Dad.

CHAPTER 6

McAlister's satellite surveillance businesses were growing at an exponential rate. Most of his customers did business in Washington, DC. For the convenience of his customers, he decided to relocate there from New York City. Not surprisingly, office space was at a premium and difficult to find.

A friend in commercial real estate called him and said, "Robert, a commercial building right off the Beltway went up for sale."

Without hesitation Robert said, "Buy it now."

"I thought you might say that, so I put a binder on it this morning. It's yours."

"I appreciate that, sir. Thank you."

Robert began to remodel immediately. He had his trusted assistant, Jacklyn Setter, handle all the details.

Robert thought, *How fortunate I am to have competent employees working for me.*

Weeks later, his secretary buzzed him. "I have the recruiter on the phone. All the biology applicants have been screened and are ready for their final interviews."

"Great. Can you make arrangements to have the interviews held at the new office? And can you ask Jerimiah, Deborah, and Becca to attend the interviews?"

"Yes, sir. I'll take care of your requests."

From hundreds of applicants, Jacklyn had selected ten of the most promising candidates. The final interviews would be conducted by the team.

Interview day arrived, and Robert was in a rare mood. He whistled and hummed as he walked down the hall. He even danced a few steps in the corridor. His dreams were becoming a reality, and he was walking on air.

Deborah, Becca, and Jerimiah were on their way to the conference room when Robert called out, "What a beautiful day!"

Deborah smiled back. "Yes, it is."

"Are you three as excited as I am? Did you do your homework and go through the applicants' files?"

The three said in harmony, "Yes, Mr. McAlister."

Everyone broke up laughing.

The interviews were intense, lasting most of the day. Five exceptional candidates were chosen: Carlton Demmings, biophysicist; Ethan Wesley, microbiologist; Bartley Cummings, ecologist; Claire Simmons, botanist; and Barbara Lewis, herbalist.

Carlton was a thirty-four-year-old single male and a genius in biophysics. He found challenges exciting and never turned one down. Carlton preferred working alone but would agree to work with a partner on occasion. He was a team player but expected his share of the kudos. When he was bored, he would look for other employment, which might have explained his three jobs in four years. Considering all the facts, he still was *the* biologist to have on board.

Ethan, twenty-four years old, was thought to be an oddball nerd—that was an understatement. He carried two pocket protectors, and most of the time, he had a calculator in his hand. He could quickly solve any mathematical problem. If he wasn't working with the calculator, he was peering through a microscope. Ethan did not like crowds or big cities. He enjoyed being on a team and thought of himself as a leader. He might have to adjust to working at McAlister Laboratories, but otherwise he would be a good fit for the organization.

Bartley was thirty-five years old and divorced. He had won many awards and had his work published in several biology journals. Two years ago he had been paralyzed in a skiing accident and was now confined to a wheelchair. He spent every free minute working out or indulging in some sort of physical activity, which kept him in great shape. He was pleasant and courteous and enjoyed participating in team projects or events.

Claire, thirty-two years old, was married with two children. She was a botanist with several degrees. She had also published a book on her research. She had one reservation—moving her family. She planned to sit down with the family and discuss the job offer. "I will get back to you as soon as I know where the family stands."

Barbara, thirty years old and single, was highly respected in the herbal community. People said she could work magic with herbs and plants. She was thrilled about the research and excited to be considered. She was friendly and cheerful. She had some minor health issues, but they were not going concerns. She could start immediately.

CHAPTER 7

With the team now complete, it was time for them to visit their new workplace and home.

The corporate jet circled the futuristic structure. It was dwarfed by giant redwoods and sequoias, deep in the forests of Northern California. The resort, as Robert liked to call it, was finally complete, despite construction delays, material shortages, and the lack of availability of high-tech scientific equipment.

The resort opened its doors to the new residents—the elite team of biologists that had been handpicked for the chance of a lifetime. They were presented with an opportunity to discover medicinal herbal remedies that would change the course of history for mankind. Once a health spa, it now had been given a new life as a high-tech research laboratory. Robert believed that a friendly and relaxing work environment inspired a creative atmosphere where biologists could work, play, and reside in relative comfort. The facility now resembled a private luxury resort / research center.

The chartered jet's wheels screeched as they touched down on a private airfield adjacent to the resort.

The ground crew directed the pilot to a designated position on the asphalt tarmac next to Elaina McAlister's private Gulfstream G-500. The sun's brilliant rays seemed to light up the resort, making it sparkle like the walls were diamond encrusted.

It had been almost two years since construction had commenced. Jerimiah had traveled worldwide with Elaina. She made the introductions to prominent dignitaries; he promoted his "Save the TREEZZ" campaign. Deborah applied for the required permits and certifications. She also ordered the specialized equipment lab supplies. Becca continued studying for her master's degree full time and helped her sister when she could.

Jerimiah, Deborah, and Becca were on hand to greet the new employees. Only three biologists exited the plane. Jerimiah looked at Deborah; she admitted to him, "I had hoped Claire could join us, but conflicts within the family changed her plans. And Barbara had a relapse of her health condition. So now we are six." The three biologists exited the plane, getting the first look at their new home. They were astounded by the ultramodern design. The manicured lawns and landscaping were trimmed to perfection. Robert was a big believer in first impressions.

"Good afternoon, ladies and gentlemen. I'm Clyde Butters, resort manager, and I'd like to welcome you to your new home and workplace. If you would follow me to the lobby, I will show you a three-dimensional map of the complex so that you can orient yourselves. The map will show the building and recreational amenities the facility provides. When you are ready, please follow me through the hall to the cafeteria and enjoy some refreshments." Once the new residents' appetites were sated, the group moved on.

Clyde continued the tour. "May I point out the focal point of the compound: the futuristic design of this circular, domed edifice? This building houses a cutting-edge biology laboratory like nothing the world has ever seen. The lab will be your workplace. Mr. McAlister hopes this unique environment will enhance and inspire many new discoveries. To the left is a heated, crystal-clear Olympic-size swimming pool. Colorful cabanas and spas dot the perimeter. To the right you will see ten private chalets, all aesthetically constructed around the shore of the primeval mountain lake. Tennis and basketball courts are surrounded by a quarter-mile paved track. A complete gym with the latest equipment is available twenty-four hours a day. Should the research become stressful, a massage therapist is on staff to provide relaxing relief for the team. Other buildings contain private penthouses, luxury two-bedroom suites reserved for Mr. McAlister and his close friends."

Clyde circled back and stood in front of the lab. "We saved the best for last." The huge automated double doors opened, triggering a burst of lightning bolts in an array of brilliant colors. Then the roof separated, allowing radiant sunlight to flood the hall. A high-tech, clear shield began to slide into place, protecting the hall from dangerous ultraviolet rays. After the oohs and aahs had ceased, Clyde escorted the group into a decontamination chamber / safe room. The biologists' cheers echoed through the hall. That excitement was followed by applause. Everyone was impressed.

Clyde said, "Your lab is unrivaled, with technical, one-of-a-kind scientific research equipment. The security system is a prototype; its design and specifications are classified."

As the team examined the equipment, three dark figures stood in the shadows, out of sight. Robert, Elaina, and Jerimiah smiled broadly at the scientists' reactions and enthusiasm. It was all Robert had hoped for and more.

Clyde had one more surprise. He pushed the button on a small remote, and the domed ceiling again split apart. This time a laser light show, complete with sound, recreated every natural event on the planet. It was magnificent and took their breath away. Thinking that was the end, the residents were treated to one last revelation. A huge telescope emerged from the floor—a stargazer's dream come true. Cheers rang out again, much to Robert's delight.

There were five doors around the hall's perimeter; each led to a private office, one for each biologist on the team. Robert, Elaina, and Jerimiah materialized from the shadows to the enthusiastic applause of the group. Robert took a bow. "Thank you for your spirited response. I trust that you approve of your new workplace?"

Again thunderous clapping and cheers reverberated through the lab. For the next few days, the residents would enjoy all the amenities the resort had to offer.

Clyde reminded the group to choose their chalets. Becca Carlsbad ran ahead of everyone and quickly claimed the last chalet; Deborah took the adjacent one. All were professionally decorated, and each chalet had its own distinctive theme. The rest of the team didn't seem to care which one they chose; to them, they were all the same. The vacant chalets were for guests.

———

Two days later Robert asked Deborah, Becca, and Jerimiah to join him in his private penthouse.

When they arrived together, Robert said, "Welcome to my home away from home. Sit down and make yourselves comfortable. I'd like to thank you for all your assistance in bringing the lab to fruition. Deborah, I have discussed at length who is best qualified to head the lab, and I'd like to offer you the position. I hope you will accept."

Deborah was completely surprised. "I thought it was already decided that Jerimiah would head the lab?"

Robert remarked, "After much consideration, we feel you are best suited for the job. Your knowledge and prior managerial experience make you the obvious choice."

She looked at Jerimiah, expecting some animosity. He smiled and nodded. "I totally agree. Your experience more than qualifies you for the job."

Deborah was honored by the promotion. "I thank you for the confidence and for your trust. I can assure you that I will do the best I can to lead this elite group of biologists on the challenge of a lifetime. Our discoveries will aid all of mankind."

Robert smiled. "That response just assured me we have made the right decision. I will make myself available day or night should you need my assistance. Also, I believe you will be pleased with your raise."

He looked at Jerimiah and winked. It was quite substantial.

The announcement was made the next day. Everyone seemed pleased that Deborah was now the lead biologist.

Deborah said, "Everyone, let's start saving mankind. Our priority is finding an herbal medicine to replace expensive manufactured insulin. We have two elements in our favor.

One, the boss has a book containing formulas and recipes dating back centuries. Some of the plants have been extinct for quite some time. We need to find replacements for the herbs.

Two, our own Jerimiah Simpson, is a world-renowned plant biologist and an expert in dendrology. He is our go-to man for questions concerning trees." She looked at Jerimiah and smiled.

———

The first week was spent researching plant life associated with diabetes. The team uncovered many formulas, which led to thousands of combinations in the required quantities. After two months without their making much headway, frustration was building—they began to think this might not be as easy as they had first anticipated. Days turned into weeks and weeks into months, and still the elusive formula escaped the biologists.

Finally the team got a break. Deb explained to the group, "Carlton was going through an ancient archive and found a reference to an herb called *ling zhi*. It's found in Alaska at the base of the deciduous trees. It's very rare—only one in ten thousand trees, to be exact. And if we need it, we'd better get there before the snow, as winter's coming on."

Deborah called Jerimiah. "We have a lead on the rare herb ling zhi, found in Alaska. I think we should send you, accompanied by another team member, up there before the snow. I'll make the arrangements."

"I agree with you; I'll start packing," Jerimiah replied excitedly.

Becca overheard the conversation. "Sis, can I go, please? All my work is done here. Please let me go with him."

"OK. As long as your work is complete, you can go."

"Thanks, Sis. I can't believe I'm going to Alaska with Jerimiah."

Deborah cautioned, "This isn't a vacation, and Jerimiah is a coworker. I know you like him, but keep that in mind."

A disappointed Becca hung her head. "Yes, Deb—I mean, Ms. Deborah."

Deborah had chartered a private jet for the two biologists to make the trip to Alaska. It would land at the resort in two hours.

Jerimiah was packed and waiting in the lobby. He looked down the hall and saw Becca and Deborah coming toward him. He quickly ducked into the men's room. *Becca's the last person I want to see—B. B., Boring Becca. Her sister is so hot. This is my chance to talk to her alone, maybe get a date.*

Deborah was a beautiful woman. She had it all—silky blond hair, the face of an angel, and a tall, slim figure with curves in all the right places. Her legs were long and sexy, and she had a great derriere. Men would turn around just to watch her walk by. She could have had any man she wanted, but she had other responsibilities, such as taking care of her sister. She was very protective of Becca. Deborah made sure that Becca didn't go anywhere without her.

Becca walked into the lobby, dragging a duffel bag on a plastic base with three wheels. He thought, *That's strange luggage for Deborah. I would expect her to have the best.*

Deborah walked into the lobby and said, "Have a safe trip, and best of luck finding the herb. Love you, Sis."

He was shocked to realize that Becca, not Deborah, was going with him. He cursed under his breath. "How the heck did I get stuck with Boring Becca? She sure isn't much to look at."

Becca was a plain Jane, with mousy brown hair that she kept in a ponytail. She wore baggy clothes that did nothing to accentuate her athletic figure, and she talked incessantly, which drove Jerimiah crazy.

The manager man picked up Becca and Jerimiah at the lobby and drove the pair up to the waiting chartered jet. The two biologists got on board. Jerimiah took his seat, hoping that Becca would sit in front of or behind him. No such luck. She sat across from him with a big smile. Excitedly, she squeaked, "This is going to be fun, Jerimiah. We might be together for weeks if we don't find the herb."

He lowered his head and groaned to himself. *Just kill me now.*

She chatted nonstop for the next hour and kept calling him "Jer." She was driving him nuts. Finally, he closed his eyes and tried to sleep. As he drifted off, she was still chattering. Sometime later he peeked and found her asleep. Relieved, he relaxed. The flight time into Fairbanks was about five hours.

"This is your pilot speaking. We will be landing in Fairbanks in fifteen minutes."

The blaring announcement jarred Becca awake. "Are we there, Jer?"

He muttered, "Yes, Becca."

"I can't believe we're in Alaska, just you and me. We're going to have a good time."

CHAPTER 8

Snowflakes welcomed Becca and Jerimiah to Alaska. The roads had a light coating of snow. Deborah had reserved a Jeep for the pair. The clerk set the keys down on the counter. Becca immediately grabbed them and began walking toward the vehicle.

Jerimiah barked, "Oh no, you don't. You're not driving. Give me the keys."

Becca adamantly said, "No. Nobody said I couldn't drive, and besides, I'm a good driver."

"Damn you, Becca. You're a pain in the ass. Now give me the keys."

"You think because I'm a girl I can't drive—well, I can."

He tossed the keys to her. "OK, you have the keys—drive."

As Becca drove, Jerimiah had a death grip on the door handle and the edge of his seat.

Becca looked over and laughed. "Are you scared?"

"Damn right, I'm scared."

"Well, watch this." She mashed the accelerator and spun the steering wheel. The vehicle began to do

360-degree turns. Then she skillfully straightened out the vehicle and proceeded to their destination.

"What do you think of that?"

Jerimiah's face was white as a ghost, and he muttered, "Damn, girl, you are a good driver."

Becca proudly replied, "My dad taught me how to drive."

The pair continued to their motel, located in the small town of White Place, where it was reported that the herb ling zhi might be found. It was almost dark when they arrived. There wasn't much to the town, just a few stores, a gas station, and the small motel. He pulled up to the building, went inside, and spoke to the clerk. "Hi. I believe we have reservations for two rooms, probably under Simpson."

The female clerk answered, "None for Simpson, but I do have two rooms for Carlsbad."

"Yes, Carlsbad. That's ours."

"I'm sorry, sir. We had a problem in the second room, so we have only room one available."

"One room for the both of us?" He thought, *Why me, Lord? Why me?*

He asked the clerk, "How cold is it supposed to get tonight? I may just sleep in the car."

"Not too bad, sir, around twenty degrees tonight."

He walked out to the Jeep to give her the bad news. "Becca, we'll have to share a room tonight; the second room is not available."

Delighted by the announcement, she ran from the Jeep, grabbed her bag, and entered the room, where she immediately marked out her side of the bed.

"What's that for?" he queried.

"That's your side, and don't cross it."

"You don't have to worry about that, Becca."

After he'd settled in, he said to her, "I'm going over to the gas station to see what they have to eat."

"That's great. I'll have some chips and dip, two Diet Cokes, a granola bar, maybe two—"

"That's enough, Becca. It's not a supermarket. We'll be lucky to get anything."

A few minutes later, he returned with a shopping bag.

"Wow, you did good, Jer. Let's see what you brought."

"My name is Jerimiah, not Jer."

She pulled out chips, dip, Cokes, four granola bars, and a bag of popcorn. "Let's eat and go to bed."

"You eat. I'm not hungry." He took off his boots, socks, sweater, and shirt and quickly climbed under the covers. He took the extra pillow and put it in the center of the bed.

She left her bra and panties on and quickly jumped into bed.

"You didn't look, did you?"

"Don't worry, I didn't look. Now please go to sleep."

"But I want to talk. I'm not sleepy."

"Well, get sleepy." With that, he pulled the covers over his head.

He thought, *How can two sisters be so different? One gorgeous, the other a plain Jane.*

"You know, Jer, I don't think you like me. I'm always nice to you, but you're never nice to me." She began to sniffle and cry.

"Oh, come on. Don't cry. If you stop crying, I'll be nicer to you."

"Do you promise?"

He groaned. "Yes, I promise."

Cheerfully she said, "Thanks, Jer. Hey, do you wanna play cards? I brought a deck with me."

"No, I think I'll just get some shut-eye."

There was silence for one minute, then she said, "Jer, are you asleep yet? I think I heard something outside."

Groggily he muttered, "It's nothing. Go to sleep."

A few minutes later, she said, "I heard the noise again. There's something out there."

"Becca, it's nothing. Go to sleep."

It was nearly midnight when she shook Jerimiah awake. "Did you hear that?" she asked in a whisper.

This time he did hear something. It sounded like paper rustling or tearing.

He slowly unlocked the door, cracked it, and peered outside. Suddenly two glowing red dots appeared in the dark, followed by a vicious, deep growl. He instantly slammed the door and locked it. The hair on the back of his neck stood up as he shouted, "Holy moly! There's a wolf out there!"

She said, "I told you I heard something."

After they calmed down, he looked around the room and then inside the trash can; it was empty.

"Becca, where did you put the garbage?"

"I put it just outside the…oh my God, I'm sorry. I didn't know. I didn't think…I'm sorry."

"Well, let's be more careful, especially at night."

"You're right, Jer. I'll be more careful."

The next morning Becca was up and looking out the window.

Jerimiah, still in bed, rolled over and asked, "Any wolves out there?"

Becca replied, "None that I can see. Do you think they're gone?"

"Yes, I believe they're gone. It was probably the food that drew them in."

The pair got dressed and went out to the Jeep. Jerimiah handed her the keys. Totally surprised, she looked at him and smiled. He smiled back. With the GPS in his hand, they headed to the last reported sighting of the ling zhi herb.

Arriving at the designated coordinates, the pair split up and began their search. He told Becca that they could never lose sight of each other. If they came across a small stalk sticking out of the light covering of snow, they got down on their knees and gently brushed the snow away to see if it was the ling zhi. Hour after hour, they continued to search, despite being cold and tired. The roar of a snowmobile could be heard approaching in the distance. Jerimiah waved as it sped by them and then disappeared in a cloud of blowing snow.

He said to Becca, "Let's call it a day." Those were the words she had been waiting for. She ran for the Jeep, started it up, and turned on the heat full blast. He jumped in, and they headed for the motel.

They arrived to find that the clerk had chicken-and-rice soup waiting for them. They had been famished. It was as good as any gourmet meal they'd had—maybe better. Both took hot showers and turned in. They were bushed. Becca was asleep in minutes; no noise would wake her that night.

Rising early, they grabbed hot coffee and egg biscuits from the gas station and then continued their search for the elusive herb.

Around two o'clock that afternoon, they heard the snowmobile approaching. This time the rider stopped. "Hey. What are you looking for?"

Jerimiah explained, "We're in search of an herb called ling zhi."

The young man laughed. "Get on, and I'll take you to it." Becca got on behind the operator, and Jerimiah climbed behind Becca. Twenty minutes later, they pulled up to a small house. The young man said, "Come with me." They walked around the back, and there was a pile of ling zhi. The pair looked at each other in disbelief.

Becca cried out, "Can you believe this? We searched for two days, freezing our butts off, and this guy has a pile behind his house."

The young man shrugged. "If you'd asked at the gas station in town, they could have told you I collect the stuff."

They grabbed what they could carry, and the young man took the pair back to their Jeep.

Jerimiah said, "Thank you. Can we give you something for the herbs? We really appreciate your help."

"Naw. I know where there's more." With that, he revved the engine and disappeared into the frozen white landscape.

The pair drove back to the motel, still amazed by what had happened. Jerimiah checked out of the room and drove to the airport, anxious to get back home.

Becca called her sister and excitedly said, "Sis, we got it! We got the ling zhi herb, and we're coming home."

"That's great, Becca. Congratulations on a job well done. Come home, and let me hug you."

A voice in the background called out, "Do the hugs go for me too?"

She laughed. "Of course. You can have a hug, too, Jerimiah. Hurry home safely, and I'll pass on the good news."

Later that evening the chartered jet touched down at the resort. The team was there to greet the searchers. Hugs and high fives abounded. Jerimiah was right behind Becca for his hug from Deborah.

"I've waited a long time for this."

They hugged for a minute. He inhaled deeply, savoring her intoxicating scent. They looked at each other. He had a huge smile on his face. She smiled back and shook her head.

As they walked back to the lab, Becca approached Jerimiah and timidly asked, "Jer, now that we're friends, would you take me out sometime? It doesn't have to be a date. Maybe just for a drink?"

He hastily replied, "I'm going to be tied up with this new herb, so I don't think I'll have the time."

"OK, maybe Friday? That's my birthday, and I'll be twenty-one." With a tempting smile, she winked at him.

He quickly turned away and thought, *Why couldn't she be Deborah?*

Becca was upset by Jerimiah's rejection. She hissed under her breath, "He'll be sorry. I'll show him. Someday he'll want me, but I won't want him."

There was excitement in the air as the team quick-stepped into the lab. Bartley cleared his work area and began dissecting the ling zhi. Ethan and Deborah formulated a solution to liquefy the plant. Carlton ran compatibility tests.

Confident of success, the biologists had a renewed sense of determination. But once again optimism quickly faded; there was still one subtle ingredient missing. The team began to search everywhere for a lead, a clue, anything. Having no luck, the biologists hung their heads, dejected and out of options.

Suddenly Jerimiah had a marvelous thought: *Maybe the TREEZZ can help us. I'll go into the forest and ask for their help.* He jumped up like the place was on fire and ran into the forest without a word to anyone. Ethan tried to follow, but Jerimiah was a man on a mission.

When Jerimiah reached the tree, he looked around to make sure that no one was following. As always, he stood in front of the majestic sequoia. He was greeted by a warm, comforting breeze. He immediately began to absorb information.

He returned with the necessary information. Grinning from ear to ear, he burst into the lab, panting heavily. "I know where the missing herb is."

Deborah sat him down. "Calm down, Jer," she said, adopting Becca's nickname for him, "and catch your breath. Someone get him some water."

After a while he explained, "The herb we need is extinct, but a sealed container of the herb is housed in the Virginia Museum of Natural History in Martinsville. It has been stored there since 1984. It came from a small museum from West Virginia that was destroyed during the Civil War. The herb is silphium, or *silphion.*"

Deborah immediately contacted the museum and explained the urgency regarding the plant. The museum cooperated fully, and the herb was sent via one-day air to the lab. As soon as the package arrived, the team began mixing the exceptional formula, working feverishly into the night. They were so close that they couldn't stop now. At the bewitching hour of midnight, the test results were positive: the team had formulated the first oral herbal insulin ever.

As Deborah gathered all the data relating to the drug, she thought, *I'm glad only two team members, Becca and Ethan, have the complete formula. That will help keep it safe.* There was no urgent need for that information. They could give it to her in the next few days.

The lab still had more tests to run on the formula, as required before FDA approval, but that was just a formality and of course required a ton of paperwork.

Euphoric, Jerimiah met Robert in the lobby; he remarked, "You're now the owner of the first herbal insulin ever formulated."

"I can't tell you how proud I am of our team. Free insulin for all humanity—my dream has materialized, thanks to an elite group of dedicated scientists."

CHAPTER 9

Lucius listened intently to the conversation between Robert and Jerimiah. It rang in his ears: "You're now the owner of the first herbal insulin."

His father listened too. Lucius remarked, "Now what do you think, Dad? If we don't do something drastic, we're doomed. We'll be out of business."

Clay, looking pale, asked his son, "Do you have something in mind?"

"If we could copy the formula, we could rush it to the patent office. Then it would be ours."

"McAlister doesn't seem to be in any hurry. I'd say we have a week, maybe two."

Lucius's eyes got big, and he jumped up from his chair. "I got it. We'll hire an expert to steal the formula, but it must be done quickly."

"That's a great idea. Nobody gets hurt, right?"

"Nobody gets hurt."

"But how do we go about hiring someone?"

"We'll use a third party."

"OK, let's give it a try."

"I'm glad you agree, Dad. I'll take care of everything. I want to keep you out of this should something go awry."

That night, on the dark web and using a third party, an ad was placed for someone experienced with industrial espionage. The IP addresses were untraceable. Within hours three people had answered the ad.

Lucius was now faced with a bigger problem: "How do we choose the right crook?"

Lucius decided to ask for references, although he really didn't think that would work. A friend of a friend gave him a name: Mr. B. He told Lucius, "Whatever you do, don't double-cross this guy, and pay him quickly. He's a very dangerous man."

Lucius Lattimore decided to make an offer to Mr. B. On a secure, encrypted satellite phone, negotiations began. Lucius explained the situation and gave as much detail as possible. Mr. B. quoted a price of $300,000 and said he would get the formula. Both Clay and Lucius gasped at the cost.

Mr. B. growled, "Don't bullshit me, boys. You know the patent is worth twice that. And another thing: I do it my way. You have no say in my methods. Understood?"

Clay asked, "No one will be hurt, right?"

Mr. B. laughed. "Of course not. I wouldn't hurt a fly."

Lucius inquired, "How long do you think it will take?"

"I figure a few days. Maybe a week."

Lucius said, "We have an agreement."

Mr. B. noted, "I don't think I have to remind you, once you have the formula, the money will be immediately transferred into my account, or I will kill you and your family."

Lucius went home, made himself dinner, watched TV, smiled, and slept like a baby.

Clay went home to his wife. She said that dinner would be ready in a few minutes. He answered, "I'm not hungry, dear. Eat without me."

"Are you OK, Clay?" she asked.

"I'm all right, just tired. I'm going to bed."

Clay didn't sleep a wink; he was having second thoughts about the dastardly deed he was part of. He felt like he'd made a deal with the devil.

———

Robert had a prototype security system installed in the resort complex; his technicians thought the resort would be the perfect place to test it. While completing the installation, a tech uncovered a McAlister Industries listening device.

The tech called Robert. "We discovered a listening device hidden in the lobby. It looks like it was installed during the remodeling." The tech laughed. "Were you spying on yourself?"

Robert thought for a minute. He didn't recall giving anyone permission to install that type of device. "Send it to our lab, and have them trace the owner. Then call me with the ID."

The tech called an hour later. "Sir, the device was sold in a spook shop located in San Francisco. The buyer paid cash."

Robert was very concerned. He wondered why someone would eavesdrop on the resort, especially in the lobby. The most valuable asset the lab had was its biology team. Suddenly it hit him. *The insulin formula. But only two biologists have the complete formula, and they've never discussed it with any other team member, let alone outside the lab.*

It didn't add up.

He called Deborah and Jerimiah into his suite. "I'll explain the situation, and you tell me what you think." Robert conveyed the story and waited patiently for their assessment.

Deborah spoke first. "I can only surmise that someone wants information they believe we have. The insulin formula is the only asset of value; it's worth a fortune if you think about it."

Jerimiah countered, "One good thing is that no one has spilled the beans about anything, or they wouldn't have a bug planted."

Robert smiled. "Thank you for making a positive point. Do you feel that we can or should take any precautions?"

Deborah suggested, "Maybe we should ask an expert their opinion?"

"That is an excellent suggestion, Deborah," Robert said.

"I second the idea," Jerimiah said.

Robert knew just the man for the job—his old friend was the best when it came to personal protection and corporate security.

Robert made the call, but it went straight to voice mail. "You've reached Vic Bowden. I am out of the country on business. Please leave your name and number. I will return your call when I can."

"Hi, Vic; it's Robert McAlister. Call me, please. It's urgent."

CHAPTER 10

Deborah wanted to have a party on Thursday to celebrate the team's success, as well as Becca's twenty-first birthday. The local deli catered the delicious food, and the bakery made a coconut layer cake, a party favorite.

The team enjoyed the feast and began dancing.

Becca was standing with her sister. Jerimiah figured this was a good time to ask Deborah to dance. He made eye contact and walked toward her. He didn't see Becca's big smile. He walked up to the sisters and asked, "May I have this dance?"

Deborah was ready to accept when Becca cut in. "Yes, you may."

The disappointment was written all over his face. *Will I ever get to be alone with Deborah?* The two danced across the floor. Becca was in heaven, and he was in hell.

———

Friday arrived, and Becca's absence from the lab was noticed.

Deborah reassured the group that Becca was fine. "She just needed a personal day."

For her twenty-first birthday, Deborah had bought her sister a complete makeover. It wasn't that Becca wasn't pretty; she just didn't seem to care about her personal appearance—she wore hardly any makeup. She contended, "It's too much work, and nobody pays any attention anyway." But she really felt she needed a change, and this was an opportunity to make that change—Becca would do anything she wanted. The spa offered some suggestions, but a girl her age said, "Let me do you over, Becca. You'll love it."

Becca nervously agreed. The girl began the make-over. Five hours later the new Becca made her appearance. The attendants and patrons alike gasped at the change. She certainly wasn't the girl who had walked in five hours ago. Her straight brown hair was now a short, spiky blond. Multicolored fingernails. Tight black leather pants. Black-and-white sneakers with pink laces. A white T-shirt and a military surplus field jacket. One might have described her attire as borderline punk.

Deborah anxiously waited for Becca to return home.

A horn honked. *Beep, beep.* "Deb, I'm home."

Becca jumped out of the car. Deborah stood on the porch in shock. "Oh my God!" she exclaimed. "You look so young; you could pass for a teenager."

Becca danced around in circles. "It's the new me—don't you just love it? Well, Sis, do you like it?"

Deborah was still recovering from the initial shock. "Well, Becca, it is different—I'll say that. But the question is, do you like it?"

"Yes, I do. I know it's a bit outrageous, but I'm comfortable with it."

"Good for you."

"Do you think Jer will like it?"

"I don't believe it's his style, but you never know."

"Well, it's too bad if he doesn't like it."

Deb smiled as she looked Becca up and down.

Becca asked cautiously, "What are you looking at? What is it?"

Deb said, "I never really looked at your butt, not that you ever wore anything to accentuate it. But, girl, you have a great butt. Not much in the boobs department, but a great butt and long, sexy legs."

"Do you really think so?"

"Oh yeah—you'll get looks now."

CHAPTER 11

As expected, Jerimiah cringed when he first saw her. But with those snug jeans, his eyes went straight to her curvy butt; he couldn't take his eyes off that tight little butt. In no time he accepted her new look and complimented her on the change. Whatever. This was Becca—take her or leave her alone. The rest of the team thought her transformation was perfect and congratulated her. She was very comfortable in her new skin.

Two weeks later Robert returned from his business trip. As always, after such trips, he went to the lab to say hi to his favorite person, Deborah. Becca happened to be in her office. Robert knocked on the open door. "I'm sorry—I didn't see you had a visitor. I'll come back later."

Deborah called, "Robert, get back here."

"I didn't want to disturb you and your visitor."

"Robert, this is Becca."

He looked at Becca and then looked back at Deborah. "Becca, is that you? Oh my, yes—it is you. You're so different."

"Do you like it, Mr. McAlister?"

"Let me look at you for a moment. Now turn around. Yes, I do believe I like it. You're so modern."

Deborah interrupted. "Becca, that's a compliment."

"Really? Thanks, Mr. McAlister."

"Becca, call me Robert."

"OK, Robert."

After Becca left, Deborah said to Robert, "I was afraid you would disapprove of her new look."

"Quite the contrary. I respect an individual's personal choices. Actually, I like her new look. It's just she looks so young."

"I will admit, she does look younger."

———

The lab was tasked with producing the herbal insulin in a concentrated form to achieve the volume required. It wasn't as easy as doubling the contents. The quantities had to be exponentially increased. Deb left the task in the capable hands of Ethan, the mathematician, and Bartley, the ecologist.

As far as compatibility, there were no adverse side effects during human cell testing.

———

Robert and Elaina had completed their business negotiations with several foreign countries. They were looking to spend some time at the resort relaxing and getting better acquainted with the team. They wanted to personally congratulate each and every member.

After the pleasantries, Robert announced, "I invite you all to join me for dinner tonight in the hall to celebrate your success."

A local company was hired to make all the arrangements, including the catering and entertainment. As expected, the team was thrilled to be socializing with one of the wealthiest men in the world, their esteemed boss. The festivities began at 6:00 p.m. with the band playing some mellow dinner music. The attendees were dressed in their best. The men wore sport coats with ties. Elaina was stunning in a sparkling cocktail dress. Deborah was elegant in a long white gown slit to mid-thigh. Becca had on a white long-sleeve shirt with a red skirt and black boots. She looked cute.

Robert tapped his glass. "Excuse me, friends. Through your tireless efforts, my dream to create a free herbal insulin medication for mankind has come true. This brilliant group of scientists has worked a miracle, a miracle that will bring people's suffering to an end, and it's free. I thank you all from the bottom of my heart. With that said, enjoy your dinner and stay safe. Just one more small item."

He handed everyone a white envelope. They opened the envelopes to find checks for $10,000. "Let's enjoy dinner and stay safe."

The food was superb and the desserts to die for. The band began to increase the tempo, and the guests moved onto the dance floor. The men lined up to dance with Elaina and Deborah. Robert noticed this and made a point to ask Becca to dance. "My dear, may I have this dance and the next one?"

Becca smiled broadly. "Yes, you may, Robert." He took her hand and led her to the dance floor.

A slow dance began to play. Becca looked at Robert. He held out his hand; she smiled. She took his hand, and instantly a magical connection was made. He experienced the same sensation—a feeling they had never felt before. It was as though their feet never touched the floor. They glided gracefully like they were the only two people in the room.

Deb watched her sister dancing with Robert and smiled, thinking, *He is the most considerate man I know.*

———

Robert was now alone in his suite with just his thoughts. *My gamble on a young team has paid off, not to mention just how much the world will benefit from this discovery. Some companies might see a reduction in profits, but that should inspire them to move on to bigger and more lucrative commodities.* Robert's look of contentment suddenly turned to one of concern. He thought, *Stay safe—was that a Freudian slip? Is my team in danger? Would someone try to harm them to get this formula?*

Robert, now fearful, knew the competitive and ruthless world of pharmaceuticals. Companies would stop at nothing to protect their huge profits, including stealing formulas and eliminating the competition by any means necessary. Robert whispered to himself, "Maybe I'm just an alarmist." He thought again about the urgent call he'd placed to Vic and wondered why he hadn't yet returned it. He hoped his friend was all right.

Robert's phone rang early the next morning.

"Did I wake you up? I hope so. I know you billionaires sleep late."

In a tense voice, Robert blurted, "Vic, thank God you called. I think my people…I think my team…"

"Robert, calm down, and take a deep breath. Now slowly tell me what's wrong."

"Vic, we're at the resort, and I think harm may come to my team."

Victorio Bowden, now forty-two years old, was still fit. At six feet five, he was a formidable opponent. He also was an accomplished assassin with several long-distance kills under his belt. Although now retired from the NSA, he'd been trained in all forms of hand-to-hand combat. He could disarm someone in the blink of an eye, or he could be a teddy bear, soft and cuddly. The last part was a rumor, as only two people could verify this: Elaina and Robert. Because of the nature of his prior undercover operations and the tragic nature in which he'd lost Alicia, he had never remarried.

Robert went into detail about the dire situation and then asked Vic, "What do you think?"

The retired agent hesitated. "Robert, give me a day to touch base with my contacts, and I'll get back to you."

Robert detected a touch of apprehension in Vic's voice, which worried him.

Early the next day, Vic called back. No pleasantries were exchanged, which wasn't good. "Robert, we need to move quickly. Double your security staff, have the biologists confined to the compound, and have security escort them wherever they go."

The philanthropist's heart pounded in fear upon hearing the urgency in his friend's voice. Robert nervously asked, "Is it that serious?"

Vic answered sternly, "I'm afraid it is. The word on the dark web is that a fortune was just offered to an assassin known as Mr. B. if he can obtain 'the formula,' and I guess you know what formula that would be."

Robert was stunned. "Will you help us? I feel terrible that I put my team in danger. What can we do?"

Vic replied with regret, "To be honest, I'm worried. We're a day late, but maybe we can catch up. I need to get to the resort as soon as possible. Another precaution we should take is to have a hypnotist stand by at the resort. I'll call you later with the details."

Robert was puzzled. *A hypnotist?* Whatever the reason, he trusted Vic's instincts. "Elaina's corporate jet is at your disposal. Whatever it takes, you have carte blanche."

As the G-5 flew back to the resort, Vic hastily reviewed information on the lab's research and team members and the resort's blueprints. He needed to hit the ground running; there was no time for preparation.

Vic had an uncanny ability to inhabit the criminal mindset. This was what made him a very dangerous adversary. He thought, *We're a day late, maybe more. My gut is telling me that Mr. B. is already two steps ahead of me.*

He knew of Mr. B., who was considered one of the most dangerous men in the world. At six feet four, Mr. B. was a big man; he was 250 pounds of muscle. His face looked as if it were chiseled from granite. His eyes appeared to be black holes. He never showed emotion and never smiled. He was a ruthless assassin, sadistic and cunning. His hobby was gambling, and his women were fifty-dollar whores.

Vic's assessment of Mr. B was correct. The dangerous villain needed to attain two crucial facts to execute his plan. First, he needed to identify the biologists working on the insulin project. They would have the complete formula. Second, he needed to extract the insulin formula from the biologists by any means.

To identify the two biologists, Mr. B. sent a phony parcel driver to the resort. A brown parcel truck stopped at the front gate at exactly 11:55 a.m. The timing was critical; it had to be precise. The fictitious parcel driver told the guard, "I have a delivery for…" The driver showed the guard a smudged name on the envelope. He indicated that it had gotten wet and apologized. Just then, Bartley Cummings came rolling by in his wheelchair. This was his routine every day, and he was very punctual. Mr. B. was counting on this.

The guard called him over. "Hey, Bart, maybe you can help this guy."

The driver showed Bartley the smudged envelope. He looked at the smear and then at the return address. "The return address is a medical company dealing with insulin products, so it must be for Becca or Ethan."

The driver thanked him for the information and was allowed to pass through. He went through the motions but never delivered any envelope. The driver grinned as he called Mr. B. "I got the names, boss: Becca and Ethan."

On the opposite side of the lake, one of Mr. B.'s men looked through a pair of binoculars. He watched intently as the biologists returned home. He noted the chalet numbers for each member of the team. With pictures in hand, he identified the pair and circled their chalet numbers. Now they knew where the biologists lived. The voyeur quickly called Mr. B. and gave him the information.

Just before dawn, two scuba divers swam across the lake. This was done to avoid the security sensors. They came ashore beside the chalets. They waited in the shallow reeds of the lake for just the right moment to attack.

Suddenly, the resort was put on alert. A wildfire had suspiciously ignited and was heading their way. Great billows of white smoke could be seen in the distance. The wildfire had been intentionally started by Mr. B.'s men to distract and confuse the security at the resort. The forest service put the resort on standby to evacuate at a moment's notice if the fire threatened them. Around ten o'clock that morning, the evacuation order was issued. Each biologist was escorted by security to their chalet to retrieve their important belongings and then taken to a waiting van.

Elaina's G-500 approached the resort's private airfield, lowered its landing gear, and touched down. The pilot pointed out to the VIP passenger the nearby wildfire. The fire immediately raised his suspicions. As the jet rolled to a stop, the brawny man jumped from the jet and ran up to the guard at the front gate.

He presented his credentials. "Vic Bowden, security specialist, assigned to the resort by Mr. McAlister."

With prior notification of Mr. Bowden's arrival, the guard opened the gates, and he was allowed to pass into the resort. He ran to the lobby office and burst through the double doors. He identified himself to Clyde, the manager. "Vic Bowden. Where are the biologists?"

Clyde, startled by the ex-agent's sudden entry, stuttered, "The...the biologists are...are being evacuated right now."

At that exact moment, two scuba divers exited the lake. Amid the thick smoke and chaos, the attackers assaulted and drugged the guards and the two biologists. The semiconscious biologists were dragged into the waters of the lake.

At the same time, Vic ran back to the front gate just as four helitankers from the forest service hovered over the lake, filling their water buckets before proceeding directly to the suspicious wildfire.

As they did this, the air traffic controller conversed with the forestry helitankers. "Helio one, you reported three choppers assigned to the resort fire. Over."

"Ten-four, control. Three buckets. Over."

"Helio one, I have four buckets over the lake. Over."

"Helio one, we sure won't send him home. I guess we have four buckets. Over."

"Control, this is bucket four. I have a low oil pressure alarm. I'm setting down in the old quarry. I'll wait there for the mechanics. Over."

"Ten-four, bucket four. Over and out."

Bucket four was a stolen helitanker. It hovered over the lake, allowing the scuba divers to put the drugged biologists into the water bucket of the chopper. The divers were next to get into the bucket. The pilot flew to the nearby abandoned quarry, where a waiting van took the biologists to an unknown location. The kidnapping had been a success.

Vic ran to the van loading the resort's occupants. He yelled over the choppers' whirling blades, "Is everyone accounted for?"

The driver shouted back, "We're missing four passengers." Vic quickly looked around and saw the chalets near the lake. Running in that direction, he searched for any signs of the missing biologists. As he got closer, he saw two security guards lying on the ground. Both had been beaten up pretty bad and drugged. He signaled the remaining security guards for help with their injured colleagues, and they were evacuated.

In the smoke and confusion, Vic glanced up to see a helitanker with a bucket heading in the opposite direction of the fire. *Strange*, he thought. But he was too busy to dwell on it. With everyone else safely evacuated from the resort, he sat down with his head in his hands. *Damn, a few minutes earlier, and I could have foiled the kidnapping.* He yelled loudly in frustration, "Just a few damn minutes!"

He looked around the vacant complex cloaked in smoke. How was he going to tell Robert that he'd failed and that members of his team were in peril? Reluctantly, he made the dreaded call.

Robert immediately picked up the phone. "Is everyone safe?"

Vic responded with regret, "I'm so sorry, Robert. I failed you. I failed the team. I lost two members. I'm so sorry."

"Don't blame yourself. It was my fault for being naive and not more concerned with my team's safety. What can we do now?"

Vic said sadly, "If you still want me, I'll start looking for answers."

"Of course I still want you. You're the only man who can bring my people home alive. Do whatever is necessary. Use every piece of technology my organizations have, and spare no expense. Just please bring them back safely."

Vic expressed his gratitude. "Thanks for your confidence. I'll bring them home."

CHAPTER 12

The heroic efforts of the firefighters brought the wildfire under control around the resort, but the fire still raged in the nearby valleys.

Elaina and Jerimiah were in the McAlister building in Washington, DC, compiling a list of applicants for the foundation's grants. They had been at it for days.

Elaina stretched. "Jer, let's take a break and get a hot dog from the vendor in front of the building." Becca's use of the nickname had spread to everyone.

He smiled. "Great idea."

The pair ordered their hot dogs and sat on a bench in front of the many oak trees that lined the street. Munching on the delicious food and looking at the beautiful tree, Jerimiah thought, *I'm sorry I've neglected you, my friends. My apologies.* The TREEZZ's response sent chills up his back and placed a look of fear on his face: "There is a wildfire near your mom's house."

His expression told Elaina something was wrong. "What's the matter, Jer? Tell me."

His voice cracked. "There's a wildfire near my mom's house."

Elaina jumped up, her phone already in her hand. "You call your mom, and I'll call Vic."

Jerimiah got a recording. "The cell tower for this number is temporarily out of service due to the recent wildfire." His next call was to the forest service.

Elaina had better luck with Vic. "Hi, Vic. We heard there's a wildfire near Jer's mother's house. Do you know anything?"

Vic was surprised. "No, I don't, but there's one raging here, and with their house so close by, it could have reached them by now. I'll get right over there."

"Thanks, Vic."

"Forest service, emergency line."

"This is Todd Bailey's son. Is there a wildfire near his house?"

"I'll check, Jerimiah...I don't have a report of one. Hold on, and I'll transfer you to the fire tower."

"Fire tower three. Can I help you?"

"This is Todd Bailey's son. Do you see signs of a wildfire in the vicinity of Todd's house?"

Tower three responded, "I'm looking right now. We've had a low cloud cover for the last three hours, so it's difficult to see any smoke. Hold on, Jerimiah. I see possible smoke rising above the cloud cover. I'll send a crew—code one."

Elaina called the pilots of the G-5. "We need to get to the resort ASAP."

Meanwhile, Vic drove the truck like he had stolen it. As he rounded a curve on the way to Mattie's house, he jammed his foot down on the brake pedal, locking up the tires. He slid to a stop right before a burning tree that was blocking the road. There was no doubt that this was a wildfire.

He called 911. "I'm reporting a wildfire on Bear Basin Road. Access is blocked in both directions. We have a residence two miles westbound of my location, which is 41-48-59 North, 123-48-27 West."

A forest service helicopter briefly saw the house, but the smoke was too thick for him to land. Vic attempted to walk there, but the unpredictable winds forced him back.

Todd's supervisor called to check on him, but there was no answer.

Standing on his porch, Todd saw the thick smoke heading toward the house. He clutched Mattie and kissed her. "Don't worry, dear. We've gotten through the fires before, and we'll get through them again." Todd's tone was reassuring, but his face was etched with dire concern. The couple took another look at the intense flames. This time their luck had run out. The intense heat drove them indoors. The interior of the house was bathed in a reddish-orange glow from the flaming inferno. In desperation Todd began to fill more plastic containers with water while Mattie soaked several blankets. The blankets would cover them and filter the smoke to ease their breathing. Suddenly, the water from the tap slowed to a drip. Mattie looked at Todd, wondering what had happened. Todd threw a wet blanket over himself and ran toward the generator. He placed his hand on top of it, but it was still; there was no vibration. The lifesaving generator had stopped. He glanced at the fuel gauge; it was empty.

Todd's heart sank. The four commercial sprinklers placed strategically on each roof corner to continuously drench the home with water stopped spraying. It had been their last resort to save themselves and their home from the deadly firestorm.

Todd ran back inside. The blanket he was wearing had completely dried from the heat. The couple huddled in the bathroom, where the tub was full of water.

Mattie looked at Todd with tears streaming down her face.

Todd said, "Don't cry, Mattie. If it's God's will, we'll make it."

She said, "Oh, Todd, I'm not crying because it's the end. My tears are tears of joy for all the good years we've had together. I had hoped there would be a few more, but I won't be greedy."

"Mattie, I love you so much. If we must go, I want to be right by your side." They embraced.

Loud crackling and heavy smoke began to filter into the home, and the elderly couple started to cough.

Outside the house, through the thick smoke, two vines crept toward the structure. The vines slithered up the side of the foundation, forcing the electrical box open. One vine attached itself to a black wire and the other to a white wire. Sparks flew as hundreds of volts charged the electrical fuse panel. Within a minute, the well pump activated and began to feed water to the roof sprinklers. Todd raised his head and looked up at the skylight to speak to the Lord. He blinked and then blinked again.

"Impossible!" he exclaimed. "That can't be water droplets hitting the skylight. I guess I'm really gone, or this is a miracle." He nudged his wife. "Look up, Mattie. Do you see water hitting the skylight?"

"I do. Can this be true? Is it really happening?"

The couple got up and went to the kitchen door, where they looked out the window. Sure enough, the sprinklers had extinguished any stray cinders—the thankful couple had been saved, along with their beloved chalet.

Vic looked to the heavens and prayed for Jerimiah's parents. No one could have survived that fire. Now the overcast sky released its bounty of rain. After dragging the fallen tree out of the way, Vic jumped into his truck and raced to their home. All he saw was charred and blackened earth. His head hung low as he turned into the Baileys' driveway. He looked ahead, and his mouth fell open. There was the house, standing amid the destruction, with just a few singed spots where the flames had licked it. He opened the truck door and ran for the house as the two occupants graciously welcomed him.

Vic said, "Let's get you back to the resort until the forest service deems the area safe."

———

Jerimiah asked the pilot of the G-5, "If it's safe, can you circle the resort? I should be able to see my parents' house."

"I'll give it a try, Jerimiah."

The plane circled, but the smoke was thick. The pilot made one more pass. All aboard strained to see any sign of a chalet; all they saw was smoke. The jet had the runway in sight and landed at the resort. Jerimiah looked out the jet's window and smiled as his tears flowed. There stood his parents, safe and sound.

Jerimiah ran from the plane and hugged his mom and dad like he had never hugged them before.

That evening Jerimiah went to visit his old friends. He walked into the majestic sequoia. Tears filled his eyes as he sobbed. "I owe you a debt of gratitude I can never repay. Thank you so much for saving my parents." As he looked around, all he saw were smiles—hundreds of thousands of smiles embedded in the bark of the trees.

In the world of TREEZZ that was their way of saying, "You're welcome." Another mystical, magical moment.

A few days later, the forest service allowed the residents to return to the few homes that had survived. Vic and Jerimiah drove Mattie and Todd back to their house. Mattie immediately began to clean up. Todd was anxious to understand why the generator had suddenly come to life to produce electricity for the well pump. Vic looked at the propane tank; it was definitely empty. The three men then looked at the electrical box. The main feed had obvious arcs where some type of power connection had been made. Vic and Todd looked at Jerimiah.

The young man said, "Don't look at me. It was the TREEZZ."

CHAPTER 13

Upon returning to the resort, the residents were afraid and confused, and rightfully so. They had trouble comprehending the reason for the kidnapping of their friends—no, their *family*. This type of tragedy happened to other people, not to them. It was a nightmare they constantly relived. Vic knew they were longing for some sort of information and assurance that everything would be all right.

Deborah took it especially hard. She was terrified that her sister and Ethan would be harmed or worse. It devastated her to think that she might never see Becca again.

The team gathered for the regular morning meeting. Vic offered to speak to the group. "Hello, team. My name is Vic Bowden, and I'm a retired agent for the National Security Agency. I want you all to know that I am an expert in situations like this. There is a very good chance that we will get them back safely."

In a calm and reassuring tone, Vic explained to the team what had happened and why. "Once the kidnappers get the information they want, they'll let them go."

Vic failed to inform them that he was also an expert at lying, and he did so now in a most convincing way.

He said to the group, "Please write down any details that you feel are pertinent to the investigation, no matter how insignificant they may seem. Robert has given me carte blanche to do whatever is necessary to get our people back. And that is just what I intend to do."

Vic was upbeat and positive, giving them hope. He wished he had the same measure of confidence; unfortunately, he didn't. Felons didn't leave witnesses.

Vic took Deborah aside and tried to comfort her. She was the one who needed it most. He asked, "Is there anything I can do? Would you like to go back to your chalet?"

Tearfully she whimpered. "Yes, but please stay with me. I don't want to be alone right now."

Vic understood. "I'll stay with you as long as you like." He walked her to her chalet and then asked her to wait outside. "I'll check the inside just to be safe." The home was clear. "Deborah, it's safe to come in."

Once there, she immediately curled up in the corner of her couch, dabbing her eyes with a tissue. He knelt in front of her and held her hand. She was trembling. He moved up next to her, putting his muscular arm around her. She was exhausted, having barely slept since the kidnapping. Resting her head on his shoulder, she fell asleep. He looked down at this beautiful woman curled up next to him. It had been a long time since he'd comforted someone in distress. He felt true compassion for her, a feeling he had buried inside him many years ago when Alicia died. Slowly he relaxed, and his eyes closed.

Hours later Vic twitched, jolting himself awake. He slowly slid his arm away from Deborah, trying not to wake her.

He quietly tiptoed to the front porch and watched the beautiful sunrise over the lake. It was hard to believe a terrifying event had taken place there yesterday.

He began planning his next move but then heard a noise behind him. Before he could think, his hand was on his weapon. He turned to find Deborah, wrapped in a blanket and barefoot. Softly she asked, "Do you mind if I join you?"

"Not at all." Then she handed him a hot cup of coffee and gave a slight smile to go with it. That was the first time he had seen her smile. It was a warm and friendly smile; he would never forget it.

"Thank you. Right now there is nothing I need more than this cup of coffee."

They watched the fog-shrouded sunrise. Both relished the serenity of the dawn. Not a word was spoken.

Eventually he broke the silence. "I have to go to work. Will you be all right here? I can get security if you'd like."

"Thank you, but I think I'll be fine. I'm sorry I was a bother. I'm sure you had better things to do than babysit me." She turned away from him and began to tear up.

"Deborah, I promise you that I'll bring Becca and Ethan home safely."

She fell into his arms. "Vic, I don't know what I'd do if something happened to my little sister."

He held her tightly, stroking the back of her silky blond hair. "It will be OK. I'll bring them home." He released her as they both walked to the door. "Thank you for the great cup of coffee. Would you mind if I check on you this evening?"

"Please do—I'd like that." He looked into her eyes; he was mesmerized by her beauty. "Vic, Vic, are you OK?"

"I'm sorry. I seem to have drifted off somewhere. Strange...I have never had that happen before."

Deborah remarked, "You probably need sleep. See you tonight."

He walked to the lobby, thinking how nice it had felt to comfort someone in need. Once there Vic went straight to the fresh-brewed coffee for a second cup. He sat down and went through the notes the team had written but came up empty. The next action was to interrogate the security personnel at the resort. Coming up empty again, he drove to the hospital in Crescent City. The tall medical building overlooked the city marina and its many boats. From the nurses' station, he got the room number of the two injured security guards. He walked in with two bouquets of flowers; this was a rare occurrence for him. He couldn't remember the last time he had given someone flowers. He thought, *I'm getting too sentimental in my old age.*

After the introductions and pleasantries, Vic questioned the guards, having obtained the doctor's permission. Karen Reagan had a fractured arm, and Susan Lloyd had two broken ribs.

"Ladies, do you think you could answer a few questions? Did you notice any labels on the kidnappers' clothing? Any odd smells, tattoos, accents, glasses, or anything that might be a clue?" They came up with zero. There hadn't been much to identify, with the perpetrators in scuba gear.

After taking notes and some more small talk, Vic asked the female guards, "Do you need anything?"

Karen asked sheepishly, "Do you think we could get a telescope? We'd love to look out at the boats."

He said, "Sure thing. I'll bring one with me tomorrow."

He looked out the window at the marina below. All types of boats dotted the harbor. One beautiful yacht stood out; it was anchored about two miles off the coast. Vic figured that it was probably too large for the marina slips. It must have been ninety or a hundred feet long. *That lucky dog*, he thought. He dismissed his daydreams and got back to business.

Vic now had to think like a criminal—to be specific, a criminal like Mr. B. *Where would I go if I wanted to hide out for a while with two unwilling guests? A very remote area, but coming and going in a remote area draws attention from the locals.* Maybe the felon had rented an RV and was traveling, never in one place longer than a day. If so, he would be very hard to track.

In reality, Mr. B. was a superstitious man. He believed in curses, spells, and strange events. All things were omens—some bad, some good. He had heard whispers about the TREEZZ and how some people had kinships with them. He wasn't going to take any chances, so he would avoid the TREEZZ if possible. He needed a location where he could extract the formula from the biologists without causing a stir. A place where he would not be bothered but where he could come and go without drawing attention. Mr. B. made his decision; he chose a location right under everyone's noses.

Mr. B. smiled at his plan to hide in plain sight. It was the perfect place to extract the formula from the kidnapped biologists and dispose of the bodies so they would never be found.

———

Vic was on his way back to the resort when he received a call from a surveillance company tech. "Vic, we may have a lead on Mr. B. It seems he likes to gamble. We picked up some chatter that a Mr. B. may be in town this week for a high-stakes poker game. We're working on a location."

"Great!" Vic said excitedly. "Stay with it, and good work." His phone rang again. "Hi, Robert. How are you?"

"I'm probably better than you."

Vic grunted. "I've had better weeks. We're not making much progress."

"I just want to tell you how comforting it is to have you here. I have complete faith in you, and I know that you'll do everything in your power to bring our biologists home. I understand that you stayed with Deborah last night. Thank you for your concern. She is one of the nicest people I have ever met. Is there anything you need?"

"Thanks, Robert, but I'm good for now." As soon as Vic returned to the complex, he went straight to Deborah's chalet and knocked gently on her door. She was still barefoot and wrapped in her blanket, just like he'd left her. "Come in. I apologize for my appearance. I don't have much motivation."

"Deborah, you look fine."

"Thank you, but I know I don't. Is there any news?"

Vic's shoulders slumped, and in a low voice, he said, "I'm afraid not."

She went back to the couch, pulled her blanket snugly, and curled up in the corner with a tissue and a blank stare, looking out the window.

Vic asked, "Is there anything I can do?"

"Sit by me. I feel safe when you're near."

He sat down next to her. They both watched the sunset bringing another day to an end. In the darkness she again rested her head on Vic's shoulder. Soon she was sleeping peacefully. He gently put his brawny arm around her, trying not to disturb her. He looked at her sleeping. He wanted to keep looking at this lovely woman, but her tranquility relaxed him, and he, too, fell into a deep sleep.

———

Vic's built-in alarm clock woke him just before dawn like it did every day. Quietly, he slipped off the couch and went outside on the front porch to await the sunrise. In a half daze, he thought he heard the voice of an angel purr, "Would you like a cup of coffee?"

He turned to see Deborah handing him a cup. She poured a cup for herself and joined him on the porch. Both enjoyed the fresh-brewed coffee. Together they watched the bright orange sun ascend above the eastern mountain tops. He turned and looked at her in the glow of the morning sunlight. Her shimmering blond hair was tangled and tossed. Her eye makeup was dried on her cheeks, yet she still appeared beautiful. Vic thought, *She is so beautiful, her radiance glowing in the morning light. I'm beginning to develop feelings for this woman.*

After a time she asked softly, "Do you think we'll get Becca and Ethan back soon?"

"I won't rest until you and Becca are reunited. That's my promise."

With a slight smile, she looked into his eyes. At that moment he thought, *I would do anything for this special woman.* He asked, "Is there anything I can do for you?"

She sighed. "I don't know. I don't know anything right now." She began to cry. He took her in his arms and held her gently. "I'm sorry—"

He interrupted her. "You go right ahead and cry."

She sobbed even harder. He looked at her; she was like a helpless little girl, vulnerable and afraid and clinging to him. He tried to be strong for her, but the sight of her anguish brought him to tears. He felt so helpless; there was nothing he could do to comfort this woman.

One of his tears fell on her hand.

She looked up at him and said remorsefully, "Now look what I've done. I have you crying too."

He countered, "Some lingering smoke must have gotten in my eyes and made them tear up." He thought, *The last time I cried was for Alisha, a lifetime ago.*

She composed herself. "I don't know how to thank you for these last few nights. I feel so safe and protected when you're with me."

He smiled. "I'm glad you feel that way." He wanted to tell her of his feelings for her, that he was falling in love with her. He angered himself. *Don't you dare make a fool of yourself. Do you really think she you be interested in an old dog like you?*

That morning he made another trip to the hospital. He brought with him a brand-new telescope. He hoped that would lift Karen's and Susan's spirits. He entered their room to find the women sitting up, laughing, and watching TV.

Karen said, "Vic, you remembered the telescope. Thank you."

He asked, "Did you think I would forget?"

The two women looked at each other and nodded. "Yes."

"Here, let me try it out." He mounted it on a tripod and peered through the lens. As he randomly looked around the harbor, he thought, *A boat would be a good place to take a kidnapped person. Nah, too obvious—or is it?*

Just then the nurse walked in. "So what do you think of our patients?"

Vic said, "They look like they're doing great. They'll be back to work in no time."

The nurse whispered, "Just shows you what a few happy pills can do."

He jokingly replied, "You don't happen to have a few extras, do you? I could use some happy."

They both laughed.

He chatted for a little longer with Karen and Susan and then left. When Vic returned to the resort, he went to check on Deborah. Jerimiah was sitting with her.

"Jerimiah, why don't you take a break. I'll stay with her for a while."

He smiled. "Thanks for caring about us, Vic."

Deborah was tense and restless; she was pacing back and forth on the porch.

He figured it would be best to let her wear herself out. He was patient as he sat in the living room. Finally, exhausted, she came in, sat down, and curled up in her favorite place on the couch. He sat next to her and put his arm around her.

She looked up at him with her big, hypnotic blue eyes. "You must have something better to do than sit here with me."

He wanted to say, *I want to be with you now and for-ever. I'm falling in love with you.* He was confused about the feelings he had for this woman. *What makes everything about her so special? I can't help myself. I admit it, I love her.*

Vic asked softly, "Would you mind if I called you Deb?"

She frowned. "I only let good friends call me Deb."
He hung his head.
She smiled. "Yes, you can call me Deb."
He grinned broadly. There was no one else he would rather be friends with.

CHAPTER 14

Mr. B. enjoyed the many amenities of the large private yacht that a third party had rented. By using a third party he avoided any monetary transaction that may tie him to this yacht. Mr.B." was in no hurry to get the information from the biologists. He sat with his feet propped up, drinking top-shelf bourbon and smoking Cuban cigars. He was doing all this in the warm California sun.

Mr. B. yawned and thought, *Life is good.* He smiled and puffed on his fat cigar. Right now he had the pair tucked away in a safe place. He didn't want them moved until tonight. The fewer people roaming about, the better.

Just after midnight, the drugged biologists were brought to the dock at the Crescent City marina. They were in burlap bags, so they were easy to carry. Because burlap sacks were used to transport all types of food and marine supplies, they would not raise any suspicion, which was just the way Mr. B. liked it. He and an associate loaded their human cargo into the small tender belonging to the yacht used to ferry passengers and supplies. Mr. B.'s associate was to act as guard and cook.

Once they were aboard, the kidnappers put them in separate cabins and tied them up, even though they were still drugged.

Later that day Mr. B. ordered the guard to bring the two groggy victims to the lounge area. As their blindfolds were removed, they quickly shielded their eyes from the sunlit cabin. When their vision had adjusted to the bright light, the pair gasped in fear at the large masked man.

He stared down at the biologists with empty black eyes. An air of death surrounded him.

In a gravelly voice, he politely asked, "Is there anything you require? Anything at all?"

Ethan shook his head. "No."

Becca angrily demanded, "Yeah. I want you to drop dead!"

Mr. B. expressed surprise. "Well, that's a poor attitude for a pretty little thing like you, especially after all the trouble I went through to get you here and make you comfortable. Anyway, just let the cook know if you have any needs. And just for your information, if you want to take a dip, it's two and a quarter miles to shore, and the cook chums twice a day, just to keep the resident sharks happy."

He looked at his associate. "Take them back to their cabins. Make sure their hands and feet are secure, and gag them." He laughed heartily, slapped the cook on the back, and laughed even louder as he left.

The biologists had been aboard for two days without food. That evening the cook made an exceptionally delicious meal and purposely let the aroma drift through the cabin area. The cook and Mr. B. thought it was funny to keep their hands and feet tied as they tried to eat. The two men laughed as the captives scarfed the food off the plates. Mr. B took pleasure in watching his prisoners attack the meal like hungry dogs. He intentionally did that to demoralize them, make them feel like animals, and wear them down. He was succeeding.

That evening the cook brought the pair back up to the vessel's lounge to meet with Mr. B. This time he kept them blindfolded just for effect.

Mr. B. got right to the point. "My friends," he uttered with a slight chuckle, "you have some very special information that I would like to have. I know you worked hard for it, and I'm sure you don't want to give up the formula. Would I be correct in that assumption?"

Becca gave no response. Ethan nodded.

Mr. B. responded, "Good. I'm glad we understand each other. Here's the thing. I have a friend who is willing to give me a lot of money for that formula. And because I love money, I really want to give him what he wants. Now, I could just ask you for it politely, and I would be very appreciative if you gave it to me. So appreciative, in fact, that I would seriously consider letting you go." He smiled widely. "Really, I would. But if you decide that you don't want to help me, well, I'll just have to torture you. I can tell you that it will be extremely painful. If you don't die, you will be scarred mentally and physically for life. I may even add some of your parts to my collection. I'll let your imagination figure out which ones." He laughed loudly. "It will be an agonizing torture, and I've had lots of practice."

He instructed the cook to take the prisoners back to their cabins and secure them. As the captives left, Mr. B. taunted them. "Now try to get some rest, and don't have nightmares about the excruciating torture or your missing parts."

The next morning Mr. B. kept them locked in their rooms until midday. He wanted them to think of nothing but his threats.

Finally, Mr. B. had them brought up to the lounge, where he sat in a recliner playing with a straight-edge razor. The cook removed their blindfolds. Ethan looked at the razor and began to tremble. Right then and there, he decided to give up the formula.

Mr. B. quipped sarcastically, "I hope you both slept well."

Ethan scoffed. "I didn't sleep at all."

Mr. B. snarled. "That's too bad, sonny. I had hoped you would be well rested. Are you ready to write down the formula? I believe you will give it to me because you're a smart young man."

Becca cautioned, "Don't give it up, Ethan. He's going to kill us anyway."

Ethan nervously asked, "If I give it to you, will you let us go?"

Mr. B. said, "That was the agreement, and I stand by my word."

Ethan picked up the pen, but he hesitated. He was having second thoughts, and he didn't trust his captor.

Mr. B. knew this was going to take a little persuasion. He took the straight-edge razor and held it up so that Ethan got a good look. Mr. B slowly ran it down the front of Ethan's pants. Exerting pressure, he sliced through the fabric. Ethan cried out in pain as the razor cut into his upper thigh.

Becca looked down on the deck; there was a small puddle of blood. She screamed, "Stop, you sadistic bastard!"

He separated the two biologists, ordering the cook to take Becca into the next room.

Mr. B. said to Ethan again, "Give me the formula." He moved the razor toward the center of his pants. "Give me the formula for the insulin."

The night before the kidnapping, at Vic's suggestion, a hypnotist had taken each biologist aside, and, under hypnosis, he had given them instructions for how to respond when a male voice said, "Give me the formula for the insulin."

The formula the hypnotist had given them left out one essential ingredient. Without that ingredient, the insulin formula was useless. When Mr. B. spoke those words, it triggered the hypnotist's preplanned response, and Ethan wrote down the formula.

Mr. B said, "You see, we could have avoided bloodletting if you hadn't hesitated."

When Ethan was finished, he lowered his head in shame. He had just given away the formula they all had worked so hard for. *My team will hate me for this. I'm washed up as a biologist. I lost my integrity, and I lost my team.*

Mr. B. ordered the cook to take Ethan into the next room and to bring Becca out. As the door closed, Ethan said to Becca, "Just give him the damn formula."

Mr. B advised, "OK, pretty girl, I need you to write down the formula. This way I can compare it to Ethan's copy and see if you two are telling the truth. I know you'll give me the correct information."

She sneered. "I won't give you the formula. You're a piece of shit, and you're going to kill us, no matter what we do."

Mr. B. responded, "I have to hand it to you—you're a brave one. Now it's my turn to have some fun." He picked up the straight-edge razor. Looking at her, he questioned, "Where will I cut?"

He walked over to her, and with a quick slash, he sliced off the two buttons of her blouse, exposing the top of her lacy bra. Looking down, he commented, "Very nice, pretty one." He put the razor up to her face. "Such a pretty face. It would be a shame to carve it up like a jack-o'-lantern."

She spits at Mr. B. "If I had that razor, I'd cut your balls off."

Mr. B. smiled. "You're feisty lass. Given the chance, I believe you would do just that."

He started to laugh and then suddenly turned around and backhanded her with a vicious blow to her face. She fell backward and hit the floor. "I hope you're happy because that's what you asked for. Don't fuck with me, bitch."

She lay on the deck, blood dripping from the corner of her mouth. He threw the pencil and paper on the deck and growled, "Give me the formula for the insulin."

Suddenly she froze; then, as if in a trance, she picked up the pen and wrote down the preplanned formula.

Mr. B. laughed. "Was that so hard?" He took the two formulas and compared them. They were exact. He told the cook, "Take them back to their rooms, and tie them up tight."

On the rear deck of the yacht, Mr. B sat back and put his feet up. The warm sun felt good. He began to relax and dreamed of how he would spend his fortune. That night he left the yacht and went out to celebrate his victory. He told the cook, "I'll be gone for a day or two. I've got a big game. Keep an eye on those two, and don't touch the girl."

Mr. B. left with the formula and drove to L&L Chemical. He gave a nearby drunken homeless man twenty dollars to stick the envelope in the mail slot in the front door. It was marked "To Mr. Lucius Lattimore."

Authentication of the formula would take about two days. Mr. B didn't mind; he had all the time in the world.

———

Back at the yacht, the sun was overhead; it was noontime. The cook brought food to the hungry pair.

After devouring her meal, Becca purred, "Sir, is there any way I could get some sun? I'm freezing down here. Just a few minutes on deck would warm me up. I promise not to try anything."

The cook said, "No."

After feeding Ethan, the cook thought, *if I let her up on deck, she might show some skin. She's got a nice ass.* He went to her cabin. "I'll let you up on deck to get some sun, but just for a few minutes."

He untied just her feet and led her topside. "Lie down on the deck so that no one will see you."

She lay down on her back and sighed. "The sun feels so good." She arched provocatively. The cook's eyes popped, and he sneered lasciviously. "Sir, could you unbutton my blouse so that I can get some sun on my tummy? It's so cold."

He unbuttoned her blouse with trembling hands. He was about to touch her when she said, "Remember what the boss said: no touching the girl."

Disappointed and afraid of Mr. B., he backed off. She was on deck for a good half hour. She listened for familiar sounds but heard none.

The cook said, "It's time to go back." When she stood up, she looked in all directions but saw nothing familiar. He escorted her back to her room.

As the cook tied her up, she whispered, "Can I go up there again tomorrow? I'll be really good, I promise." Then she winked.

He asked, "Do I get to see some skin or not?"

"Yes, but that's all."

"I'll think about it," he replied.

The next day the cook brought food to the captives. Becca looked at him and smiled. "Will you let me get a little more sun? I'll be good, just like yesterday."

He untied her feet. "OK, but I want to see skin, or back down you go."

"Maybe you could stretch some?" She looked at him and winked.

He brought her up on deck.

She whispered, "I would remove my blouse if my hands were free."

"You don't have big boobs, so take off your pants—you have a great ass."

He quickly untied her hands, and she slowly unbuttoned her jeans. She wiggled her butt, sliding out of the jeans. She had on a white pair of panties. The cook's eyes were fixed on them.

She asked, "Are you happy now?"

Without moving his eyes, he nodded. While he ogled her, she raised her hands as if stretching, hoping to draw someone's attention. Becca went through a stretching routine for almost an hour. She was exhausted. *All that work, and I couldn't signal anyone for help.* She did see the marina in the distance, and behind it was a large building, an office or a hospital. Otherwise she recognized nothing.

The cook's phone rang while Becca was still on deck. It was Mr. B. She overheard part of the conversation in which Mr. B. said that he wouldn't be back until late tomorrow.

All this time, poor Ethan was stuck in his room, but he was thankful that he had all his parts and a little food.

———

Vic got a call from the surveillance techs; they were excited. "We have some good news for you."

"I sure could use some."

"We have Mr. B.'s name—Bogart Gibbons. He made a call, and we intercepted it on the encryptor. He's ex-military and a very dangerous assassin. He's going to a high-stakes poker game tonight. We're trying to get a location."

Vic said to himself, *Bogart Gibbons, I'm coming after you, dirtbag.*

CHAPTER 15

It was a warm, sunny day in Northern California, great for lying outside and getting some color. At the hospital Susan had the telescope set up on her bed. She was examining the marina and watching a cruise ship pass by in the distance. As she scanned the horizon, she saw a tiny figure on the big yacht. Susan quickly centered on the boat. She hoped to see the lucky owners or some friends aboard, maybe a celebrity or a famous person. She focused on a woman standing on the upper deck, stretching, her short blond hair barely moving in the wind.

She adjusted the lens and got a clear view of the woman. Gasping in disbelief, Susan looked away and then refocused. Her mouth fell open. She whispered to herself, "Becca?" The more she looked, the more she knew it was her. Susan was stunned. "It's Becca!"

She immediately called Vic, between gasps, she cried, "I see Becca! I'm looking at Becca. She's alive!"

He didn't know what to think. *Was it a picture? Maybe someone who looked like her?* "Susan, calm down. Where do you see Becca?"

She said excitedly, "I'm looking at her standing on a yacht in the harbor."

He was dumbfounded. "Are you sure it's her?"

"I'm telling you, it's Becca."

"I'm on my way. Don't take your eyes off her."

As Vic raced to the hospital, he looked up and thanked the Lord. Twenty minutes later he burst into Susan's room. "Where is she? Show me."

Susan said, "Look through the telescope at the big yacht."

He peered through the lens, and there was Becca, being led below deck by a man. Shocked, he began to assess his options. He thought, *the hell with options—I'm going to that yacht.* He told Susan, "Call the coast guard and the security team. I'll call harbor patrol."

By the time he reached the marina dock, harbor patrol was waiting with their boat. He jumped in and told them to head for the yacht. He filled them in on the way. Vic pulled his weapon as they closed in on the vessel. He jumped on the swim platform and began to climb aboard. The cook appeared, pointing a gun at him. In a flash the harbor police aimed their weapons at the man; five laser dots appeared on his shirt. At five to one, the odds weren't very good, so the cook dropped his weapon and raised his hands in surrender. Vic grabbed the man by the throat and demanded, "Where are Becca and Ethan?"

The cook pointed to the cabins below. Vic leaped down the stairs and smashed in every door until he found them. As he untied them, relief flooded through him that they were both alive. Becca hugged her rescuer even though she didn't know him. Ethan hugged him too.

Vic called Deb and handed his phone to Becca. "Oh, Deb, I love you so much!"

"Becca! Thank God you're safe. Are you hurt? Are you OK?"

"I'm fine, but Ethan's been cut."

"Oh my God! How bad?" she asked.

Becca handed the phone back to Vic. "Deb, this is Vic. They'll both be fine. Ethan just needs a few stitches, and Becca's physically OK."

Becca looked at him. "Who are you, and where do you get off calling my sister Deb?"

He laughed. "It's a long story, but your sister and I are friends."

Not trusting anyone right then, she said, "I know all my sister's friends, and you're not one of them."

"I'm a new friend." Vic handed the phone back to Becca.

Deb said to Becca, "Give that big man a hug and kiss for me."

Becca was a bit confused, but she obeyed her sister.

Happily he remarked, "If that's the reward for rescuing you, I'm going to do it again tomorrow."

The EMTs checked Becca and released her. Vic took her hand. "Come on. I'll take you home."

Deb was on the porch when Vic drove up. The sisters ran to each other and hugged like they'd never hugged before.

Deb pushed Becca back to look at her. Satisfied that she was all right, the siblings embraced again. Vic escorted the sisters to Deb's chalet. The retired agent checked to be sure it was clear and then let them in. He was taking no chances. "I'll let you girls have some alone time."

Becca said, "Please don't go. I'm still afraid."

He looked at Deb, and she nodded, indicating that it was OK for him to stay. Hours later the sisters were asleep in each other's arms. He quietly left the chalet but posted two security guards, one at each door. He also had security activate two surveillance cameras focused on Deborah's chalet.

Vic's next call was to the boss. "Robert, Becca and Ethan are safe and out of danger."

Robert's voice cracked with joy. "Thank the Lord for this miracle. And thank you for bringing my people home safely."

Vic said, "When you get the details, you'll see that the Lord was with them. The rest of us are just his servants."

Robert asked, "How are the sisters doing? Are they together?"

Vic smiled. "Yes. They're together, and security is posted at each door of the chalet."

"Will you stay with them at night until they feel comfortable? I know they feel safe in your presence, especially Deborah."

Vic was surprised. "And just how do you know that?"

Robert answered, "Because she told me. That beautiful woman is very fond of you, my friend. I assume you feel the same."

That information gave Vic a whole new outlook. He smiled and rubbed his chin.

The next day Vic walked to Deb's chalet and touched base with the security personnel. They reported that all was quiet.

She saw him approach and ran to the door, smiling. "Hi, Vic. Please come in."

Once they were inside, she wrapped her arms around his neck and gave him a big kiss. "That's what I call a warm welcome," he happily replied.

Becca squealed, "I'm next!" She proceeded to hug and kiss her white knight.

"I'm the luckiest man alive. Kisses and hugs from two beautiful women."

They all enjoyed a good laugh.

Deb offered , "Please come and sit down. Is there anything I can get you?"

"No, thanks. I just wanted to check in on you both. I'll be back tomorrow." Vic wanted to stay, but he figured they needed private time together.

That day Deb began noticing subtle changes in Becca. Her sister hesitated when going into another room. A door closing or a strange sound caused her to freeze and fold her arms in nervous fear. She never completely closed her bedroom door. Becca methodically went about her assignments in the lab and welcomed any task, putting on a happy face in front of the team.

That night Deb awoke to find Becca sitting up with her arms around her knees and tears in her eyes. Sometimes when she closed her eyes, she saw his evil, ugly face. Deborah knew this was the result of the kidnapping and the sadistic villain still being out there.

Deb thought *I know it's wrong, but I wish that man were dead. If this dark horror continues, Becca may need help. I'll speak to Robert tomorrow.*

———

Robert called Vic early the next day. "Good morning, Mr. Bowden. How are you on this fine day?"

"I'm well and enjoying the sweet morning air. But I thought you rich folks slept in."

Robert laughed. "I sleep in when I have company."

Vic chuckled. "Then you very rarely sleep in."

"Very funny, Mr. Bowden. I called to see if you could take over as director of security at the resort for a while. I know your presence puts our team at ease, which pleases me."

"Yes, I can stay and oversee the new security system. I wouldn't want to miss Bogart's reaction when L&L Chemical finds out that the formula is useless."

"I'm concerned that there will be retaliation and that you and the resort will both be targets."

Vic said, "I'm hoping he'll try for me. He has two reasons to take me out. First, I disgraced him in front of his peers. Second, he knows that I'll dog him until one of us is dead. I'll be the bait to lure him out."

Robert cautioned, "Take no unnecessary risks. Be careful, my friend, and thank you."

CHAPTER 16

Two days had gone by, and Vic anxiously waited for the preverbal shit to hit the fan. L&L Chemical would now know that the formula wasn't complete and would refuse to pay Gibbons. This would infuriate the criminal. He hoped that Gibbons wrath would be taken out on him. He knew the kidnapper would be livid about the trickery, and angry people make foolish mistakes. Vic would be ready for his slip-up.

With no word from Lattimore, Gibbons grew impatient and contacted Lucius. "Where the hell is my money?"

Lattimore barked back, "For what? A useless formula not worth the paper it was written on?"

Gibbons was speechless thinking *is this guy trying to stiff me, or did McAlister's people pull a fast one?* He regained his voice. "Bullshit. Don't cross me, asshole."

Adamantly, Lattimore said, "I'm telling you that the formula is no good. Go ask another biologist."

Gibbons muttered, "I'll get back to you."

Two days later Gibbons did something he had never done before—eat crow. He called Lattimore and admitted, "I underestimated McAlister's main man, Bowden." The brawny felon choked on his words. Under his breath he vowed, "I'll kill Bowden for this."

Lattimore said, "You want Bowden dead, and I want Simpson dead. Maybe we can work out a deal."

Gibbons answered, "I'll get back to you."

Bogart Gibbons began to do surveillance on Bowden and Simpson. He needed to know how difficult the assassinations would be. Gibbons subscribed to McAlister's satellite surveillance computer software package. He could this program to his advantage.

He wore an evil smile as he used a stolen credit card to pay for the service. Then with a sick laugh, he thought, *I'll use McAlister's own system to kill his friends.* Simpson would be easy. He walked each morning at the same time, almost to the minute. Bowden would be a challenge as he was unpredictable. He very rarely let his guard down. He was disciplined and wary. Again Gibbons smiled as he thought, *I need a challenge like Bowden to sharpen my skills.*

Days later Gibbons got back to Lattimore. "One hundred thousand to take out Simpson."

Lattimore balked at the sum. "Come on, Gibbons. For Simpson?"

"That's the price. Take it or leave it."

Lattimore reluctantly agreed. "All right, as long as it's done soon."

He chose his custom-made sniper rifle, a silenced 7.62-mm-caliber rifle. He scouted his location carefully, selecting a rise with high weeds that looked down into the resort compound. His camouflage matched the surroundings. The escape route was a one-lane paved road leading to the main highway. Every day at 7:00 a.m., the target would walk the track several times for exercise.

The weather report predicted a slight haze in the morning, giving way to bright sunshine and a light breeze.

Gibbons smiled and then laughed. "What more could a sniper ask for?"

At 3:00 a.m. the assassin drove his car to the target site. With his rifle set on its tripod, he calmly relaxed and bided his time. At ten minutes to seven, he looked in the scope. The wind was minimal, so it wouldn't be a factor. Jerimiah Simpson was right on time; Bogart would let him make one lap. The second lap would be his last. The sniper picked his location and gently placed his finger on the trigger. Simpson's head was in the center of the crosshairs. He squeezed the trigger, knowing that the target's head would instantly explode.

Bogart stayed focused on the crosshairs, but Jerimiah kept on walking. Bogart's eyes bulged at what he didn't see. His natural reflex was to reload and get off another shot. He did so, put his target in the crosshairs, and fired. In the compound a tree limb could be heard snapping.

"This can't be. I couldn't have missed him. This isn't happening. I killed the guy!" He looked down into the compound and saw that Simpson was still walking. Stunned and unable to explain the miss, he quickly packed up and left.

About that time Vic came out of the lobby and joined Jerimiah on his walk. "How are you doing, buddy?"

"Just fine, Vic, but look out for falling limbs. Two of them nearly clobbered me."

Vic joked, "Did you upset the trees?"

"Not that I know of," Jerimiah replied seriously.

Minutes later he pointed out the broken limb lying on the ground. Vic picked up the good-sized branch and looked at the break. He knew right away that a projectile had severed the limb. Twenty feet away lay the second limb, and it had the same distinct marking, indicating that it had also been severed by a projectile.

He said to Jerimiah, "Get in a building right away, and stay away from the windows."

Jerimiah laughed. "Are you serious?"

Vic's expression was very serious. "Please get inside now." He called security and told them that a sniper was in the area.

Vic lined up the severed limb and tried to get an idea of the trajectory that the shot had taken. He narrowed it down to a rise on the west side of the resort. He grabbed one of the security guards and had him drive to the location. Looking around, he quickly found crushed leaves and could smell the spent gunpowder. He looked down the line of sight; there wasn't a tree limb within ten feet of the path of the projectile.

Vic was stumped. He had never seen anything like it. It was as if the limbs had purposely deflected the bullets away from Jerimiah. *No, I'm not buying that the bogeyman or the TREEZZ are his friends. There must be a logical explanation.* This was Vic's introduction to the magical, mystical world of the TREEZZ.

Jerimiah called, "Vic, how long do I have to stay in the building?"

"I'm on my way. Sit tight." Vic went back to the resort. "Do you mind if I call you Jer? It's a little easier on an old dog like me."

"I guess so." He moaned. "That's what everyone else has been calling me, thanks to Becca."

"Jer, I have to ask you this, but please don't get upset: Can you think of any reason why someone would want to kill you?"

"If this is a joke, it's not funny. I wouldn't have a clue why anyone would want me dead."

"OK, OK. I had to ask. I believe the broken tree limbs deflected the bullets and saved your life."

Jerimiah was speechless. He sat down and turned pale.

Vic said, "Jer, I'm probably way off base here—you know me; everything's a conspiracy. Don't give it another thought." Vic called Robert and explained what had taken place at the resort that morning. "Can we get Jerimiah out of town for a while?"

Robert said, "Elaina will be reviewing applications for grants. She could use his help. And he could rehearse his first deal for a forest preserve using the slogan 'Save the TREEZZ.'"

"Great. How soon can you send them off?"

"If you feel that it's urgent, they can leave in the next few hours."

"It's urgent, believe me."

Two days later the G-500 landed in Santiago, Chile. A handful of dignitaries greeted the McAlister representatives. After the formal introductions, Elaina and Jerimiah were taken to their hotel.

He fell on the bed and stretched just as Elaina walked through the adjoining door. "Jerimiah, don't get too comfortable. We have a reception to attend this evening."

"Darn, I forgot. Do I have to go?"

"Yes. You're my escort, so look your best."

The reception was cordial, with plenty of delicacies. The McAlister representatives were gracious and diplomatic, as always. The gathering ended at eleven o'clock, and Elaina and Jerimiah were happy to get to their rooms.

He quickly undressed and got in bed. A short time later, Elaina called. "Jerimiah, could you come here for a minute?"

He jumped out of bed and pulled on his pants. He opened the door to see Elaina trying to unzip her dress. "Will you be a dear and help me?"

He pulled the zipper several times before it released. He walked back to the door as Elaina whispered softly, "Thank you."

As he turned to answer her, she let her dress slip off, revealing a tiny pair of panties and no bra. She smiled. "Oops." Elaina enjoyed flirting with her new partner. She had a reputation for innocent teasing. His face immediately turned pink, but he got an eyeful of the very sexy Elaina. Needless to say, he dreamed of his partner that night. Jerimiah took no offense at the teasing; he rather enjoyed it.

Intense negotiations began the following day. Several organizations were vying for the grant, but only one would be victorious. That's where Jerimiah came in. His job was to convince the government to set aside thousands of acres designated as a forest preserve that was never to be inhabited or cultivated. Whichever organization Elaina chose, they would agree to use their influence to secure land for the Save the TREEZZ campaign. The McAlister Foundation insisted that the grant be perfectly legal and that they make all the stipulations public. Robert didn't need or want any implication of a scandal.

Days later a worthy applicant was awarded the generous monetary grant. Now it was time for Jerimiah to earn his paycheck. Late that night he walked into the forest and looked around; no one had followed him. He quickly stepped into the TREEZZ.

As he was greeted by a warm welcome and the familiar bright-white light, his mind began absorbing the telepathic message of the TREEZZ. He emerged minutes later. He always felt confident, proud, and thankful after his meetings with the TREEZZ.

At 10:00 a.m. the next day, Jerimiah made his plea before a panel of conservationists and ecologists. The government's experts were astonished by his knowledge of the TREEZZ. They listened intently as he described the damage to the forest and the repercussions that would follow. Serious conversations ensued, which pleased him.

One gentleman on the panel asked, "Is it true that McAlister Laboratories is working on herbal insulin?"

He looked at Elaina before answering. She gave him a nod. "I am pleased to say that they are."

The room suddenly erupted in applause. Elaina smiled, delighted with Jerimiah's first presentation. The TREEZZ were also pleased with the new rain forest preserve and with the man they'd groomed to save the TREEZZ, Jerimiah Simpson.

CHAPTER 17

Bogart Gibbons was in a state of depression. Every time he looked in the mirror, he saw a loser, a failure, a has-been. Clay Lattimore took pity on the villain and let him stay in a tiny storeroom on the edge of L&L Chemical's property. The room had electricity, a kerosene heater, and, most importantly, an internet connection. As Bogart lay in his room, looking up at the peeling paint on the ceiling, he began reviewing his life. How had he ended up in a hole like this?

His parents were considered middle income. They owned their home and had a fairly new car. They both worked, and they seemed to enjoy the arrangement. Young Bogart was named after Humphrey Bogart from the classic movie *The African Queen*. Bogart was a large man and was not close to being considered handsome. In fact, he was scary to look at. The only time he had a friend was when they wanted someone threatened or beaten up. He knew it was wrong, but he desperately wanted a companion. Of course those friendships didn't last long. When they finished with him, he was cast aside and made fun of. Finally, he realized that people only used him. As he got older, he used his size to intimidate others for monetary gain. He began to enjoy this lifestyle. In high school he was known as the enforcer. Gangs would hire him to make collections, rough people up, and just be a badass. Several gangs vied for his talents. Eventually, the police heard of his illegal activities and arrested him. When he was brought before the judge, he pleaded guilty. The judge had a soft spot for folks telling the truth and gave him a choice: jail or the military. Bogart wisely chose the military.

Marine First Sergeant Johnathan McGee took one look at the new recruit and cringed. That was, until Bogart stood at attention. The sergeant's eyes popped, and he thought, *This man could be the poster boy for recruiting marines*. He walked up to Bogart and pushed him hard. Bogart didn't budge. The sergeant pushed him even harder, and again, Bogart didn't move.

The sergeant said, "Now push me, you sad sack."

Bogart pushed the sergeant hard, and he landed on his back. All the recruits moaned and groaned. Bogart was in for it now. The sergeant jumped up, his face twisted in rage. Calmly he stuck out his hand and barked, "Marine, you and me are gonna be good friends."

Bogart loved the marines, and he advanced quickly through the ranks. He and his sergeant stayed together for years. As a team they couldn't be beaten. They both signed up for Operation Desert Storm. The pair excelled in any and all missions they were given. They were especially proficient as a sniper team, gaining worldwide recognition for executing the most difficult shots.

A young captain from another division resented the men's notoriety. One day the captain confronted

McGee. Harsh words were spoken, and McGee swung at the captain. The man, who was much younger, severely beat the sergeant. When Gibbons found out, he became enraged. Without thinking, he beat the captain and two fellow officers, putting them in the hospital. Months later he was court-martialed and dismissed with a dishonorable discharge.

Bogart Gibbons only employment experience was security and assassination. Now he was in hiding from the police, facing kidnapping and attempted murder charges after the botched abduction of Becca and Ethan. The ex-marine was running low on cash after failing to receive his payment from Lucius. L&L Chemical was giving him some routine security work in addition to the hits on Bowden and Simpson. As far as Bogart was concerned, it was charity, and it disgusted him. He wondered what had happened to the elite sniper he once was. Bogart became angry and cursed Vic Bowden. It was he who was responsible for Bogart's downfall. Being a superstitious man, he believed in Lady Luck, as well as in good and bad omens. He knew that to change his luck, he needed to kill Bowden. He began working on a plan to redeem himself and to prove he was the best. Killing Bowden was the only way to redeem himself and get his respect back. He would take pleasure in this assassination.

CHAPTER 18

With Jerimiah thousands of miles away, Vic began his investigation into the assassination attempt. He pondered where to start. *How about the beginning? Duh.*

He got Jerimiah's parents on the phone. When Todd answered, Vic asked, "I was wondering if I could ask a few questions about Jerimiah's younger years."

"Sure, Vic. Shoot."

He needed to pull something out of his hat quickly. "This is a standard security check. It's just part of my job."

"OK. What would you like to know?"

"Did Jerimiah have many friends growing up?"

"Not really. We live pretty far out."

"Can you remember any of their names?"

"I can only remember one, and I wouldn't necessarily say they were friends. He and Lucius Lattimore were competitors all through school. I remember after one run-in they had, Lucius promised to get even with him for some reason. Other than that, I can't think of anyone else."

"Thanks. This is a big help. Have a nice day."

Vic mused. *Lucius Lattimore, part owner in L&L Chemical, a major supplier of manufactured insulin and syringes used to inject the insulin. I believe I have found the motive and another link to L&L Chemical.*

The former NSA agent knew that Gibbons wouldn't stop pursuing him until he'd made his kill. With his reputation as an assassin on the line, money was no longer an incentive.

Vic decided to try to lure Gibbons out with a challenge. He posted a note on the dark web goading Gibbons: "Hey, big man. Anyone can take out an unarmed, naive young man. Why don't you try me? Victorio Bowden."

For two days he waited for a response from Gibbons. He was beginning to think that maybe Gibbons was getting old and tired. The next morning he checked his email and saw that he had a message from an unknown sender. Curious, he opened the email. It read, "Victorio Bowden, I did some background on you. Impressive, very impressive. I'm honored to finally have an adversary worthy of my attention. You threw the gauntlet down. Now will you accept my challenge?"

Vic smiled as he thought, *Thank you, Bogart.*

The following day, a FedEx envelope arrived addressed to Victorio Bowden. He knew right away that it was from Gibbons. He opened the envelope and read the invitation.

The GPS coordinates indicated that the challenge would start in the middle of the Mojave Desert—nothing but sand and sweltering heat.

He thought, *Not a tree within twenty miles. Gibbons isn't taking any chances this time. No trees, no limbs.*

Gibbons gave him four hours to reach the starting point. That gave Vic just enough time to pack. There were no weapons allowed.

He jumped in the Jeep and headed in the direction of the desert. On the way he called Robert and explained what was going on.

Robert became extremely upset. "That is the most foolish thing I have ever heard. Do you have a death wish?"

"Robert, Jerimiah's life is in danger as long as Gibbons walks this earth."

"You're right, as usual." He sighed. "Is there something I can do?"

"Yes, there is. I heard a rumor that your advanced weapons division is experimenting with a special suit."

"That's highly classified. How did you find out?"

"I don't sit around reading the newspaper all day. I'm a nosy rascal. Anyway, can you get me that suit?"

"I suppose I can, but it's a prototype, so it's not been completely tested."

"I have no choice. I need an edge, and I need it dropped to me while I'm driving to the desert. Gibbons has me on satellite. It's one of your satellites, I might add; he has a subscription."

"Sorry about that. I'll see if we can do something."

As Vic traveled to the GPS coordinates, Robert's drone flew overhead and dropped a small camo bag into the Jeep. It was the suit. Vic hoped this would be enough of an edge.

DAY ONE

Vic arrived at the coordinates. Stopping in front of a barricade, he found a small box. Inside were a bottle of water, a light sleeping bag, a compass, and a note directing him to walk two hundred feet to the south. Just as he'd reached that distance, an explosion destroyed his Jeep. Gibbons had planted a bomb just in front of the barricade. If it was meant to instill fear in the retired agent, Gibbons was sadly mistaken.

Vic did, however, lose his proverbial edge. His ace had just disappeared in a cloud of smoke. He read the rest of the note: "Strip naked, so I know you have no weapons or other items to assist you."

With the surveillance drone hovering, Vic stripped, held his arms up, and turned around. *I hope you like what you see, dirtbag.*

Out of the corner of his eye, Vic noticed a small camo bag. He couldn't believe his luck—it was the bag with the suit. It had been blown clear of the Jeep. All he had to do was get to the bag. Now dressed, he took his water bottle and walked toward the camo bag. He unzipped his pants and urinated, intentionally dropping his water. He bent over and retrieved the bottle and the camo bag. He stuffed the bag in his pants and zipped up. The note directed him to walk fifteen miles on a zigzag course; at the end he was to stop and rest for the night.

Around midnight he pulled the camo bag from his pants and opened it. Inside was a balled-up piece of a strange mesh material. He spread it out and found a total bodysuit; the head, face, hands, and feet would all be shielded. He smiled. *This suit is just what I need.* He quickly tucked it back into his pants. Exhausted, he crawled into his sleeping bag and fell asleep.

DAY TWO

Vic was up before sunrise. He watched the orange ball rise up over the parched desert sand. He was now motivated to end this game. He began the tough climb, weaving his way up the steep mountain slope. The third day would be the scheduled rendezvous, with the two adversaries meeting face to face.

Gibbons was amazed that his prey had gotten this far and in reasonably good condition. He began to have second thoughts, wondering if he'd underestimated the former agent. Vic wasn't to be counted out, not just yet. He had a few tricks he planned to use to even the playing field.

By the time he stopped for the night, Vic had reached the next coordinates. He could barely move. Every muscle in his body ached. He was covered in scrapes and bruises. He painfully climbed into his sleeping bag, hoping for relief. He found none.

The next morning would mean that there was just one more day to go before the big day—the showdown, the finale, the termination of one opponent. He was at an elevation of forty-three hundred feet. The night air chilled him, and he pulled the light sleeping bag over his head. About midnight, he heard a buzzing noise coming toward him. He recognized the sound as a drone. It hovered over him. The drone was fitted with a camera, a heat sensor, and a weapon that could be fired automatically by preprogrammed parameters. He knew that Gibbons would be watching him from now on. He smiled at the drone and gave it the finger. That was the first time he'd smiled that day. It felt good.

DAY THREE

The sun rose over the mountain crest, and the bright rays blinded Vic for a moment. Shielding his eyes, he looked around. There was nothing. It was a barren landscape unfit for man or beast. *I'd give a thousand dollars for a hot cup of Deb's coffee; I'd give a million if she were here to give it to me.*

He closed his eyes and envisioned Deb standing in front of him smiling, her blond hair mussed, handing him a cup of coffee. He reached out for it, but nothing was there.

He broke camp and continued his agonizing journey. Barely reaching the next point, he stumbled and fell, rolling several times before grabbing a rock to stop his slide down the steep slope. He knew that Gibbons was watching, and Vic wanted him to think that the fall had injured him.

He slowly crawled to the next waypoint. The drone's hum decreased in intensity; it needed a recharge. Now was his opportunity to get the upper hand. Hiding behind a large boulder, he quickly undressed and donned the special suit. It was a very tight fit, almost like a second skin. He cringed in pain as the porous material scraped across his wounds.

Meanwhile, Gibbons replaced the batteries and relaunched the drone. He guided it to the other side of the boulder, expecting to get a visual on Vic, but the man had disappeared into thin air. Gibbons panicked as he maneuvered the drone, hoping to find a heat signal. He got nothing.

The suit was a prototype cloaking device, shielding the wearer from heat sensors. It also had special pixels that made it blend in perfectly with the surrounding environment. The wearer was virtually invisible.

Unnoticed, Vic began to move toward Gibbon's position. Gibbons drone searched in vain for a heat signal. The assassin had made a fatal mistake: he'd adjusted the sensors for close range. Vic saw the drone hovering. He pulled the face covering off for a split second, alerting the drone's heat sensor. The drone's weapon turned to the heat source, but then it lost the signal and disengaged. Gibbons grabbed his weapon and took up a position at the best vantage point. He felt Vic's presence. He could smell that his prey was near, but where? Gibbons was sweating profusely. Things were not going his way.

Suddenly, the drone picked up another heat signature. Vic watched it closely as the droned hovered between him and Gibbons. He pulled the face covering down and then back up. The weapon quickly swung in his direction. Once again, the source was lost, and the weapon disengaged.

Without warning, the weapon turned in the direction of Gibbon's heat signature. His eyes popped, and his ugly face contorted with fear. The weapon engaged and discharged. Five projectiles ravaged Gibbon's body. He had assassinated himself.

Vic collapsed as the last drop of adrenaline surged through his veins. He lay in the morning sun, exhausted, having spent his last amount of strength.

After an hour, he regained some of his vigor. Vic loaded Bogart Gibbon's body and his equipment into the dead man's Jeep and drove to the town of Needles. There he reported the incident to the sheriff.

After the sheriff reviewed all the evidence, the video from the drone, and the satellite photos, Vic was released pending a complete investigation. Months later he would be cleared of any wrongdoing.

Dirty, tired, and hungry, he called Robert from the police station. "Hi, boss. Scratch one bad guy."

Robert gasped. "Thank God. Are you all right?"

"Yes. I've probably lost a few pounds, but that's a good thing. I'll give you the details when I get back to the resort."

"I'll be waiting for you, my friend."

The retired agent felt good, like he was ten years younger. *I love that rush of adrenaline, the deadly cat-and-mouse game, using every trick I know and having an edge.* He looked to the sky and roared, "Yes! I'm the man!"

Vic caught a flight into Washington, rented a car, and drove straight to McAlister's advanced weapons facility.

Tom Martin, the chief engineer, greeted him. "Glad to see you're still among the living. How did the equipment work?"

"The suit saved my life. I'm in debt to you and your people." He handed the suit back to the engineer.

"That's our job. While you're here, I have something else I think you'll like."

Vic smiled. "I love surprises." He followed Tom to the underground testing bunker.

Tom instructed Vic, "Stand right here while I get the weapon." Tom unlocked a vault and removed what looked like a ray gun from a Buck Rogers movie. "I'm setting this on the lowest setting. Be prepared to have the wind knocked out of you."

Vic inhaled, held his breath, and then nodded that he was ready.

Without a sound, an invisible energy pulse thumped him, causing him to hold his stomach as he buckled over in discomfort. Growling, he said, "What the heck was that? I didn't see or hear a thing."

Tom laughed. "You weren't supposed to. This is our new weapon; we call it APEP, for antipersonnel energy pulse."

"If that was the minimum setting, what does the max setting do?"

"It emulsifies all internal organs." He handed it to Vic. "Here, shoot me."

Vic hesitated. "Seriously?"

Tom said, "Go ahead and pull the trigger."

Vic pulled the trigger, but nothing happened. He looked at Tom, puzzled.

Tom laughed. "It will fire only when the assigned personnel's handprints and eye scan activate the weapon."

Vic grinned. "That's really slick. I love it. You guys are the best."

As Vic left the building, Tom said, "Hey, Vic. Be careful, and say hi to Mr. McAlister for us."

"I'll do that, Tom."

Vic got in his car and smiled as he drove back to the resort. Suddenly he had a hot flash and began to perspire. He cringed, "OH no, I didn't call Deb to let her know I'm safe and on my way home. Well I'm not that far thinking, its better I explain what happened in person and not over the phone.

———

The retired agent pulled up to Deb's chalet. He wore a false grin hoping for a warm welcome. Instead, the two sisters were standing on the porch with their arms folded and stern expressions on their faces.

His mind raced. *What did I do now?* He walked up to the porch with a puppy dog look. "Hi, girls, how have you been for the last few days?" He was met with nothing but silence. He smiled and tried again. "Did you miss me?"

Deb sounded cross. "Vic Bowden, the question is: Where have you been? We've been worried sick about you. You could have told us that you were going away for a few days. But no, there was nothing—no note, no call, nothing. I guess we aren't that important to you."

Becca echoed her sister. "Yeah, what she said."

He hung his head in shame. "I'm so sorry. I should have called. You two girls are the most important people in my life. But if you let me explain, I think you'll understand."

The girls looked at each other. "I guess we could hear him out." Becca said with a disgusted sighed.

Deb replied, "OK, but it better be good."

As he related the story, the girls sat there in disbelief, their mouths wide open in horror.

In a state of shock, Becca repeated, "Gibbons is dead. Gibbons is really dead." She slowly fell to her knees, covered her face with her hands, and began to sob. Deb and Vic helped her to a chair and comforted her. A short time later, Becca collected herself, saying, "I know I shouldn't feel this way, but I'm glad he's dead. He'll never hurt anyone again."

Vic whispered, "Yes, Becca. He can't hurt anyone now."

They all hugged.

Deb said, "I'm sorry we were angry, but we care for you very much. We should have known that you wouldn't just leave unless it was very important. But," she warned, "don't ever do it again."

Just then she got a call from Robert. "How are you and Becca doing?"

"We're fine now that the desert wanderer is home."

Robert said, "Yes, everyone's glad he's back. I'll be at the resort in a few hours to get the details of the incident."

Deb was surprised he nonchalantly dismissed Vic's dangerous adventure. He must have something else on his mind.

"I was wondering if I could meet with you and Becca?"

"Sure. Just give us a call when you're ready."

"Great. See you soon."

Later that afternoon Robert called Deb and asked if he could come to her chalet.

"Of course," she replied. A short time later, he knocked on the door, and Deb greeted him. "Come right in, and make yourself comfortable."

Becca walked out of the kitchen. "Hi, Robert."

"Hello, Becca, pretty as always." He chuckled as he said, "Love your outfit." Her shorts were full of holes, and she wore one of Vic's old shirts, three sizes too big, and a mismatched pair of socks. Becca wasn't sure that was a compliment or an insult. She gave Robert a big hug anyway.

"Hi, Deb."

"Hi, Robert."

"Make yourself comfortable."

After the pleasantries the trio sat down and discussed the latest news.

Robert became serious. "Becca, my deepest apologies for the unthinkable incident that happened because you worked for me. Words cannot express my regret. Is there anything I can do for you? Anything at all?"

"Thank you, Robert. I feel I'm getting better every day."

"That's good," he said. "I have a good friend, Carlie who went through a similar experience. If you ever want someone to talk to who will understand, just let me know. She's a wonderful person; I think you would like her. The offer is open, anytime, anywhere."

Trying to muster a smile, she answered, "Thank you. I just may take you up on that offer."

"And, Deb, as always, if there is anything that you require, I am at your service."

After he left, the sisters praised their boss. Deb said, "He is the nicest man—so thoughtful, compassionate, and kind."

"He's very handsome for an older man. Did you feel his hands? They're so soft and gentle. A girl would be lucky to catch him."

"An older man? Seriously, Becca? He's in his prime."

CHAPTER 19

McAlister Laboratories was completing the last tests for the herbal insulin to receive approval from the FDA. But McAlister Laboratories wasn't the only lab discovering new products to benefit mankind.

Lucius Lattimore perused the morning newspaper; he choked on his coffee as he read an article in the *Los Angeles Times*: "Bogart Gibbons, a known felon, has died. His body was found by a hiker in the Mojave Desert. Sources say he was testing an experimental weapon when it malfunctioned and accidentally discharged, taking his life. This was the information the police made available to the press. This reporter will follow up if more information becomes available."

Shocked by the news of Bogart Gibbon's death, Lucius broke into a cold sweat. *Did Bogart say anything or leave any incriminating evidence before he died that would implicate me in any way?*

Lucius decided to keep a low profile and worked incessantly. He was in the middle of testing his newest product. Soon he expected to apply for a patent for the growth hormones. This genetically altered cell, made with a human growth hormone and a vegetable cell, would speed a plant's size and growth, thus increasing crop yield. Of course only three chemists knew about the altered cell—Lucius, Horace Riley, and Thacker Croft. The product, if successful, would earn L&L Chemical billions in revenue. Out of professional curiosity, Jerimiah followed L&L's progress on the growth hormone.

During a casual conversation, Jerimiah commented, "Vic, I've read in a biology journal that L&L Chemical is working on a growth hormone. I went to school with the son, Lucius. His father owns the company."

Vic donned his best fibbing face. "You don't say. Are you friends with Lucius?"

"No, we aren't friends."

Vic asked, "Would you mind keeping me informed on their progress? This could be a good investment."

Jerimiah agreed. "I'll do that. Will you excuse me? I have to meet an old friend."

———

Jerimiah went into the forest and up to his favorite sequoia. Looking up, he smiled at its great height. "Hi, TREEZZ. I'm here for a visit."

Immediately he felt the friendly ambience and a sense of tranquility. He was besieged with information regarding his friends the TREEZZ. They were concerned that human hormones were being injected into plants and small trees. Every biologist knew that this was forbidden territory, but they threw caution to the wind, and the experiments continued. This biological testing was being conducted in a remote area of India due to the country's confusing drug laws. The name of the village was Kottappadi, which was located near the Elimbileri Rain Forest Resort.

Jerimiah called Robert. "We have a situation that has the TREEZZ very concerned. Human hormones are being injected into balsa wood trees and surrounding crop-yielding plants. The TREEZZ and I feel this is a dangerous situation that needs to be addressed immediately." Robert concurred. An hour later, the team had a conference call. Jerimiah was stressed; his tone conveyed urgency. He gave the team all the information he had.

Deb immediately was taken aback. She commented, "Everyone knows this was strictly forbidden. I can't even imagine the horrible implications this experiment might unleash on both man and trees."

Elaina suggested, "We have to be in India for a scheduled meeting with government officials. We might use this business deal as a cover to find out more information."

Robert was all for that. Deb began to assemble a team to investigate. He reminded them all, "Take no chances, and stay in touch."

Deb quickly chose Carlton to take samples, and Vic was security. They were acutely aware that time was of the essence.

A chartered C-130 landed at the resort to pick up its passengers. A corporate jet would draw undue attention in such a remote area. The flight time to India was twenty-two hours.

———

Landing at an airport near Kozhikode, Vic and Carlton rented a vehicle and proceeded directly to Kottappadi.

Vic followed an overgrown, unused trail that led them to an abandoned camp.

Carlton took some samples of balsa tree resin. He noticed some areas of distress on several balsa trees. He took samples of this possible infection. Vic collected several hypodermic needles he found thrown into the thick brush. As he did so, he saw a shadow fly overhead. He looked up and saw vultures circling several hundred feet away. He made his way through the thick brush and then detected the rancid odor he would never forget. It was the putrid smell of decomposing bodies. He knew that scent well. He dug a shallow grave and placed two bodies in the hole. He said a quick prayer and left. While Carlton categorized the samples, Vic went into town to see what the locals had to say.

Bar tongues wagged freely. He questioned several young men who had been out to the abandoned camp. They were paid well to let the doctor extract growth hormones from their pituitary glands for research. They did have concerns about two missing brothers. Vic had all the information he needed. The two men returned the rental and boarded the waiting C-130 to their destination, California.

Upon their landing, the samples were hastily taken to the lab. It didn't take Ethan long to find a very odd-shaped cell. It was nothing like he'd ever seen before. He called his colleagues over for their opinion. Bart commented, "It looks like a pregnant cell."

That response raised eyebrows. What if it *was* a "pregnant" cell?

CHAPTER 20

Becca began to think about Robert's offer. Maybe she did need to talk to someone. Maybe she wasn't aware of the emotional scars the horrible incident had left.

She took out her cell phone and called him. "I'm sorry to bother you. I've been thinking about your offer. I'd like to meet your friend."

"I'm so glad you've decided to talk to Carlie. I'll ask her to come to the resort for a few days so that you can get acquainted."

Becca asked, "Are you sure it won't be a bother to her?"

Robert said, "Absolutely not. It was she who made the suggestion."

A few days later, a private jet was heard circling the resort. This was the first time its passenger had seen the complex, and she wanted a bird's-eye view. Impressed, she was anxious to see Robert and to meet his young friend Becca.

The plane's door opened, and a well-dressed woman who appeared to be in her early thirties (but actually was in her early forties) disembarked. She was handsome but not a goddess—tall, with auburn hair and a fine figure. She obviously took very good care of herself. Her skin was flawless, which was why she looked so much younger.

She smiled as she saw her friend. "Robert, it's been much too long. Come kiss me."

He smiled sheepishly as he complied. Their warm greeting and body language indicated that they were more than just friends.

"You look beautiful, as always," he said. "Come. I'll show you to your suite, and you can freshen up."

Standing on her porch, Becca observed the friends' reunion. She thought with a hint of jealousy, *They must be awfully good friends to kiss like that. I'm curious, I just may do some snooping around.*

Becca's snooping proved to reveal some interesting facts regarding Carlie and Robert. Seems they were a hot item some years back. Rumors had it they were about to get engaged. Then something happened and the relationship ended.

Robert called Becca that afternoon. "I was hoping this was a good time for you to meet Carlie."

A bit nervous, she agreed. "Yes, this is a good time."

"I'm assuming you would be more comfortable at your place?"

"You're right; I would. Thank you."

"We'll be right over."

Becca quickly put on a pair of casual shorts and a loose-fitting T-shirt.

On the way to Becca's, Carlie complimented Robert. "Robert, I'm impressed; this oasis is beautiful— the mighty redwoods and sequoias, the chalets on the shore of the pristine mountain lake. Yes, you have quite a private resort here."

"Thank you, my dear. You do know you're always welcome?" Minutes later he knocked on the chalet's door. "Hello, Becca."

"Hi, Robert,"

He said, "This is my friend Carlie. Carlie, this is Becca."

Feeling slighted, she thought, *Hey, I'm his friend too.* The women shook hands as Becca invited them in. Carlie had changed into comfortable attire.

Becca gasped. "I recognize you. You're Carlie Andrews! I can't believe I just shook hands with you. My sister and I have always admired you, and we love your products."

Carlie smiled. "Thank you for the compliments. I'm so happy that you like them."

Robert said, "I have to get going. I'll let you ladies get to know each other."

Becca said, "Carlie, please sit wherever you'd like."

Slipping her shoes off, Carlie curled up on the couch. Becca sat in a chair with her knees up; she was already shoeless. Carlie expressed her sympathy for the tragic event Becca had endured. Becca thanked her. Each woman eyed the other. Carlie thought, *How pretty and intelligent for someone so youthful.* Becca thought, with a hint of envy, *Carlie is rich and famous. Robert's a lucky man. I wonder why they broke-up.*

"Becca, whenever you feel like talking, just go ahead. We have all the time in the world."

The girls chatted about Carlie's line of cosmetics.

Becca's curiosity got the best of her. "Do you mind if I ask what happened to you?"

"Not at all. You need to know so that we can relate and share our deepest feelings. My business was flourishing, and I was launching a new skin care line, so I decided to buy some jewelry to celebrate. I went to a famous jeweler in LA, where I purchased a one-hundred-and-fifty-thousand-dollar necklace. When I got home, I put it right in my safe. Suddenly I heard a noise. Two masked men had followed me home. They had observed me purchasing the jewelry. They both had guns and demanded the jewelry and my cash. I gave them everything they asked for. They started to leave when one walked back into my bedroom." Carlie's voice quivered.

Becca said softly, "You don't have to go on."

Carlie sniffled. "I must." She composed herself and continued. "One of the men grabbed my blouse and ripped it down the front. Then he tore my bra off. I covered myself with my hands. He pulled down my skirt. I remember his eyes; they were black, like two holes. They looked empty and dead. He yelled at me to drop my hands, so I did. He pulled down my panties. Both of them stared at me. I felt numb. I closed my eyes, hoping that all they wanted was the jewelry and the cash. It wasn't. The one who ripped my clothes off began to unzip his pants. I begged, 'Please don't do this. Please don't hurt me. Take anything you want, but please don't hurt me.' He paid no attention to my plea. He pulled his pants down, and I closed my eyes. I didn't want to see that disgusting piece of shit. He threw me on the bed and attacked me."

Becca began to cry. "*Oh*, Carlie. I'm so sorry. I can't even begin to imagine what that was like." She got up and went over to Carlie and hugged her.

Carlie dabbed Becca's tears and then her own. She continued. "I vaguely remember that his breathing became rapid and that his breath stank. I prayed that the attack would end. He let out a loud moan and then lay on top of me for about a minute, I guess; I had no sense of time. I didn't open my eyes until the door slammed shut. I stayed there for a few minutes just to make sure they were gone. When I thought it was safe, I got up and called the police. Then I got in the shower, where I sat down and cried and cried. The police found me there. They covered me and called the EMTs. A tech working for Robert heard the report and called him right away. Thank God he was in town; he rushed to the hospital. I don't know what I would have done if he hadn't been there. He stayed with me for days, never leaving my side."

Becca dried her tears. She went to Carlie and hugged her again.

"I'm sorry I had to tell you that awful story, but you needed to know that I do understand how you feel."

Becca asked, "Would you mind if I just curled up next to you for a while?"

"Not at all; I'd like that." They both dabbed the tears flowing from their eyes.

The session had been very stressful for both women. It had left them drained, and they fell asleep holding each other in the warm rays of the late afternoon sun. Hours later, the girls awoke just before the sun began to set.

Becca said, "I'll be right back." She returned with a bottle of wine and two glasses.

Carlie said, "Do you mind if we go out on the back porch and watch the sunset?"

Becca grinned. "Yes, let's do that. It's so beautiful here."

The girls finished the bottle of wine just as the sun disappeared below the horizon.

"That's just what we need. I hope you have more."

Feeling the wine, Becca giggled. "I do, as a matter of fact."

The girls tapped glasses, and Carlie said, "Here's to us and our new friendship."

Becca smiled, thinking, *I really like this Carlie. She's a special lady.* They each had another glass of wine as darkness fell over the posh resort.

It was time for Carlie to take her leave. "I better be going and let you get your rest."

"Don't walk back to your suite. You can stay here. I would feel much better if you stayed."

"Really? You wouldn't mind?"

"Not at all."

Becca showed Carlie to the guest bedroom. Impetuously Becca leaned toward Carlie and kissed her good night.

Carlie smiled, and Becca blushed at her impulsive behavior.

"I'm sorry. I don't know what came over me. I had this desire to kiss you."

"I didn't mind; in fact, I enjoyed it."

As she lay in bed, she thought, *I've never kissed another woman, except Deb, of course. I don't know why—I just wanted to kiss her and thank her.*

———

Early the next morning, Vic lightly knocked on Deb's door, hoping that she wasn't sleeping. He was just about to leave when the door opened. "You wouldn't happen to be looking for a free cup of coffee, would you, mister?"

"No. Actually, I came to see you, but if coffee is available, I could go for that too."

Vic watched Deb, who was dressed in his long-sleeved shirt, walk toward the kitchen. *God, she is sexy. A great set of legs—and that butt. Oh, that butt.*

"Let's watch the sunrise," she proposed.

As they sat on the front porch in the dawn's light, they noticed a figure leaving Becca's chalet. Deb and Vic were very curious and strained to see the person. As the figure got closer, they could see that it was a woman.

Deb was flabbergasted by who she saw. "What's Carlie Andrews doing leaving my sister's house this early in the morning?"

Vic questioned, "Who is Carlie Andrews?"

"She owns Carlie's Cosmetics. You know…she's in some of her ads for skin cream and her perfume, the one you like, Saints and Sinners?"

"Oh yeah, Now she looks familiar. Those ads are the ones with the hot models." Deb turned and looked at him with a frown. "But not as hot as you, Deb."

"Lucky save, Mr. Vic."

CHAPTER 21

The lab buzzed with the rumor that the cosmetic magnate Carlie Andrews was at the resort. Everyone wanted to meet her. Robert knew that the team would get very little work done until they met Carlie. At 9:00 a.m. he escorted Carlie to the lab. The room filled with excitement and applause as she entered. She was accustomed to her celebrity status and knew all the right words to say.

Robert introduced the team. After making small talk with the group, Carlie wanted to speak with Deb and get to know her. Deb was thrilled. The two women talked for over an hour. Deb thought, *That is one of the nicest women I have ever met. I feel like I've known her for years.*

Carlie remarked, "I hope we can make some time and continue our conversation."

Deb happily agreed. "Yes, I would enjoy that."

———

The next day the lab was back to normal. Carlton and Bartley were running tests on the balsa tree and samples and the "pregnant" cell.

Bartley called Deb over. "Take a look at this."

She peered into the microscope and adjusted it several times. Then she looked back at Bartley. "This must be your week for discovering new cells. I've never seen a cell quite like this one. It's completely different from the last one. Try to isolate it and look for more."

She immediately went to her library to see if she could identify the odd cell. She had no luck.

By the end of the day, Bartley was rechecking the cells before they were secured in isolation. His eyes bulged; the pregnant cell had split. He quickly called the team. They all agreed to store the cell away in a cryogenic freezer for further examination.

Early the next morning, he removed the odd cell for further testing and let it thaw to room temperature. Later he placed it under the microscope and was shocked to discover three identical cells. He alerted Deb, and the lab went on lockdown. Protocols called for complete insolation. He hurriedly locked it up in a sealed chamber and put it back in the freezer. Luckily only Bartley had risked contamination. After a chemical wash-down, he was cleared to leave the isolation chamber.

Now dressed in a protective suit, Bartley carefully removed the stored cells and returned them to room temperature. He looked to see if the cell had split again. Unfortunately all three cells had expired. Any hope of identifying them was now lost unless they could be reproduced, a daunting task, to say the least.

Deb was disappointed that they hadn't been able to identify the cell. It was clearly deadly, and it was much too dangerous to have it floating around in a forest. The biologists knew that this cell had to be reproduced if an antibody were to be found.

Deb's mind kept going over scenarios of how, where, and why the cell formed. It looked like she wouldn't get any sleep that night. A knock on the door broke her train of thought. When she opened it, she was delighted to see Vic standing there with a bouquet of flowers and a bottle of wine.

Deb smiled broadly. "You're just what the doctor ordered. Come in, and make yourself comfortable—that is, after you pop the cork."

The couple sat on the back porch, sipping wine and watching the sunset. Vic made a daring move and took her hand. She looked at him and squeezed his in return. He breathed a sigh of relief. They got cozy and watched TV for a time. Then they both drifted to sleep. Deb woke up and turned the TV off, which woke Vic.

He apologized. "I guess I fell asleep. Sorry."

She said, "If you're comfortable, stay right here for the night."

"Are you sure? You don't mind?"

"Yes, I'm sure. I can trust you."

She kissed his cheek and wished him pleasant dreams.

He whispered, "If I dream of you, I'm sure they'll be pleasant, but to be on the safe side, lock your door."

Both laughed loudly.

―――

The next morning Carlie was up early and out for a jog. When Becca saw her run by, she quickly dressed and joined her.

"Good morning, pretty girl," Carlie said.

"Good morning to you, Carlie. Do you mind if I join you?"

"Not at all. I'd enjoy your company."

At the lake they stopped to take a breather. They gazed out over the water, admiring its beauty, its surface like glass, so serene.

Carlie turned and noticed a vine creeping up Becca's leg. She jumped back, speechless, and pointed to the vine. Becca looked down and touched the vine. She said calmly, "Good morning, little one. This is my friend Carlie. Little one, say hello to Carlie." The vine slid over to Carlie and wrapped around her wrist. Carlie didn't move a muscle. "It's OK, Carlie. The trees are my friends. This vine is just saying hi."

Carlie was shocked; she didn't know what to do. Finally, she was able to speak. She cleared her throat and asked, "Becca, are you some kind of magician or witch or shaman?"

Becca laughed. "No, the TREEZZ are really my friends, and now they're your friends."

Carlie touched the vine, and it gently squeezed her hands. She giggled like a child. "They like me."

Becca said, "Carlie, I can't explain it, but can this be our secret?"

"Of course."

Although Carlie was skeptical, she trusted Becca. This secret led to a special bond that brought the women closer. They opened up and shared their deepest secrets, wants, and desires. Theirs was a special trust, formed by a mystical, magical bond.

The ladies continued their conversations until the subject of intimacy arose.

"Becca, would you care to broach the subject?" Becca was silent. Carlie suggested, "I think this may be a good time to explore your feelings on this very private issue. Becca, has your recent incident changed your feelings about sex?"

Becca gave the question serious thought. "Yes, I have sexual needs and wants, but right now I can't even think of a man touching me. I find it repulsive—his rough hands, his impatience, his selfish demands. Then, when he is satisfied, he goes to sleep, and I'm left cold and empty. I want the caress of his soft, gentle hand. I want tender kisses all over. I want to be slowly brought to orgasm. That may be too much to ask, but that's what I want. If I can't have that, I'd rather not have sex."

Carlie was taken aback by Becca's candor.

Excitedly she whispered, "Becca, I had those same feelings, and I still do. After the attack it took me a long time to even think about sex. I know that this will stay just between us. Robert was the only man who gave me what I needed. His patience and sensitivity made me want him. When I gave in, it was his tender touch, his soft caresses. He pleasured me before himself. He gave me all the same things you desire. I could swear the man read my mind. I looked forward to our intimate times. But that was years ago, and we both have moved on. I often wonder if I made a mistake not marrying him."

Becca was silent and began fantasizing about being with Robert and how he might satisfy her sexual needs and desires. Suddenly she came back to reality. "Oh, Carlie, our intimate conversation has given me a new direction, new hope, a new beginning."

Immediately everyone noticed a new attitude, a zip in her step, and a smile on her face. She was slowly enjoying life again. And of course her fantasies of being with Robert continued. Deb made it a point to speak to Carlie to thank her for all the help and support she'd provided to her sister.

She said, "I'm a bit jealous of you spending all that time with Becca. But you have helped her immensely, and I thank you for it."

"Becca's fortunate to have your love, support, and understanding. And let's not forget Robert, so gentle and caring."

Deb agreed. Yes, Robert—she noticed he looked at Becca differently. And Becca was extra attentive when he was present. She wanted to look her best.

———

In her office at the lab, Deb was filling out the paperwork regarding the mutant cell. She was disappointed that the cell had expired before it could be identified. She decided to hold a meeting with the team to get their thoughts.

With the group assembled, she stated, "This is where we stand. We know that L&L Chemical is experimenting with a human growth hormone. We know that cadavers were supplying the growth hormone gland, and we can assume that the balsa tree was chosen because of its softwood. Other crop-producing plants also showed signs of hormone injections. The question is: Why inject the tree with the hormone?"

Carlton spoke up. "Maybe they wanted to see if there would be any harmful effects?"

Bartley applauded Carlton's deduction. Maybe, just maybe, the tree/human combination had produced the mutant cell.

She noted, "Now we're getting somewhere. Keep it going."

Becca asked, "Why India?"

Ethan answered, "Probably because the growth hormone is considered a controlled substance in the United States and is highly regulated by the FDA. Other countries may not have the resources to enforce the ban and look the other way."

Bartley asked, "What's our next step?"

Deb replied, "We need to finish the paperwork on the herbal insulin and start producing it in volume. That's our priority. We can concentrate on the growth hormone later."

She assigned Becca and Ethan to find a way to increase the volume of herbal insulin. The pair started in the nursery. Both biologists enjoyed the quiet, calm serenity of the space. It was just the atmosphere the kidnapping victims needed.

As Becca was pruning a small tree the next day, a tiny branch wrapped itself around her hand and wrist. She giggled at its touch and whispered, "Hi, little one. Did you come to say hello?" The little branch tightened a bit. "Oh, you're so sweet. Thank you." She quickly looked around to see if anyone had noticed what had just taken place. No one had, and she breathed a sigh of relief. This became normal, and whenever she entered the nursery alone, a different plant would greet her with a touch. For now this was Becca and Carlie's secret. Their caresses seemed to calm and relax Becca. She began to spend more and more time in the nursery.

Deb approached Jerimiah and asked his opinion about the cell. He had a suspicion and replied, "I'll get right back to you."

Jerimiah entered the forest, making certain that he wasn't followed. He walked into the tall sequoia and returned a minute later, more knowledgeable and confident in his quest to save the TREEZZ. Hurrying back to the lab, he went directly to Deb's office. "I have some great news. The TREEZZ informed me that we need to make a triple graft between the hybrid poplar trees. They will be the best tree because of their speed of growth. The ling zhi will be needed for the herbal insulin, along with a strain of Chiapas corn, for the size of its stalks. By doing this, we will triple our production yield of the herbal insulin."

Deb stood there dumbfounded. "I've never heard of such an outlandish suggestion. But if the TREEZZ said to do it, well, we'll do it. We would have never found the right combination if not for the TREEZZ."

Jerimiah continued. "The TREEZZ also said that they would help Becca make the grafts. The resin from the tree will be used for this. It's a very rare sap and will be used to control rejection."

She frowned. "And just where do we find this resin?"

He answered, "On Three Kings Island in New Zealand."

Deb called Robert and explained the circumstances. He asked, "Is Becca up for such a mission, or should we get someone else?"

Deb replied, "The TREEZZ asked that she handle this unusual graft."

"Is she physically and mentally able to complete this assignment? Is she ready?"

"I'll speak with her and will get back to you." Deb went into the nursery. "Becca, can we talk for a minute?"

"Sure, Sis. What's on your mind?"

"The TREEZZ gave us a way to increase insulin production. We will need resin from a very rare tree found only on Three Kings Island."

Becca said excitedly, "I know that tree. It's called the *Pennantia baylisiana*, and it is very rare."

"Do you think you're up for it? Please take some time to think this over."

Becca stopped and closed her eyes for a moment before replying. "I need to do this, and I want to do this."

Deb called Robert. "Becca agreed to get the resin. She said she's ready for the mission."

"What a trouper. I'll get Elaina to clear it with the New Zealand government."

Elaina persuaded the government to give them a two-day permit to retrieve the rare resin. She also generously offered her jet to Becca and Vic. "I wish you both a safe and successful trip."

The team quickly put together a kit for tapping the tree resin, including specially designed containers and a unique cream sealer to close the tap incision.

Vic was overjoyed that he was getting out of town and didn't even ask where they were going.

Becca had one very important call to make. "Hi, Carlie. I have to go out of town for a few days. Please tell me that you'll be here when I get back."

"Becca, I'm so sorry, but I need to return to LA for the monthly board meeting. I'll try to get back as soon as possible. You know I'll be thinking of you the whole time I'm gone."

"I'll be thinking of you too, Carlie," Becca cooed.

At midnight the G-500 lifted off, its destination Wellington, New Zealand. The estimated time of travel was twenty-three hours.

CHAPTER 22

The Gulfstream landed with no fanfare. Only a courier was waiting with a packet addressed to Vic Bowden. Vic grinned. He preferred to come and go discreetly. He opened the packet; inside was all the documentation needed to secure the resin. The permit expired in two days. He thought, *If the weather holds, we'll be fine. If the weather goes south, we're out of luck*. He passed the information to Becca. She read it and raised her hand with her fingers crossed.

The pair weren't dressed in expedition khakis. Becca didn't fit the profile of a beautiful adventuress: flawless makeup, perfect hair. No, she was dressed in tight jeans, sneakers, and a hoodie. Vic looked like an extra for the movie in his wrinkled pants and a worn-out hat.

At the bottom of the packet, Vic found a note. It stated that a professor of biology would accompany the team on behalf of the government, which was a standard precaution. *Standard precaution, my butt. He's a damn spy.*

Becca and Vic walked over to the waiting helicopter that would transport them to Three Kings Island.

The pilot asked, "Where's the third passenger?"

Vic replied, "The hell with him—"

As he spoke, an elderly man crossed the tarmac, carrying his hat, an umbrella, and a suitcase, and called, "Wait for me!"

Vic and Becca helped the older man into the chopper. The copilot buckled him in and gave a thumbs-up.

The chopper lifted off, and the three passengers were on their way to the island.

The conversations were kept to a minimum due the noisy rotating blades.

The helicopter landed two hours later, and the three passengers disembarked. After the whirlybird departed and the dust settled, Becca stuck out her hand to their companion. "Hello. my name is Becca Carlsbad. And your name is?"

In a low grunt, he mumbled, "Professor John Smith, senior biologist."

He gave Becca the once-over, thinking, *You can't be serious. She's still in high school. Who are they trying to fool?*

While Vic looked for a place to set up the tent, John Smith accosted Becca and dragged her to the side. Vic's eyes were fixed on Becca. *One more aggressive move like that from Mr. John Smith, and I'll be all over the old coot.*

Smith questioned her. "Miss, what makes you think you can tap the resin in this rare tree? I personally protected this tree for the last forty years, and I'm not going to let some…some schoolgirl touch my trees."

She humbly said, "I can assure you, sir, that I am highly qualified and have the expertise to successfully tap the trees."

The older man became loud and boisterous. "Do you really expect me to believe that? How old are you anyway?"

Becca said, "My age has nothing to do with tapping this tree."

Smith countered, "I insist that I oversee this operation on the government's behalf."

Becca sought to calm the man. "I'd be honored to have such an esteemed biologist oversee the procedure."

That seemed to quiet the irate man. With all parties in agreement, the mission was on for the following morning.

———

The sun had just cleared the horizon, and the old professor was sitting on his bags, waiting for Becca and Vic to exit their tents. He looked at his watch and shook his head.

Becca said to Vic, "I can see this is going to be a fun trip."

He smiled and agreed. "With luck, he can be our entertainment."

The island was windblown and barren except for the *Pennantia baylisiana*, a small shiny-leaved tree. She and John made a preliminary examination of the tree. While running her hands over the leaves, Becca noted that the trees were in good health and thriving on the island.

The elderly biologist confirmed her observation and asked sarcastically, "How can you assess the health of the tree by just touching it? Do you have a crystal ball, or are you psychic?"

Vic became upset with the insults.

She whispered, "Vic, he's old, and these are his babies. Let it slide."

She took out her instruments, and Vic retrieved the collection container. She made a small incision in the soft bark to install the tap. Instantly the resin began to flow, a few drops initially and then a small stream. In minutes the container was full. She opened her bag and took out a unique cream. She covered the incision with the salve, and the resin stopped flowing. Almost immediately the tree began to wilt. The government biologist threw his hands in the air. "You're killing the tree. I order you to cease and desist."

Vic looked at Becca. "Is this normal?"

She nodded and walked to the next tree. Smith ran up to Becca and pushed her away from the tree. Vic grabbed the senior biologist by the back of the neck and lifted him off the ground. "Are you going to calm down, or will I have to thump you?"

"I demand that you put me down this minute!"

Vic growled, "Only if you promise to be good."

"I will not!"

"Then hang there awhile."

Finally the professor gave in. "Very well. I'll be good."

John Smith walked back to the tree. He couldn't believe his eyes. In all the years he'd cared for the trees, he'd never been able to seal the damaged soft bark. Insects would enter the tree and eventually kill it. The biologist rubbed his chin. He was beginning to have second thoughts regarding this young girl's skills.

Darkness descended quickly on the camp, and the three visitors retired for the night. Becca lay on her back, her eyes wide open. Her thoughts drifted to Carlie. Tonight she would dream of her, of her tender caress and her arms holding Becca tight. She turned over and closed her eyes. Those pleasant thoughts relaxed the young biologist, sending her to slumber land.

Vic was the first one up and was waiting for day-break. Becca rose after smelling the coffee. The pair sat next to each other and enjoyed a spectacular sunrise. John awoke and was surprised to see that Becca and Vic were up before him.

She handed him a cup of coffee and then looked at her watch. "Sleeping in today, John?"

He smiled for the first time. "Touché."

Becca grinned. John quickly finished his coffee and went to examine the tree and the mends Becca had made. To his astonishment, the tree looked healthy, and the tap hole had healed. John hadn't believed in miracles until then. He looked at Becca. "My dear, I sincerely apolo-gize for my actions and insults. I humbly ask your for-giveness. You are a brilliant biologist. I will no longer impede your mission."

With his head lowered, he slowly shuffled to his tent, dejected and ashamed.

Feeling bad for the man, Becca called out to him, "John, I need your help. Will you assist me with this next tap?"

John turned around. "Do you really need me?"

"Yes, John. Please help me."

He ran over. "What can I do?"

She said, "I need you to seal the tap hole with this cream."

John took the cream and got to work. He looked at Becca. "Thank you."

On the next tap, John watched intently. He was learn-ing again, something he had avoided in the last few years.

She took the scalpel and placed the knife on the bark. A small branch wrapped around her hand and guided the blade a fraction of an inch higher. There she began the incision. John backed away, stunned by the sight. "I have heard tales of a tree princess who would be welcomed by the TREEZZ, and I think I have just met her." John was in awe. He felt blessed and would forever cherish these two days.

By the end of the second day, the team had plenty of resin and began to pack up. Late in the afternoon, a chopper could be heard in the distance, approaching the island.

———

The next morning the G-500 was waiting on the Wellington airport tarmac, ready to take the pair back to the resort.

On the return trip, Vic said to Becca, "I have to tell you, it's an honor to work with you. Sometimes we get caught up in our missions and take each other for granted. I don't want to let that happen. I love you like a daughter, and I'm proud to be part of your team. I hope we're able to work together for many years."

Becca's eyes watered. "Vic, that's so sweet. You are my man of steel, my bodyguard, my friend." She wiped a tear away. "I love you too. Thank you for telling me. I know it is not easy for you to express your feelings. I love you for that too."

The two friends hugged, and Becca kissed his cheek. Smiling, she whispered in his ear, "You know I'm not the only Carlsbad who thinks you're special."

He smiled. "Do you really think I have a chance with your sister?"

Becca teasingly punched him in the arm. "Ask her before someone else does."

———

This day was very special for the biologists. They all gathered on the resort tarmac to celebrate the World Health Organization's first shipment of the free herbal insulin bound for the continent of Africa. The C-130 turboprop taxied down the runway. Upon liftoff, loud cheers and clapping echoed across the resort.

After the drone of the powerful engines faded, Robert held up a glass of champagne and toasted everyone on a job that many had thought impossible. "I can't thank you enough, my friends, for the dedication you have shown in bringing my dream to fruition. But this is just the beginning of many more herbal medicines we will discover as we travel through the uncharted world of the TREEZZ."

CHAPTER 23

L&L Chemical was having great success with what they designated a plant-growth enhancer. In reality, it was a mixture of human growth hormones combined with plant life. The company was paying for pituitary glands from cadavers to harvest the hormones, which were then added to a liquid emulsifier and some cheap plant food. This chemical was sprayed on the crops. Testing showed a 30 to 40 percent increase in crop yield. The other benefit was that the size of the crop also increased. This was a major breakthrough in feeding humanity; in time, hunger might also be eliminated. The side effects were unknown in the early stages of testing.

When they intermixed certain hormones, two cells mutated into one. That cell evolved and destroyed the human cells. The deadly cell was isolated and stored in a cryogenic freezer for safekeeping. Someone well paid leaked this information to a foreign agent.

L&L Chemical needed to speed up its testing, and in doing so, it bypassed several safety procedures. This went undiscovered because the FDA regulated the growth hormone, and the Department of Agriculture regulated crop enhancement.

Unbeknownst to L&L Chemical, there were two very powerful people with different objectives. Just before making their big announcement, Lucius and his father, Clay, were contacted by a well-known Chinese biologist, Wang Ti Lu. He requested a private meeting with the two owners and his specialized team of biologists. Wang Ti Lu said, "This meeting may prove to be very lucrative for your company." The Lattimore's were reluctant at first, but greed prevailed.

The second person interested in their product was a Brazilian biologist, Ingalls Smutch, who worked for a wealthy landowner in Brasília. Smutch was there to observe and listen. He paid attention not just to the product but also to others interested in purchasing the item. And if the product was all it was reported to be, he was to place a very large order. Mr. Smutch oversaw huge coca fields. The coca was grown for the sole purpose of making cocaine.

Wang Ti Lu was interested in examining the test results concerning the mutant cell. He also asked if he could speak to the chemist who had discovered it, Horace Riley.

The Lattimore's summoned the low-level chemist. "Gentlemen, this is the chemist who found the cell. Unfortunately, the cell has expired."

The Chinese team asked if Riley could reproduce the mutant cell. "Yes, I can reproduce the cell, but it is extremely dangerous. Should it be accidentally released into the atmosphere, it could have deadly consequences."

Wang Ti Lu asked, "How fast? And how many can you create?"

Horace Riley answered, "I could have maybe a hundred in two days."

"Excellent," said Wang. "We will take as much as you can give us. There is, however, a stipulation; *we* must be shown the procedure to replicate the cell."

Horace looked at the Lattimore's. "I don't think you realize how dangerous this mutant cell is. Under laboratory conditions, a deadly virus could be produced. And why would you want to—"

Lucius interrupted him. "Gentlemen, gentlemen, we are all men of science. We have discovered a new cell, and it must be investigated in the name of progress. I'm sure that Wang's team is highly qualified." Lucius looked at Horace and instructed him to fill the order. "You know, Wang, that this will be expensive?"

Wang smiled. "We will pay you very well."

Horace Riley knew that Lucius was interested only in the money. He had to warn someone of this danger. He could think of only one person who would understand: Deborah Carlsbad. He called Deborah but got her voice mail. Instead of leaving a message, he abruptly ended the call, deciding to try again the next day.

Meanwhile, Lucius knew that he had to dispose of Horace Riley as soon as he delivered the deadly cells to the Chinese.

With the final paperwork completed, the Department of Agriculture approved the application. L&L Chemical sent out invitations to join the company in a celebration of their new product. To give the appearance that the company had nothing to hide, it sent Deborah Carlsbad a VIP invitation to the festivities. Many reporters from large news agencies attended as well, promoting the new product. One young independent reporter named Sylvester "Sly" Tabor knew that other news outlets had it covered.

Sylvester was a twenty-two-year-old junior journalist. He was of medium height, with an athletic build, dark hair, and glasses. Secretly he considered himself a ladies' man. Unfortunately, he was the only one who thought so. He loved the newspaper business and hoped to someday be a senior reporter. He just needed that one Pulitzer Prize–winning story.

While sitting in L&L Chemical's lobby, he read an item that mentioned Ms. Becca Carlsbad as a young, successful cellular biologist performing highly advanced tree grafts. When he saw her picture, he was smitten. He immediately decided to pursue her story. The young reporter learned that Becca worked in a lab not far from his location. He would prepare himself for the interview by studying the process of tree grafting, Becca's specialty. Hopefully his knowledge would impress her.

He drove to the resort and approached the front gate. "My name is Sylvester Tabor, and I'm a freelance reporter. I'd like to do a story on the biologist Becca Carlsbad."

The guard took his number and told him that someone would contact him. The guard called Vic and gave him Tabor's number. Vic called the reporter, knowing that he needed to blow this guy off. "Mr. Tabor, my name is Vic Bowden, head of security. Did you fill out the 2-125 form?" he asked, although no such form existed.

Sly replied, "No, sir. I didn't know about that form."

"Give me your email address, and I'll have one sent out."

Tabor did so, but Vic never wrote it down; he figured that would get rid of the young reporter. He didn't realize the fledgling journalist's persistence.

That night Tabor hid in the nearby forest, hoping to get candid pictures of Becca going about her business. Security called Vic. "Sir, we have a trespasser on the grounds."

Vic rushed to the office, and there on the surveillance feed was the pesky reporter. He understood that Tabor was just trying to get a story, but he didn't want him snooping around the resort, especially in light of the sensitive research. Vic called Jerimiah. "I hate to bother you at this time of night, but we have an unwanted guest in our forest. A pest, you might say. I'd like to give him a little scare."

Jerimiah laughed. "I think we can arrange that for you."

Vic smiled. "Thanks, partner."

Tabor camped out with his camera equipped with a telescopic lens. For all his patience, he captured only one picture of Becca. It was a dark night. The moon peeked through the clouds every so often to create mysterious, haunting shadows. Sly, cold and hungry, thought, *This would make a good Halloween night.* He became drowsy after midnight, and his mind started playing tricks on him. He began imagining monsters from his childhood.

A passing cloud blocked the moonlight, and he felt something wrap around his leg. At first he thought it was a snake, and he almost screamed. He hated snakes. The cloud passed, and in the dim light, he saw a vine curling around his ankle. He tried to get free, but the vine tightened. A second vine wove around his other leg. Then several other vines came out of nowhere. Sly panicked and began struggling to free himself, but he couldn't. The vines began pulling him toward an old, twisted tree. Fear was etched on his face. He looked back, and the huge tree trunk cracked open. He was going to be eaten by a tree.

He struggled and started to scream. "God help me—I don't wanna die!"

But the vines kept pulling him toward snapping yellow teeth, waiting to devour him. *This is it. I'm going to be eaten by a tree.*

Suddenly, a bright light appeared. He shielded his eyes and saw a menacing shadow.

A deep, raspy voice asked, "Are you all right, young man? Let me help you. What are you doing out here?"

"Oh, mister, thank you! You saved my life. The tree was going to—" Tabor caught himself just in time.

"Going to what?" the man asked.

"Oh...uh...going to fall on me. Yes, I thought it was going to fall."

"Let me take you over to the resort lobby so that you can get cleaned up."

"Thanks, sir," the reporter answered.

On the way to the lobby, Vic introduced himself. "My name is Vic Bowden." He stuck out his hand.

Sylvester shook it. "I'm Sylvester Tabor, independent reporter. Hey, you wouldn't be Vic with the security staff?"

"Yes, I am, and now I remember. You wanted to do an interview with Ms. Carlsbad."

Now safe, Tabor found new courage. "Did you see the monstrous vines attacking me? I had most of them thrown off, and I killed a few...I think. I probably scared them off just before you came."

Vic said, "You're safe now. They don't come out in the daytime." Vic choked several times as he held back his laughter.

The reporter hugged his liberator in gratitude. "You can call me Sly, sir."

Vic said, "Well, Sly, sometimes we imagine our greatest fears. Are you afraid of snakes?"

Sly nodded. "I hate snakes and anything that looks like a snake."

The ex-agent said, "There you have it. Your sub-conscious thought the vines were snakes. To tell you the truth, I didn't see any vines near you or a man-eating tree. But that doesn't mean they don't exist. Personally, I don't go into the forest at night." Again, Vic struggled to hold back his laughter.

Feeling much better, Sly announced, "I don't know what happened, but you saved my life. I owe you. Is there anything I can do?"

"No, thanks…wait a minute. There may be some-thing you can do for me. As head of security, I always like to know what the competition is doing. Do you plan to attend the celebration at L&L Chemical?" When Sly nodded, Vic continued. "Maybe you could keep your eyes and ears open for anything interesting. Well, I don't have to tell you; you have a nose for news." Both men enjoyed a good laugh.

"I'll get back with you tomorrow," Sly stated.

———

Sly flashed his press pass and entered the L&L reception hall. There were well over one hundred guests. One, in particular, drew Sly's attention. She was a very attrac-tive, tall blonde. He made several passes by her. On one, he caught the scent of her perfume; he inhaled deeply, enjoying the aroma.

While getting a breath of air, Sly noticed a Chinese delegation entering a side door of the plant. They were escorted by a big, nasty-looking man. His mean expression and demeanor signified that he was a tough hombre. Sly knew that he'd seen this man before, but right then he was too busy to give it much thought. He recognized one of the other men as a high-level government biochemist. Sly had a feeling that this was important and made a note for Vic. He went back inside and looked for the tall blonde.

As Sly walked by her for the fifth time, she turned and asked, "Are you following me?"

Sly stuttered, "Uh…why, yes I am. I was wondering what perfume you're wearing. I'd like to get some for my girlfriend."

The blonde purred, "Take Me Tonight."

Sly turned three shades of red.

The blonde clarified. "Don't get your hopes up. That's the name of the perfume." She turned and left, and he watched in pleasure as she walked out the door.

———

The first signs of light came out of the east. The sun's brilliant rays would soon follow. Sly passed through the front gates of the resort and parked near the lobby. He walked into the building, expecting to see no one.

Much to his surprise, Vic was standing near the coffee machine. He handed Sly his first cup of the steaming brew.

Vic cheerfully said, "Good morning, young man. Did you have a productive night?"

Sly responded, "Actually, I did. I saw something that you may find interesting and someone who I found interesting."

"Don't keep me in suspense," Vic said.

"I recognized a prominent Chinese biochemist. This man is seldom seen and rarely leaves his country. So I would say this was a big deal."

Just then Deb walked through the doors; Sly didn't see her come in. Looking at Vic, she mouthed, "I know him from last night."

Vic nodded. He asked Sly, "Who did you find interesting?"

Sly became animated. "Vic, you should have seen her; she was beautiful. A tall blonde—hot, and I mean hot."

With his hands he outlined her killer shape. "And the way she walked, with those long—you just…"

Vic stopped him. "Hold on, kid. Was her name Deborah?"

"I believe that's what her name tag said."

Deb suddenly appeared and walked up to the pair. "Good morning, gentlemen."

Sly's face turned crimson.

Vic smiled. "Let me introduce you to Deborah, my girlfriend."

Sly was embarrassed and speechless. If there had been a hole big enough, he would have crawled in it.

Deb, on the other hand, backed up. With a bowled-over look on her face, she stared at her new boyfriend. "Your girlfriend . . . Uh…yes, I'm Vic's girlfriend." Still staring at Vic, she asked, "Vic, did I get a promotion?" Then she looked at Sly. "Thank you for the compliments. I'm glad Vic interrupted when he did. You may have stepped on your tongue."

Deb and Vic laughed, and Sly mustered a slight grin.

Vic asked Deb, "Do you think Becca would give our friend the reporter an interview on tree grafting?"

"I think we can arrange that."

Sly's color returned to normal. Then he remembered something. "One more thing. I saw this big guy running security for the Chinese delegation. I remember his picture from the paper. I think he was involved in a kidnapping earlier this year."

CHAPTER 24

Becca's interview with Sly went as well as could be expected. She conducted herself professionally, even though Sly undressed her with his eyes several times. With the interview complete, she started back to the lab.

"Becca—I mean, Ms. Carlsbad—would you like to have dinner with me?"

Becca said, "I'm sorry, but I was involved in a terrible incident, and I'm not dating."

He said, "I understand. I'll call in a few months and see how you feel. It was a real pleasure to see you—I mean, meet you. Thanks for the interview."

She walked away but knew his eyes were fixed on her butt. She whispered, "That little pervert."

———

The herbal insulin program was running like clockwork. Now it was time to move on to the next mission: an herbal blood pressure medication. For years biologists worldwide had tried many formulas but had never hit on the right one. Deborah and Robert hoped that would change now that the team had an edge—the help of the TREEZZ.

Vic had his tech research the Chinese biochemist and his projects, which turned up some interesting facts. He was the head of China's Biochemical Testing Laboratories outside of Beijing. To Vic, that translated to chemical weapons. Vic's conspiracy mindset kicked in, and he began forming theories.

Out of the blue, Deb received a startling call. "Hello, my name is Horace Riley, and I'm a chemist at L&L Chemical. Is this Ms. Deborah Carlsbad?"

"Yes, it is, Mr. Riley. How can I help you?"

"Ma'am, is this line secure?"

"Yes, it's very secure."

"I thought it would be. I've uncovered a dangerous mutant cell—a cell that could become a deadly virus for humans."

Deborah described the mutant cell in detail.

Riley was shocked. "How did you know about it?"

She replied, "Right now that doesn't matter. We need to talk. Can you meet me somewhere?"

"I can meet you at the Crescent City Library at four p.m. today. I'll be wearing a yellow baseball cap with a fish on it. We'll converse through the bookshelves. We can't be seen together."

"I'll be there at four." Deb immediately called Vic. She got his voice mail and left a message with the details of her meeting with Horace Riley that afternoon.

She entered the library a little before the appointed time. The woman at the desk asked all patrons to please turn off their phones while in the library.

Vic got out of his tech meeting and checked his messages. As he listened to Deb's voice mail, a sense of alarm raised the hairs on his neck. He tried to call but to no avail. He jumped into his vehicle and made a bee-line for the library. He continued to call her number but received the same message: "The customer you are trying to reach is unavailable at this time."

Deb walked through several aisles, looking for a yellow hat with a fish on it. As she turned the corner, she saw a yellow hat at the far end of the aisle. She walked up and whispered, "Horace?"

"Yes. Deborah?" Gruffly he said, "Let's talk."

She thought, *How strange. This doesn't sound like the man who called me. Maybe it was the connection?*

Horace asked, "How much do you know about the cell, and who else knows?"

With her suspicions raised, she said, "You were going to tell me about the cell hosts."

"Yes, I was coming to that, but right now I need to know who else knows about the cell."

She sensed that something was wrong. "I'm sorry. Call me tomorrow, Horace." She started for the door.

The man pulled a gun and stuck it in her back. "Use the side door, and don't try anything, or I'll shoot you."

Once they were outside, he pushed her to his car, unlocked the door, and shoved her in. He closed the door, which was the last thing he would remember. Vic hit the man in the head with a vicious blow that rendered him unconscious.

Deb cried out, "Vic! Thank God you're here!" She got out of the car and fell into his arms. "I'm sorry. I didn't think this would happen. I should have known better."

"You're OK, hon. You're safe now. Let's get you into my vehicle. I'll send someone to drive your car back to the resort."

Once Deb was safely in the car, he walked back to the unconscious man with size-eleven shoes. The man moaned in pain.

Vic growled, "Who do you work for?"

"Lattimore," the thug cried.

"When you see him, tell him Vic Bowden sends his love."

Deb asked, "Did you forget something?"

Vic chuckled. "Just making sure we only left our footprints and nothing else."

"You're always thinking, Vic. Now I just want to get home so that I can cuddle up next to my hero."

He smiled broadly. He was all for that.

Back at the resort, Vic took Deb to her chalet. He stepped outside and called the techs. "Run a check on Horace Riley, who is employed as a chemist at L&L Chemical. See what you come up with, and call me."

Deb was shaken up about the library incident, knowing that it could have turned out very badly. However, she felt that she'd learned an important lesson: leave the cloak-and-dagger business to the professionals. That evening she curled up next to Vic. She always felt so safe, so protected, by his side.

She purred, "I didn't get to thank you for the promotion to girlfriend."

"I'm sorry, Deb. I just didn't want Sly getting any ideas that you were available."

"Are you saying that you'd like us to be a couple?"

"If you'll have me, I would love for us to be a couple."

Deb kissed him passionately. "Does that answer your question?"

"Deb, I can't believe that a beautiful, intelligent woman like you would be interested in a ruffian like me."

"You know the old saying: 'Opposites attract.'"

The new couple cozied up and watched a movie together. It was almost the end of the movie when Vic said, "This is the good part, then I'll go back to my place."

She announced, "OK. I'm going to get ready for bed. I'll be right out to kiss you good night."

A short time later, she sashayed out of the bedroom in a sexy nightie, leaving just enough to his imagination. She whispered, "Is this the good part you mentioned?"

Deb looked better than he ever could have imagined. "You are so beautiful, so sexy. There's no other way to describe you. I love everything about you; I love you."

"I'm glad you like what you see." She took his hand and led him to her bedroom, where she slowly disrobed. "Still like what you see?"

"My God, woman. You're so hot. I can't believe I'm here with you."

"Now it's your turn, mister."

He quickly began to strip.

"Slow down, babe. We have all night. Let me enjoy your nakedness."

He stood in front of her, totally nude and a touch embarrassed. He covered himself with his hands. He had never been ogled by a woman.

She eyed him with a sly smile, "You really do like me, don't you?" She winked. "Come make love to me."

It had been a long time since either one had experienced a night of total bliss. It was wonderful, and they hoped many more would follow.

CHAPTER 25

The sun was just breaking through the mountain mist as it rose over the eastern horizon. Deb and Vic watched the sunrise from the front porch. The couple savored a delicious cup of coffee, her secret blend. The two lovers had a glow that rivaled the sun's soft morning rays. She nudged him. "You better get ready for work. You have a big day."

He looked over at the lab building and walked her into the bedroom. He would be late for work this morning. He put his arms around her, pulled her close, and kissed her. He whispered, "I love you, Deborah."

She looked down at his shorts. "You sex machine. You want to go back to bed?"

"I was just thinking about last night and how perfect it was, and I was wondering if we could do it again."

They were in a passionate embrace, and he started to kiss her neck, which she loved. He began to move lower when Becca knocked on her sister's door. "Hey, Deb. Are you up?"

Vic's deep voice boomed, "Becca, this probably isn't a good time."

"Oh my God. I'm so sorry. I didn't know. Oh, I'm sorry. I'm leaving now. Go back to…I mean…oh hell. Goodbye. Enjoy!"

———

The two lovers strolled into the lab around two o'clock. Vic tried to focus on L&L Chemical, and Deb began to address some overdue reports.

He peeked into her office. "Deb, how are you doing?"

"Not too good. I can't seem to get started. How about you?"

"Same problem. I close my eyes and see you, so I close them to see you again."

Becca walked by, laughing. "Isn't it time the both of you go back to the chalet?"

"Becca, mind your own business."

"Yes, big sister."

That night, Deb and Vic enjoyed a replay of the previous evening.

Alone in her chalet, Becca lay in her bed and thought, *I'm so happy that my sister and Vic finally got together. Now I'll keep prodding him to marry her. Then there is Sly…no, that would never work. But Carlie. I really like her, and I feel a kinship with her. Could I have a romantic encounter with her?*

She grabbed a pillow and hugged it. Drowsy from the sandman's spell, she pulled the pillow close and kissed it. She caressed it, imagining that it was Carlie. She smiled as she fell into a deep sleep.

———

Given that Horace Riley didn't show at the library, Vic had his techs run a trace on him. Using satellite surveillance, he discovered that the last visual of the employee showed him walking into the plant. That afternoon a flatbed tow truck removed Horace's car from the parking lot and took it to a garage in town. He knew that wasn't good. It meant that Horace was probably dead.

Vic immediately ordered twenty-four-hour surveillance on Deb. When he informed her of the surveillance, she wasn't pleased, but she knew it was for her safety. It was not up for discussion.

Later that week the techs uncovered some interesting facts.

Vic knew it was time to have a meeting with Robert. He called him. "Good afternoon, Robert. How are you?"

Robert groaned. "I was doing fine until your name popped up on the screen. It gave me the chills."

"Sorry about that, boss, but the chills may be warranted."

Robert said, "OK, I'm sitting down."

"I believe this information calls for a face-to-face."

Robert agreed. "I'm in Washington. This will be a good excuse to get me out of the city. See you tomorrow."

———

Ethan had been assigned to find an herbal blood pressure medication, and he was making some progress. One promising plant was the horsetail herb. Using it in combination with several other herbs, such as those from the Acanthaceae, Apocynaceae, and Boraginaceae families, had worked well in preliminary trials. Something was still missing; even so, the biologist was confident that he was close to success.

———

Carlton and Bartley were running tests on the human growth hormone for enhancing crop production.

Jerimiah had just returned from his regular visit with the TREEZZ. He had some disturbing information. The forest in India where some experiments had taken place was now experiencing a deadly virus. This virus was a human strain against which the TREEZZ had no defense. Jerimiah expressed great concern. "We need to make this a priority and find answers. *Now.*"

The biologists agreed. Deb quickly began making arrangements to get part of the team to the affected forest. Carlton and Ethan were chosen to discover the deadly cell, isolate it, and destroy it. They were up against the clock. Every day more of the forest was dying. It was a daunting assignment, to say the least. After a week the biologists had had little success. The future of the forest looked bleak. Deb had but one option: incinerate the deadly cell before it could contaminate more of the forest. That meant burning the forest in all directions for at least five miles to be safe.

Deb explained to Elaina and Jerimiah the only choice they had. The pair relayed the dreadful news to the Indian government. The Indian government accepted McAlister's recommendation, and the forest was intentionally set ablaze. Shockingly, all this destruction took place in a short period.

Now they prayed that all the deadly cells would be destroyed. Carlton and Ethan stayed for a time, checking for any signs of the virus. Thankfully, the results were negative.

Twenty miles away, residents of a small town watched in horror as great billows of smoke and ash rose high into the sky as their forests were purged of the deadly virus. Vic's techs monitored the burn and were amazed. The forest was incinerated quickly and with an intensity never seen before. In hours most of the infected forest was destroyed. One man followed the events in India with much interest—Ingalls Smutch. Should anything go awry with the coca fields, heads would roll, and his would be first.

CHAPTER 26

Elaina and Jerimiah had just finished the legwork for a grant to fund a library on the outskirts of Paramaribo, the capital of Suriname. Jerimiah was in negotiations to preserve a section of the country's rain forest. The Suriname government had done a great job of protecting its forest. About 95 percent of the country was rain forests, but pressure from private landowners was building to deforest some of the land. The Save the TREEZZ campaign would fund an educational program to save the rain forest trees. Jerimiah chose a remote part of the rain forest for the preserve. This pleased all the country's leaders.

Back at their hotel, Jerimiah called Deb. "I found the mysterious, rare kudzu root you need."

Deb was thrilled. "That's great. We believe that it's the final ingredient for the formula."

Jerimiah said, "I'll send a text to you with the location. Once again, the TREEZZ came through for the team."

Becca was in the nursery, a small branch wrapped around her wrist. "Little one, I must go to work now, so you'll have to release me." Slowly, the branch unwound and freed its willing captive.

A short time later, Deb walked into the nursery. "Becca, are you in here?"

"I'm over here."

"Are you up for an expedition to find the elusive kudzu root?"

She jumped with excitement. "You found the root?"

"We did. I'll give you and Vic the details later." She called Vic. "Hey, Mr. Bowden. Can you come to my office? I have a mission for you."

"I can't pass up an invitation from such a pretty lady."

"Not that kind of invitation, Mr. Bowden."

"Oh well. I'll be a few minutes then."

Becca and Vic met in the hallway and walked into Deb's office.

"What do you have for us, Sis?"

Deb replied, "Jerimiah found the rare species of kudzu root. It's in a place called Nantahala Gorge in North Carolina. I have the general location. Becca, when you get close, the TREEZZ will guide you to the root, so this should be a piece of cake."

Becca and Vic looked at each other. In sync they replied, "We've heard that before."

The trio enjoyed a good laugh.

Elaina and Jerimiah had the G-500, so Deb had to charter a jet for transportation. Robert called an hour later. "I'm sorry, Deb. My flight was canceled. I won't be there until Thursday."

"Don't worry about it; we're all good. I'll pass on your new arrival date to everyone."

He thought, *The heck with this. I'm buying two new jets: one for the missions and a small jet for me. I waste so much time at the airport. It's crazy.*

Vic loaded the chartered jet with their special equipment. He carried an oddly shaped bag with a lock on it, which he kept close to him. Becca thought, *He carries that bag like it has a million dollars in it.* She handed the copilot her bag and boarded the jet. The pilot finished his checklist and fired up the Rolls-Royce turbine engines. He taxied the jet to the active runway and pushed the throttles forward. In seconds the jet was airborne. Their destination was Western Carolina Regional Airport, and the estimated flight time was six hours.

Aboard the plane, Becca kept looking at Vic and smiling. Finally, he asked, "Do I have egg on my face?"

She shook her head.

"Then why are you staring at me with a sly grin?"

"No egg, but you do have a glow about you." Her smile got bigger.

He growled, "That's personal."

"Come on, Vic. The three of us have no secrets."

"I will not discuss our private time."

"Vic, I'm just so happy for you both. I was wondering if you guys saw fireworks. I want everything to be perfect for each of you. When are you going to marry her? You are going to marry my sister, right?"

"Calm down, Becca. One step at a time. I'll ask her when I'm ready."

Becca was all smiles. "OK. Now that I know that, I'm going to grab some shut-eye."

Vic whispered, "Good. Finally, some peace and quiet."

———

The resort was preparing for the boss's return the following day. Deb finished her paperwork and kicked back in her chair. With a cunning smile, she thought of the previous night with Vic. It was all she'd expected and more. She began to think of Vic's return; she would plan something special.

When she heard the sound of a jet approaching, Deb frowned. *We aren't expecting visitors, and the boss isn't due until tomorrow.* The plane was getting closer, and she realized that it was going to land at the resort.

She quickly called security. "Do you have a plane scheduled to land?"

"Yes, ma'am. We have two planes scheduled to land. Security is standing by at the runway."

She jumped into the golf cart and drove directly to the runway. The first jet, a Lear 23, rolled to a stop and taxied to the parking area. The second jet's wheels screeched as it touched down on the asphalt runway. It was a Gulfstream G700 corporate jet. A small group had gathered to see who was on the planes. The door to the first plane opened, and out of the shadows stepped a beaming Robert. No one had ever seen him this excited. He called to the group, "Come over and have a look. Aren't they sleek?"

Everyone admitted that the two jets gleaming in the bright sunshine were something to see.

Robert turned to Deb. "I hope I didn't ruin your schedule, but I couldn't wait to get back to my family—and you most of all. I must congratulate you and your new beau, Vic. I'm so happy for you, my two favorite people. Oh, I better include Becca too."

Deb remarked, "Yes. She would be very upset if you didn't."

CHAPTER 27

McAlister's corporate jet passed high over the runway at the Western Carolina Regional Airport. The pilot gave his passengers a bird's-eye view of the picturesque Great Smoky Mountains National Park. Lakes and rivers dotted the mostly green landscape. After landing, the pair rented a car and drove to a nearby motel.

They checked in, and then Becca asked, "Vic, would you mind if I came over to watch some TV with you?"

"Of course not—come on over."

A short time later, he realized that she was sound asleep in the recliner chair. He gently placed a blanket over her, and then he went to sleep.

Awake before sunrise, as usual, he had a cup of coffee in his hand. He sat outside of the room, admiring the scenic views. The fog hung low in the valleys, creating islands in the mountainous terrain. As one would appear, another would fade away. The predawn rays from the rising sun lit up the timberland. Ground fog set an eerie scene in the low valleys and hollows.

Becca opened the motel door, stretched, and yawned as the morning sunlight greeted her.

Vic said, "Let's get going. We're burning daylight."

"OK. Right after my shower." Sometime later she came out of the motel room, with her hair still damp but ready to work.

"Come on, little girl."

Becca hissed, "You know I hate being called a girl. You and Robert insist on calling me a girl."

"I know. That's why I said it. Remember, to us, you are a girl." He laughed heartily and then shook his head and threw her the keys. "I heard you're a good driver…little girl."

She looked at the keys; she was stunned. "Vic, you trust me. Thank you."

He just smiled. Stopping first at the local restaurant, the kudzu hunters enjoyed a tasty country breakfast—biscuits and gravy were musts.

Vic said, "OK, partner. You drive, and I'll give directions."

Becca was all smiles as she climbed into the Jeep. Vic guided them onto a dirt road. They followed that until it became impassable.

He said, "We go on foot for the next mile." He grabbed his oddly shaped bag and unlocked it. He took out a strange-looking hand piece. It had a handle like a pistol, with a telescopic lens on the side. The barrel was finned. He said, "Becca, this is a prototype hand energy-pulse weapon. It's like no other. It can fire only when it recognizes the authorized person holding the weapon. Now hold the weapon, and I'll authorize it for your use. Do you want to see how it works?"

"Of course I want to see how it works!" she shrieked.

"I'll place it on the lowest setting. You'll feel a little discomfort; it will buckle you over and take your breath away. Do you still want to try it?"

"Yes. I'm not a little girl or a chicken."

"OK. Get ready." Vic pulled the trigger.

The pulse hit her without a sound. She grabbed her stomach and fell backward, almost hitting the ground.

He ran over to her. "Becca, are you all right? I'm sorry. I shouldn't have done that. I'm so sorry."

"Vic, don't worry. It just knocked the wind out of me. I'm fine. I needed to see how it worked; besides, I'm tough. I won't break like a little girl."

Much relieved, he said, "What do you think? Pretty neat, isn't it?"

She agreed. "It sure is. Where did you get it?"

"Robert's arms company loaned it to me. We won't need it, I'm sure, but one never knows. What do I always say?"

She repeated in a snotty tone, "Expect the unexpected."

"Good girl. Now let's get going."

"Always with the *girl*."

An hour later she spied a leaf identical to the one in the picture she had. She took a test kit out of her bag and put a drop of fluid on the leaf. In less than a minute, the leaf tested positive for the kudzu vine. Now she needed samples of the root. While Vic bent over to help her, two men quietly approached. He stopped digging. The hairs on the back of his neck rose, and he slowly reached for his weapon.

The man grumbled, "Don't move, dickhead, or you're dead. That goes for you, too, girlie."

Vic froze. He didn't know if the man was armed, but he had to assume that he was.

"What are ya'll doing on our mountain?"

Vic said, "We're looking for roots. We didn't know this was your mountain."

"Wrong answer, asshole. Them are our ruts."

"Sorry. We'll put them back and leave."

"Wah ya think, Jeb?"

"They seem harmless. Just an old guy and his daughter."

"OK, you can git up now."

Vic and Becca slowly rose and turned around. Standing in front of them were two plump, bearded young men. They had no weapons. Vic breathed a sigh of relief, as did Becca.

Vic said, "Hey, fellas, we didn't mean any harm. We're just looking for an odd root."

One of the tubby men said, "Show us what you're looking fer." Becca showed him the root. "Oh, heck. Them ruts ain't worth a plugged nickel." He pulled a handful of roots out of his bag. "Now these ruts are worth money."

Becca recognized them right away. "Say, boys, those are some nice ginseng roots you got."

"That's what we be huntin' fer."

She said, "I can show you where a bunch are."

One of the men asked, "Really? Would you show us?"

"Sure. It's just down the hill a ways."

The men followed her down the slope. The group began to look around. A very small vine reached out and wrapped around her wrist; she stopped. The vine gently turned her around and pulled her hand up. She pointed to the thick brush.

"Right behind that thicket, boys."

They walked around the other side, and sure enough, there was the ginseng plant.

"Ma'am, we surely do thank you. We passed that a hundred times and never saw it. We'll help you dig some of your ruts if ya want."

"That would be nice. Thank you."

The two young men dug like backhoes. Before long, Becca had all the kudzu root she needed. She also took some live vines and roots for the nursery's inventory.

The four of them shook hands. "It was nice meeting you folks. Goodbye, and thanks."

Vic was dumbfounded. "How did you know the ginseng was behind the brush?"

She answered, "The TREEZZ, Vic. The TREEZZ."

On the way back to the airport, he said, "I thought we were in trouble, but it turned out well."

"See, Vic? Not everyone's a bad guy."

"And not everyone's a good guy," he countered.

Back on the plane, Becca looked at him with a slight grin.

"Don't go there, Becca."

"There is no way you know what I'm thinking."

"Try me!" Vic barked.

"OK. I'm thinking about something back on the mountain."

"Right. You're wondering why I let two fat guys sneak up on me?"

"Damn you, Vic. How did you know that? You're a mind reader?"

"Remember that the next time you see a sexy guy."

Becca turned crimson, and the conversation abruptly ended.

The chartered plane landed and taxied between two shiny jets. Vic said, "We must have some VIPs visiting. Those jets are big money."

Becca joked, "Maybe Robert bought them for us?" She and Vic laughed loudly.

CHAPTER 28

Seeing the jets, Becca thought, *Maybe one of those is Carlie's. That would be wonderful. I wanted to think of her the whole way back, but Vic, the mind reader, was there. Oh, I hope Carlie's here.*

Vic thought, *Private jets mean security work. I was planning to spend some romantic time with my sexy lady. I still can do that. I'll multitask.*

Robert greeted the two successful hunters.

Vic stuck his hand out to shake. "What a surprise. I wasn't expecting you for another day. I thought your flight was canceled."

"It was, so I bought these two planes. One for Becca and one for me."

Vic's mouth fell open. "Are you serious?"

Robert looked at Becca. "My dear, may I present to you your own plane?"

She was astonished and thought it must have been a joke. But when she looked at him, he nodded.

"Go on in inside, and look around. If there's something you don't like, we'll change it."

She walked toward the small Lear 23.

"No, no, my dear, the other one," Robert said.

She nervously took her sister's hand, and they walked up to the G700. It was a big jet, bigger that than Elaina's. They walked up the stairs and into the cabin. It was breathtaking. Neither one of the ladies was able to speak. The pilot opened the rear cabin door; behind it was a bedroom and a bathroom, complete with a shower and tub. They both fell backward on the bed.

Deb said, "Now this is luxury at forty thousand feet."

Becca asked, "Deb, can you believe this?"

Deb was still amazed. "No, I can't."

Everyone enjoyed a tour of the multimillion-dollar aircraft.

Robert told Vic, "As soon as you can break away, come to my suite." Robert was anxious to hear what Vic had uncovered. The two men weren't taking any chances; they went to a secure, windowless safe room in Robert's suite. The room was cold, with artificial light and huge LED screens on each wall. It wasn't a room; it was a bunker.

Vic began. "We've uncovered several disturbing facts that I believe are somehow tied together. We believe that L&L Chemical inadvertently created a deadly mutant cell while developing a growth hormone for crops. Against all biological research guidelines, L&L combined a plant hormone with a human hormone. This, in turn, is the building block for a deadly human virus."

Robert's face turned a ghostly white. Vic stayed silent while the boss tried to comprehend what had just been said. Robert hoped that Vic was wrong, but he knew better.

"It gets worse. A chemist at L&L contacted Deb. He knew the danger of this cell and tried to warn her of the deadly virus. He never had the opportunity; we believe he was killed."

Robert was taken aback. "I didn't want to believe they were that ruthless."

"Robert, I'm not finished," Vic said with regret. "We also believe that L&L got careless and bypassed some biological ground rules, which is how they accidentally created the deadly virus. This virus destroyed a large section of forest in India."

Robert asked, "What about the USDA testing and review? Their guidelines are stringent."

"That's right, but because it was a chemical and not a drug, the USDA approved the growth hormone for crops."

"Vic, this has to end," Robert pleaded.

"There's more. Deb was held at gunpoint for a minute or two when she went to meet L&L's informer.

"Oh God, no! Is Deb all right? She didn't get hurt, did she?"

"If she had, there'd be a lot of dead people. I neutralized the perp."

"You didn't kill him, did you?"

"No, but he won't be handling a gun for a while."

"Vic, where do we start? What do we do? Are my employees in danger?"

"There's no immediate danger that I can see, but we do need a plan, and I'll need your help."

"You have it, my friend. Whatever you think is best. You're the expert, and I trust you completely."

Vic patted Robert on the back. "Give me a day to draft a plan, and we'll go from there."

Vic's phone rang. "Boss, I don't know if this is important, but we've been monitoring L&L's shipping invoices and noticed an extremely large order bound for a warehouse in Brasília. The name on the order is Evergreen Farms. We did some checking, and Evergreen Farms is a shell company. I'll make some calls and see what shakes loose or pops up."

Vic was confident that one of his connections would have some information. He was wrong—no one knew anything, or if they did, they weren't talking. This was someone very powerful, someone who was feared. Vic thought, *In my experience, it is either someone in the government or someone running a drug cartel. Either way, it may prove to be dangerous.*

Vic explained the situation to Robert, who smiled. "I have a good friend in Brazil, Eduardo Morales. I've known him for years, and he's quite influential. I'll give him a call to see what he knows."

When Robert called Eduardo, he excitedly responded, "I can't believe it's you, Robert. It's been a long time. To what do I owe this honor?"

"Hello, my friend. How are you?"

"I'm fine, just fine. How about you?"

"Enjoying everything life has to offer."

"Glad to hear that."

"I was calling to see if you knew anything about a farm near Brasília called Evergreen Farms."

Eduardo thought for a minute. "No, I can't say that I've heard that name. But my memory is not what it used to be."

"Well, if you do hear anything, give me a call."

"I will. Now that business is over, let's get to pleasure. When are you coming down to visit? I would love to see you and any friends you might want to invite, if you get my meaning." They both laughed.

"I'll try to get away and come see you, and I may have a friend."

"Very good. We can reminisce while we still remember." They laughed again and hung up.

Robert looked at Vic sadly. "He couldn't help us. Sorry."

Vic thought, *I hate to accuse him of lying, but men in his position know everything.*

CHAPTER 29

Becca and Ethan tended the nursery while Bart and Carlton ran hundreds of formulas with the new kudzu root. The mutant cells were safely stored in the cryogenics freezer for now.

Deb hadn't had a chance to speak to Becca privately and used this break to express her concern. "Becca, can you spare a few minutes?"

"Sure, Sis. Would you like to take a walk? I could use the exercise."

"That will be fine."

Out on the walking trail, Deb questioned, "How are you feeling? Have you been sleeping well?"

"Actually, I have. Now when I close my eyes, that awful man Gibbons is gone. He's dead and gone."

"I'm so happy to hear that."

Becca blatantly asked, "How are you and Vic doing? How's the sex?"

"Becca!" She chastised her. "That question is inappropriate. Shame on you."

"Sorry. I just want everything to be perfect for you two."

"I forgive you because I know in your heart that you want the best for us." Then she looked at Becca, smiled, and winked.

Becca grinned. "*Oh*, I also asked him when he was going to marry you."

Deb was about to chastise her sister again when her phone rang; it was Robert. "Hi, Deb. I have some good news for your sister."

Deb said, "She's right here. I'll put her on."

"Hi, Becca. It's Carlie; I just called to tell you I'll be arriving tomorrow. I hope you don't mind?"

"*Oh*, Carlie, that's great news. I can't wait to see you."

Carlie put Robert back on the phone. "I thought you would be excited; she's pretty special."

"Yes, she is very special. Thank you again for introducing me to her."

"Enjoy the rest of your day," he said cheerfully.

That night Becca couldn't sleep; she kept thinking about Carlie. *It will be so good to see her. We'll have so much fun. Maybe she'll sleep over.* She thought about their last visit and the mixed feelings and unanswered questions she had about herself. *Right now I just don't know. Hopefully Carlie will have the answers.*

A little after ten the next morning, a plane circled the resort and landed. Becca ran from her chalet to greet Carlie.

The two women hugged and kissed. "Becca, you look fantastic."

"Thank you. Carlie, I missed you so much. And look at you, lovely as always. Come over to my place, and we'll catch up."

Clyde Butters had a boy get Carlie's luggage. "Ms. Andrews, where would you like us to put your luggage?"

"In my suite, please."

Becca said, "No, no. Put her luggage in my chalet."

"Yes, ma'am," the boy replied.

The two women got comfortable and spent the next two hours laughing and telling tales of their recent adventures. It was a beautiful day, with not a cloud in the sky.

Becca suggested, "This is a perfect day to go to the pool and get some rays."

Carlie agreed. "That's a great idea. Let's do it."

Becca waited on the porch for Carlie. She soon walked out of the chalet in a sexy two-piece.

Becca smiled. "Very nice. It fits like it was made for you."

Carlie whispered, "It was. And look at you, my pretty, showing just enough skin to tease."

With a sly smile, Becca replied, "I'm glad you approve."

With the lab busy running formulas and Vic tackling the mutant cell debacle, the women had the pool to themselves.

Carlie asked, "Would you like me to put some sunscreen on you?"

"That would be nice, thank you."

Carlie put some on her hands and began to rub on the lotion. Gently, she coated Becca's back and arms. Lastly she slowly rubbed Becca's long, sexy legs. Becca moaned slightly. Carlie continued up to her firm buttocks and down her thighs. Again she moaned, louder this time.

Carlie whispered, "Would you like to do me?"

"Oh yes, I would."

She put some lotion into her hands and began to cover Carlie's back, her arms, and her legs. Following Carlie's lead, her hands caressed her tight buttocks and down the inside of her thighs. Now it was Carlie's turn to moan.

"Does that feel good?"

Carlie sighed. "I love your hands caressing me."

Becca continued for a few more minutes and then took her place next to Carlie.

Becca questioned, "Carlie, is it very wrong for me to have sexual fantasies about us?"

Carlie answered, "It's perfectly normal to have those kinds of fantasies, especially after that person just rubbed lotion all over you. I had them about you as you rubbed me."

"*Oh*, good. Could we take it further? It's been so long." Becca moaned.

"Becca, I know you want to be loved, to be touched and caressed. But that would just be sex. You need something more. You really need to think about it."

"You're right, Carlie. I will think about it. I'm being impulsive and selfish."

About an hour later, one of the handsome young pilots walked toward the pool area. As he came closer, he took off his sunglasses and stared at Becca and Carlie.

His thoughts: *Wow, two hot women. I'll turn on my Latino charm and maybe have a threesome.* He snickered lecherously.

Becca yelled, "Look out!"

It was too late—the young man tripped over a lounge chair. "I'm so sorry. How clumsy of me. I was distracted by two very attractive women. My name is Carlos Ortega."

"Hi, Carlos; this is Carlie, and I'm Becca."

"It's a pleasure to meet you, ladies. Say, I'm on my way to get a drink. Can I get you anything?"

"Yes, thank you," Becca replied. "I'd like water, and my friend will have a Sprite."

"Very good. I'll be right back."

Carlie looked at Becca. "Nice butt," she commented.

"I've seen better," Becca said and glanced provocatively at Carlie.

Carlie saw Becca look down; she just smiled.

Carlos returned with their drinks but then got a call. "Ladies, please excuse me. Duty calls. I hope we will meet again when we have more time. Adios, senoritas."

"Carlos is a hottie, isn't he, Becca?"

She smiled. "He's cute, and yes, he has a nice butt. But 'Adios, senoritas'? Ugh!"

Carlie leaned over and kissed Becca. "I like yours better."

The women left the pool area and decided to have an early dinner. Becca had selected a small Italian restaurant in town. After showering and dressing, they drove into town.

It was about eight o'clock when they returned to the chalet. "Carlie, would you care for a glass of wine?"

"Yes, that would be nice."

Becca walked out and handed a wineglass to Carlie. Three glasses later the women were a bit tipsy.

Becca stretched. "I'm a little sore, but I have no idea why."

Carlie noticed a massage table in the corner. "What you need is a massage to loosen you up."

Becca agreed. "That would be wonderful."

"Go get ready, and wear something—the last thing I need is to see you naked."

"Am I that bad to look at?"

"No, you're that good to look at." Both women laughed.

Carlie finished the massage. Becca thanked her and asked, "Can I do you?"

Carlie declined, saying, "Not tonight. Especially not tonight."

Each woman was so close to saying yes. The two of them sat for quite a while without saying a word, obviously in deep thought.

Finally Carlie asked, "Do you ever talk to the TREEZZ about your private life?"

Becca was puzzled, thinking, *Why don't I talk to the TREEZZ about my private life?* "That's a great question. I'll have to ask the TREEZZ if they have some form of sex."

"And since we're on the subject, do you ever have sexual thoughts about Robert?"

"One time I was dancing with Robert. He held me so tenderly, so caringly. He made me feel I was the only woman there. His hands were so soft, his mannerisms so gentle. Yes, at that moment, I thought about being with him, being intimate with him."

Carlie said, "Well, it probably will never happen, but it's good to know you thought about it. Remember that, should the occasion present itself again."

Becca offered, "You know, his age doesn't matter to me. He is a handsome and sexy man. But he thinks of me as a little girl, so I won't have to worry about being with him. Great. Now I have to choose who I will fantasize about tonight—you or Robert."

The next few days were spent shopping, sightseeing, shopping, eating, and shopping. The women laughed until their sides hurt. They chatted constantly. The last night in town, two guys struck up a conversation with the ladies. They were handsome young men in town on business. They asked the ladies to join them at a fancy restaurant where they had reservations for four—their friends had backed out. Carlie looked at Becca, giving her a slight nod to accept. Under one condition: It would be a Dutch treat. After much protesting, the men gave in and agreed. The meal was fabulous, the conversation stimulating, and the drinks flowing free. The men were total gentlemen the whole evening. At the end of the night, the gentlemen escorted the ladies to their room. Becca looked at Carlie and whispered, "They were so nice—I think a kiss would be appropriate." Carlie agreed, and the ladies gave the men kisses. They seemed pleased with their reward.

Throughout the three days, intimacy was never part of the conversation. Carlie was scheduled to fly out the following day; this was their last night together. Carlie went over to Robert's suite to say goodbye.

While she was gone, Becca went over to her sister's.

"Welcome back, Sis. How were your days off?"

"We had a great time. I'm sad to see it end."

"You and Carlie are very good friends; there will be more days spent together."

"Deb, I have to tell you something."

"It sounds serious."

"It is. I have had fantasies about Carlie—sexual fantasies."

"I don't think that's wrong. We all have had sexual fantasies."

"Deb, I want to sleep with Carlie. I want to be intimate with her."

"Becca, are you in love with Carlie?"

"Yes, I am, but not in the sense of wanting her for a mate. I find her sexy, caring, and tender. I tingle when she touches me. I guess I want to experience intimacy with her."

Deb asked, "And how does Carlie feel?"

"I think if I ask her, she will say yes."

"Do you think you are exploring your sexuality? Are you curious what it would be like with a woman?"

"That's part of it, but I want us to have a special moment, a special time we can always remember."

"If that's your mindset, then you must ask her for that special time. As far as the curiosity, well, that should be settled before you enter into a serious relationship."

"Deborah, I can't thank you enough for your advice; you have helped me make my decision." She kissed and hugged Deb and left.

Carlie came back after saying goodbye to Robert. "Becca, I must say I haven't had that much fun in a long time."

"I feel the same way. We should have a special moment together to remember this wonderful time."

Carlie asked, "Do you have something in mind?"

"Yes, I do; I want tonight to be very special. I want to be intimate with you."

Carlie was stunned. "Becca, what brought on this idea?"

"Carlie, I want this visit to be something special, a memory we can cherish forever. A moment in time that will be ours alone. Will you help me make that moment?"

Carlie walked over to the window and stared out. A minute later she said, "Becca, I will give you that moment, a moment to always remember. It will be my moment too—a special night that I, too, will cherish."

Carlie walked over and took Becca's hand. The couple walked into Becca's bedroom, and the door closed.

CHAPTER 30

The sun wasn't even up, and Vic was already busy in his office. Robert stepped in with two cups of coffee. Deb wasn't far behind. James Coffer was a new player at the meeting and a very important member; he ran the surveillance division for Robert. Vic and James often collaborated on special projects. This meeting would prioritize the missions by urgency. The mutant cell topped the list. The next was L&L Chemical.

Vic said, "This operation will become fluid, and we must be ready to change our plans at a moment's notice. I know you're all thinking that it can't be done, and you're right; it's impossible. But, my fellow comrades, we do the impossible. That's the bottom line. Because we adapt, and we win."

One could have heard a pin drop. Vic's attitude and confident tone made people believe him, no matter how impossible things seemed. Deb saw a different side of him—the hunter, the slayer, the victor. She was very proud of him. James Coffer thought, *I'm sure glad he's on our side. He gives the order, and you carry it out. Why?*

Because he's got your back. He had great respect for Vic, and James enjoyed working with him.

Vic ordered night-and-day surveillance of L&L Chemical. He needed to locate the deadly mutant cells. He assumed that they were being prepared for shipment to China. Customs was on alert for any suspicious packages heading there.

Vic received a call that stunned him. "Vic, intelligence just learned that the deadly cells were transported out of the country with Wang Ti Lu's entourage. They had been given diplomatic immunity. The cells left the United States undetected and are now in a lab in China."

Vic put his phone down and looked at his desk. It was piled high with shipping information on all exporting ports. In anger he swiped all the papers off the desk and onto the floor. Then he kicked them everywhere. Ashamed that he'd lost his temper, he sat back down to compose himself. He whispered one of his favorite personal quotes: "you get mad, you make mistakes.' I just broke my rule."

Becca walked by Vic's office and looked in. "Vic, you sure have a messy office. You might want to clean it up." She looked into his eyes; they were shooting daggers. "Actually, the room's not that bad." She walked quickly down the hall.

Deb assembled the biologists and told them, "Team, this is our chance to repay the TREEZZ for their invaluable assistance with our research. Time is of the essence. We don't know if the TREEZZ's virus survived. It may turn up in another forest. Here's the bottom line: we have a deadly TREEZZ virus derived from a human cell. And we have a human virus derived from a plant cell. Let's divide the team by expertise; one team will take the TREEZZ virus and the other the human virus. And keep in mind, the cells need a host to survive. This could be any kind of bacteria or parasite. Are you ready to go to work?" There wasn't much of a cheer, but she wasn't booed either. Deb took it as a win.

The following morning, the team had more answers.

Carlton reported, "The most common shipping container is the fifty-five-gallon metal drum, but the preferred container is the plastic fifty-five-gallon drum. This is because it can be altered and the plastic welded if alterations are needed. In the end, I would go with the plastic drum."

Bartley noted, "If the proper host is used, and I'm sure it will be, the mutant cell can survive for weeks—three at the most."

Ethan spoke up. "I just can't figure out why China would want to destroy us. We're their golden goose."

Vic said, "It's not China. Iran is the enemy. China just supplies the weapons—or, in this case, the virus. Thousands of humans can perish from the virus, but the infrastructure will remain intact. China would like that."

Deb said, "OK, team. Let's get back to work."

A tech contacted Vic. "Is there a way to get a drone near the Hunan laboratories?"

"What are you getting at?"

"If we can get a small drone near the lab, we might be able to fly it inside."

Vic said, "That's a great idea. Get with our advanced weaponry guys to see what we can come up with."

The next day the advanced weapons facility took Vic's tech to a high-security warehouse, where the developers showed him a working replica of a beetle with a tiny camera in it. The developer said, "This might be just what you're looking for."

Upon hearing this, Vic commanded, "Take it to the airport. A special operations plane will be waiting. The plane will fly close to the China border and launch a drone. The drone will fly very low to a predetermined location, where the bug will take flight. From there it will be in the hands of the operator."

———

At the lab in Hunan, the beetle sat on the windowsill, the camera focused on the secure room.

Later four men in white protective suits retrieved a sample from one of the drums. They handled the sample like it was extremely dangerous and took every precaution.

Days later each drum was taken into a secure room. Vic asked the team to view the video and give their opinions as to what was going on. The consensus was that the liquid in the drums was going through a delicate mixing process. Everyone agreed that whatever it was, it was very hazardous. This was confirmed by the special contamination room being used and the warning labels attached to each plastic drum.

The bug focused on the drums and would alert the operator if there were any movements. Vic smiled for the second time that day. So far he was pleased with the mission.

Days passed before the alert was sounded. Movement had been detected. Vic rushed to his office to view the video. The door to the secure room was opened, and a forklift began to load the four drums into a covered truck.

Vic asked the operator, "Can you fly down to the drums and read the shipping label and destination?"

The beetle hovered over the drums while Vic read the label:

Government Laboratories #5
Tehran, Iran
DANGER—CORROSIVE CHEMICAL
DO NOT PUNCTURE

Suddenly, the screen got fuzzy; the last thing Vic saw was the bottom of a large work shoe—and then nothing. The beetle was squashed to little pieces by a worker's boot.

Vic notified surveillance, "We have lost our visual on the target. Dedicate one satellite to tracking the drums day and night."

Later that day the satellite captured pictures of the drums at Hunan's international airport, where they were loaded on a plane. The flight plan listed Iran as the final destination.

Vic called Robert with an update. "Do you want the good news first or the bad news?"

"The good news first."

"The good news is that we've tracked the drums to Iran. The bad news is that our beetle is dead. Someone stepped on it. Sorry."

Robert bellowed, "Sorry? Sorry doesn't put one hundred thousand dollars back in my bank account."

Vic felt terrible. "I'll make it up to you somehow."

Robert laughed heartily. "Just kidding, Vic. We have insurance for just such an occasion. Don't give it another thought." Robert chuckled. "Gotcha, didn't I?"

Vic frowned and thought, *Payback's a bitch, boss.*

Vic needed to know what was going on in the Iranian biological lab. He went to the advanced weapons facility to see if they could help him.

"Hello, Tom. Good to see you."

"Vic, come on in and have a seat. What brings you here today?"

Vic explained his predicament, hoping Tom had a trick up his sleeve.

Tom rubbed his chin, which was a good sign; it meant that he had an idea. "I think we may be able to help you. Give me a few days."

Tom called three days later.

"Good morning, Tom," Vic said. "Do you have good news for me?"

"I have some good news and some bad news. What's your preference?"

"The good news first, Tom. Always the good news first."

"We designed a drone hummingbird. It's small and fast and looks identical to a real one. The bad news is that we had to go with a smaller battery because it's so small, which shortened its effective power phase. We need to build more powerful batteries or find a way to recharge the unit in the field. Solar is out because there is not enough surface for the solar panel. But don't worry; we'll come up with something."

Later that day Vic, Jerimiah, and Robert happened to be walking by the pool at the same time. Vic explained the dilemma to the pair.

Jerimiah said, "I may have a solution. Give me a few minutes."

Vic and Robert glanced at the pool to see Elaina, Deb, and Becca sunning in their bikinis. Vic said, "The women sure do look good."

Staring in their direction, Robert said, "They sure do."

Jerimiah returned. "I may have something." Surprisingly he received no reply. He cleared his throat and loudly repeated, "Men, I may have something."

"Oh, sorry, Jer," Vic said. "We were distracted for a minute. You were saying?"

Jerimiah looked over at the women and focused on Elaina. "Yes, well, I can see the reason for your distraction."

Just then Elaina saw the men looking their way. She stood up, waved, and adjusted her swimsuit. That was Elaina, always the tease.

Robert said, "You were saying, Jer?"

"The TREEZZ indicated that a small electrical charge runs through all the trees. If the designer could incorporate an electrical pickup to absorb the current and recharge the battery, our problem is solved."

Robert and Vic looked at each other. Robert smiled. "I like the simplicity of the solution."

Vic called Tom immediately. "Tom, we've got it." He went on to explain the idea.

Tom ecstatically replied, "Pure genius. Kudos to the problem solver."

As the men left the pool area, they couldn't resist one more glance. Vic smiled as he looked at Deb; he just loved her long legs and butt. *She is my dream. I still can't believe that she is my woman.*

Jerimiah gazed at Elaina. *My partner is so hot, and I'm so horny, but she is my business associate. It would be inappropriate for me to make a sexual advance. I guess I'll just look at her from a distance and dream.*

Robert eyed Becca. He now looked at her differently. *What a pretty young woman. I'll make sure to tell her.* Then he realized he had referred to her as a woman, not a girl. He began to view her differently—she was a woman, a desirable one in his eyes. Robert started to walk away and then abruptly stopped. A little voice in his head said, *Ask the young lady to dinner.* Emboldened by his wish to spend time with her, he walked over, and in front of the women, he asked Becca, "May I take you to dinner sometime?"

Becca stood there dumbfounded. *Did I just hear Robert ask me to dinner?*

Robert said, "I'm sure you're busy. Maybe some other time."

"Oh, no, Robert, I'm not busy, and I'd enjoy having dinner with you."

"That's wonderful—whenever your schedule allows."

Without thinking, Becca boasted excitedly, "How about this evening? I'm free this evening."

Robert stuttered. "Ah...this evening...yes, of course, this evening will be fine. Say sevenish?"

"Yes, that would be fine."

He walked away as all eyes turned to Becca. Elaina smiled. "I think the boss has a girlfriend." She winked at Becca.

Deb said, "I don't believe he will address you as 'girl' anymore."

Becca was stunned. She didn't know what to think. Should she be honored and read something more into his invitation? Or was he just looking for a partner for dinner? Either way Becca was pleased they would spend some private time together.

CHAPTER 31

Evergreen Farms of Brasília, Brazil, was more than happy with the performance of L&L's crop growth enhancer. Their first coca crop was an overwhelming success. The owner was pleased, which delighted the farm's overseer. The owner told the overseer, "The workers did well. A celebration is in order."

It was a festive event. The workers and their families enjoyed a bountiful feast. Wine flowed like water. The overseer sat on the porch of the plantation house in a rocker. He puffed on a Cuban cigar and sipped his favorite rum.

Evergreen Farms put in another large order of the growth enhancer for the next growing season, hoping for an even bigger and better crop yield. About a month after the second treatment of the enhancer, complaints began jamming L&L's customer service phone lines. Their clients reported that the crops were overproducing and destroying the plant. It seemed that the yield was so great that the plant snapped under the weight. Consumers were irate and wanted answers or some form of compensation. The callers were so angry that the company couldn't keep phone operators.

The Lattimore's struggled to find an answer. They called their chemists together to see if a solution could be found. One furious chemist stood up. "We told you that more long-term testing was needed, but you refused, telling us that we didn't know what we were talking about. I have no idea how this debacle can be resolved. But I do know this: I quit." Several other chemists expressed the same mindset.

The next morning, two men dressed in $2,000 suits, looking like gangsters, waited at the entrance to L&L Chemical. Clay and Lucius hesitated before getting out of their car. With no other options available, the L&L owners had to confront the two men.

One man with a Brazilian accent did all the talking. "Are you the Lattimore's?"

Reluctantly Clay answered, "Yes, we are. Can we help you?"

"Is there someplace private we can talk?"

Lucius went on the defensive. "Just what the hell is this all about? See our receptionist and make an appointment."

The two men pulled their suit coats back, displaying their handguns. "Will these get us an appointment?"

Trembling, Clay and Lucius nodded. "Yes."

In Clay's office the same man stated, "We represent a very unhappy customer. His coca plants are all broken and dying."

Lucius panicked. He stopped breathing. *Coca plants? Oh shit, they're cocaine growers.*

"He believes your growth enhancer may be the reason why his crop is now destroyed. Is it possible he is right?"

Clay stuttered. "Uh…well…"

Lucius countered, "Just tell us how much you want, and we'll pay you and be done."

The man removed a sheet of paper from his pocket and handed it to Lucius. His eyes bulged, and his mouth fell open. He looked up at the man. "There must be a mistake."

The man answered, "You are right, senor, and you made it."

Lucius handed the paper to his father. He, too, was shocked by the figure: $8 million. "How can that be?"

The man demanded, "You have one week to get the money." The two men turned and left the building.

Clay and Lucius sat in their office, stunned by what had just taken place.

Finally Clay asked, "What will we do, Son?"

"I'm afraid we've gotten ourselves into a serious bind. Those men will kill us if we don't get them the money. And with the rapid decline in orders for the enhancer, we'll be out of business."

His father said, "I have four million that I can get my hands on. Can you come up with the rest?"

"I'll have to sell some things, which might net me two million. That leaves us short two million dollars. We're in big trouble, Dad."

———

A week later Clay walked into the chemical plant with a large box. Inside it was $4 million. It was all the cash Clay had. Lucius entered the plant a short time later with his head low and a fearful look on his face.

His father knew that expression. "You didn't get all the money, did you?"

"No, Dad. All I could get was two million, as I originally thought, and that was by maxing out all my credit cards and borrowing from the bank."

The two men sat nervously, pondering their fate. Suddenly the intercom buzzed; the dreaded moment had arrived. "Sir, there are two gentlemen to see you."

"Please show them in."

The two well-dressed men walked in.

"Please sit down."

"No thanks. Do you have the money?"

Lucius said, "Yes, we have the money right here." He slid the two boxes in front of the debt collectors.

The man quietly counted the money. His expression quickly changed to a menacing frown. He looked at the Lattimore's and then at his partner before shaking his head. The other man became infuriated. "We don't take payments. It's all at once, or both of you are dead."

"Please," Lucius pleaded. "It was my fault entirely. My dad didn't know anything. Please don't hurt him. If I had more time, I know I could get the rest of the money."

One man left the office and made a phone call. He returned a few minutes later. "Do you have something of value or a special skill?"

"I've always been a chemist. Do you need one?"

"The boss has a use for you. You're going with us now. Grab the money."

Lucius and his father hugged and kissed, probably for the last time. Both had tears flowing. As Lucius was escorted out, he took comfort that his sacrifice had saved his father's life.

A private jet waited for the three men. Their destination was Brasília.

Just before landing, one of the men said to Lucius, "Wake up. We're almost there." Then he quickly put a black hood over Lucius's head.

After the plane landed, the chemist was taken to a waiting vehicle, driven to an abandoned warehouse, and locked up in a cold, dank, windowless room. Unable to see, he jumped at any sound, expecting to be executed. He was cold, hungry, and afraid. Yesterday he had been warm, full of food, and had no fears. *How could my world have completely fallen apart in twenty-four hours?*

Three days later two different men let him out. They took his hood off and led him to a table with food on it. He ate like a hungry dog. When he finished, the black hood was replaced, and he was taken to a room with a table and four chairs. About an hour had passed when he heard several men approaching. Again he began to shake with fear.

"Mr. Chemist, I must warn you, if you cannot be of service to us, we will kill you; it's that simple. So with that in mind, what special talents or knowledge do you possess? Think carefully, senor. Your life depends on it."

Lucius thought harder than he ever had. *What knowledge do I have that they would find useful?* He perspired profusely, racking his brain.

"Senor, time is up." Lucius heard the sound of a semiautomatic being cocked. He waited for the end.

Suddenly he remembered the effect that the tree virus had had on the forest in India—how quickly the dead trees burned, making it much easier to clear the land.

"Wait, I know how to clear the land very quickly. It will save you time and money."

"Not interested. Goodbye."

He quickly yelled through the hood. "Don't shoot! I have something else."

One of the other men put the gun to his head. "Let's get this over with."

The head man said, "This better be good, gringo."

"I have a formula for designer meth. This will make you millions. You know the market for meth; it grows bigger every day. Just give me a lab, and let me cook some for you."

The man stepped outside the room. He returned quickly. "Why do you have this formula for meth?"

"Because I own a chemical plant, I have the perfect environment to make a potent meth formula. I have access to any chemical I would require. This was my backup plan to save the business. The authorities would never have a clue. Listen, you have nothing to lose and millions to gain. And regarding the growth hormone, the tree virus will destroy the trees and vegetation in two to three weeks. The dead trees will burn like gasoline, making it much quicker and easier to clear the land. The land barons will pay big money for this service. The more land cleared, the more coca plants they will grow."

"I'll be right back." When the man returned, he said, "You are very lucky, senor. The boss would like to speak to you."

CHAPTER 32

It was a cold and rainy morning at the resort. The team was depressed by the lack of progress toward finding an antidote for the human virus. The inclement weather didn't help the mood.

Each day that went by, Deb reminded them, "The virus is on the move, and the clock is ticking." Deb didn't relish the constant reminder, but that was her job.

———

Elaina and Jerimiah were in Brasília negotiating with the Brazilian government on a variety of issues. Before they met with the government officials, one of the committee members, a wealthy older gentleman, approached Elaina. "My dear, you're looking enchanting today. May I extend an invitation to lunch or maybe dinner?"

She could feel his eyes undressing her. To him, this was just a game, a subtle form of blackmail. Elaina enjoyed the game and was an excellent player.

She smiled. "Dinner sounds lovely, Umberto."

"Yes. A little wine, a little amour." His smile was lecherous.

Jerimiah touched Elaina's arm. "The meeting is about to start."

She smiled. "Thank you. Your timing was impeccable."

The committee had whittled the grant list down to five. The McAlister Foundation would choose the deserving recipient.

Next on the agenda was Jerimiah's request to have the government set aside two hundred square miles of a remote section of the Amazon rain forest as a preserve. As usual, the first question was, "What's in it for the government?" Jerimiah dazzled them with his explanation and knowledge. He also pointed out the benefits to mankind and demonstrated that this would be a great example of the government leader's progressive thinking. The preserve would also be a wonderful legacy for the many generations of Brazilians to come.

Jerimiah continued, "At the risk of sounding too bold, I suggest that the preserve be named after your esteemed president, Juan Carlos." This was met with applause and cheers.

He looked over at Elaina for her blessing. She smiled and winked. He'd done well.

Elaina had saved the best for last. "If a deal can be reached for the preserve, the extinct trees propagated at McAlister Laboratories would be a gift to the people of Brazil." That sealed the deal for the preserve, and the meeting was adjourned.

Elaina and Jerimiah were walking on air. Each had a successful end to their mission. As they exited the lobby door, an unbelievable shower of tiny, beautiful flowers greeted the pair. It was the TREEZZ's way of saying, "Thank you."

Elaina and Jerimiah slowly walked back to their hotel, enjoying the beauty of the tree-lined street. Life was good. They stopped at a park bench and sat, basking in the success of a job well done.

Elaina glanced at her watch. "We need to go. I promised Antonio that I would have dinner with him."

They hurried to the hotel, and Elaina got ready for the evening. When she walked into Jerimiah's room, his eyes popped. "Wow! Elaina, you look beautiful."

She struck a sexy pose and spun around. "Do you really think so?"

"Oh yes, Elaina. You're stunning."

"Thank you for the compliment." She smiled widely. "You know, Jer, ladies can never get enough compliments."

"Enjoy your dinner," he said with a touch of sadness. *I wish I was the one taking her out.*

There was a knock on the door, followed by a voice. "Room service."

Jerimiah opened the door and was greeted by a member of the hotel staff. "Here is your chilled bottle of champagne, as requested, sir."

Jerimiah thanked him and handed him a generous tip. He walked out to the balcony. The sun had sunk below the horizon. He looked down on the street, watching couples holding hands as they went merrily on their way.

Depressed, he grabbed the bottle of champagne, popped the cork, and took a swig. He immediately wrinkled his face. *This is awful.* He took another swig; it seemed to taste better. Jerimiah wasn't a drinking man, so it didn't take much to make him a bit tipsy. He grabbed the bottle for another swig, but it was empty. In a panic, he picked up the phone and ordered another bottle. *Elaina will be very upset if she doesn't have her champagne.*

Jerimiah was just dozing off, the effects of the champagne catching up to him, when the door opened. "Elaina, did you enjoy your dinner?"

"Yes, thank you. It was delicious. How was your evening?"

"Oh, it was fine. Can I pour you a glass of champagne?"

"Please do."

He spilled a little as he filled her glass. "Oops, how clumsy of me." He hiccupped.

As he handed her the glass, she asked, "Jerimiah, are you all right?"

At that moment he leaned forward and attempted to kiss her cheek. She could smell the alcohol on his breath and instantly backed away.

Shocked, she asked, "Jer, have you been drinking?"

He giggled. "Well, maybe a little."

She countered, "Maybe a lot."

He pulled her close. Slurring his words, he whispered, "Did I ever tell you how much I like you? No, let me rephrase that: how much I love you." He took another big swig from the bottle.

"Jer, that is so nice to hear, and I like you very much."

"Do you really?"

"Yes, I do."

He wobbled. Elaina quickly steadied him and guided him to the bed. "You should sit down for a while."

As he fell backward, he pulled her on top of him. He smiled and ran his hands over her sexy derriere. She struggled to get off him, but he held her tightly.

After another hiccup he asked, "I really like hugging you. Can we go to bed?"

She finally freed herself from her intoxicated partner. In a firm tone, she said, "You're going to bed right now, and you're going alone."

He reached for the half-filled glass of champagne, spilling it on his pants, before again proclaiming his feelings. "But I love you." He closed his eyes and passed out.

Elaina smiled, thankful that he was asleep. She looked at his wet clothes. "I can't leave him like that." She undressed him and covered him up.

The next afternoon, Jerimiah finally stirred.

"Hey, sleepyhead. Ready for some strong coffee?" Elaina asked.

"Ow, my head. I feel like shit."

She handed him a cup of coffee. He took a sip and closed his eyes. "That helps some."

He was starting to get out of bed when he suddenly realized that he was in Elaina's room. Confused, he looked at her. "What am I doing in your bed?"

He looked under the covers and saw that he was naked.

Elaina watched him with a sinful grin on her face. "You don't remember last night? The two of us in bed?"

He sheepishly replied, "I'm so sorry. I have only a few memories. Did we...did I...did you..."

"Relax. Nothing happened. You spilled your champagne, so I took off your wet clothes. I undressed you and put you to bed, and you passed out. What a party pooper!" She laughed loudly.

Apologetically he replied, "I'm sorry. I don't remember. You didn't look, did you?"

"Of course not. What kind of girl do you think I am? Nice mole, by the way."

Jerimiah turned three shades of red.

"OK, Mr. Simpson, here's a robe. Go take a shower; it will help." She giggled. "If you need assistance, call me." She broke out laughing again.

CHAPTER 33

Running into dead ends on the virus, the team refocused on testing the blood pressure medications. Deb was pleased with their progress. Yet the virus wasn't turning up anywhere. Deb had to assume the virus naturally disappeared without the presence of a suitable host.

Ethan had another week of paperwork before he could begin the application for the herbal blood pressure medication. The final test results would be attached to the application. With that completed, it was now ready to be presented to the FDA. That would initiate the certification process. It sounded complicated, and it was, but Deb had done this so many times that she breezed right through it. The FDA inspectors knew Deb's work and respected her, which was a big help.

The next research would be dedicated to heart disease. This would be a great challenge for the small lab. They were competing with pharmaceutical giants worldwide, but that didn't faze the team. They had the TREEZZ on their side, as well as Robert's adopted mom's herbal treatments. At the end of the day, Deb sat back and reviewed the team's progress. She smiled, knowing the effort that had been put forth, and thanked the Lord for these blessings.

———

The Iranian connection had been a nonissue for quite a while. Surveillance had been cut back since it was seemingly a dead end. Vic had a gut feeling, though, and wanted it kept open. Some of the younger techs, unaware of Vic's background and experience in the NSA, criticized him and called him an old dog. He just shrugged it off and thought, *An old dog with big, sharp teeth.*

Months later the surveillance team picked up light chatter by known Iranian terrorists. This was not unusual, except for two words that had been intercepted: *mutant cell.* That got the attention of an alert tech, who quickly called Vic. "Boss, we may have something coming out of Iran."

"I'm on my way over." Vic hoped that their persistence was about to pay off. As he walked into the surveillance room, he could feel the renewed enthusiasm. Morale was at an all-time high. "Did the chatter originate in Iran?"

The techs informed him that it had come from Colombia, South America. That caught Vic by surprise. There was never chatter between Iran and Columbia. This was a game changer and required new surveillance.

Suddenly, the younger techs had a newfound respect for the old dog. Unfortunately, the chatter ceased, and morale dwindled.

That weekend Deb and Vic invited Becca and Robert over for a barbecue. While they waited for the food, the couples enjoyed some light conversation.

Vic announced, "Food's ready. Come and get it." He had just put the burgers on the plate when his phone rang. Deb gave him a look.

"Sorry, but I have to take this call. It's the surveillance tech."

"Boss, we have four plastic drums leaving a biological facility in Tehran. Sorry to bother you, but I thought you'd want to know."

"I'm on my way." Vic addressed his guests. "I'm sorry for the disruption, but I need to get to my office." He looked at Deb. "Save me some dinner, hon."

Deb was annoyed. "Don't count on it."

Vic rushed to his office and brought up the video. "Yes!" he said excitedly. "I know they're our drums. Dedicate a satellite to track them. Whatever it takes, I want those drums monitored at all times. And by God, don't lose them."

Hours later Vic returned to the chalet. Becca and Robert had already left. He cringed at the reception he would receive from Deb.

"I'm so sorry. I—"

She quickly cut him off. "It's fine, Vic. That's your job, and it's a very important one. We all understand, and we commend you for your dedication."

Vic was relieved; he hated it when he and Deb had words. "I'm the luckiest man in the world to have you in my life. You're not only beautiful but also understanding and thoughtful. What can I do to repay you?"

Deb flashed a sinful smile. "I'm glad you asked. If you promise to shut off your phone, I'll meet you in the boudoir."

Vic didn't need to be asked twice. He was half undressed by the time he ran through the bedroom door.

After leaving Deb's chalet, Becca invited Robert over for their favorite after-dinner beverage: Baileys on the rocks. Becca and Robert spent most nights together, he on the couch and she in her bed. They would take turns selecting movies, enjoying a butter-filled bag of popcorn and then giving each other foot massages.

They were a good match. Robert's maturity and gentle mannerisms countered Becca's spontaneity and her youthful energy and excitement. They, in fact, appeared to be the perfect couple. Robert was old school—no quick roll in the hay for him. Becca would be courted properly. However, flames of passion were fanned by a sexual desire harbored by both. Robert tried to conceal his desire, but inside him a volcano was about ready to erupt.

On most nights the couple would pick out a movie to watch. Becca had heard the movie *9 Songs* was pretty explicit. She hoped it would light the fire of passion, so to speak. Getting comfortable, they cuddled next to one another and started the movie. Halfway through, some of the scenes made him a bit uncomfortable. He shifted and turned, crossing his legs for obvious reasons.

This didn't go unnoticed by Becca. "Robert, are you OK?"

"Yes. It's just that the explicitness caught me off guard. It's a little different from our regular movies."

"We can choose another one if you like."

"No, I'm sure I'll survive." He chuckled nervously.

During one explicit scene, Becca moved very close and kissed him. She unbuttoned his shirt and ran her hand across his chest. He shifted again, but he had now reached the point of no return. Becca noticed his excitement; he didn't try to hide it. She passionately kissed him again. He returned her kiss hungrily.

He whispered, "Becca, I'm falling in love with you. I tried to deny it; I told myself it wouldn't work. But I love you."

"I love you, Robert. Show me your love. I beg you—make love to me."

He could no longer resist this pretty young woman. He ran his hand over her firm breasts. She moaned softly. Her hand caressed the inside of his thigh, gently stroking him.

"Oh, Becca, how I've longed for your touch, your kiss. I've dreamed of being with you."

She unbuttoned her blouse, and he removed her bra, exposing her perky breasts. Ravenously, he kissed and caressed her bosoms. She fell back on the couch with the burning desire to be taken by the man she loved. He slowly removed her tight jeans, kissing every inch of her exposed silky soft skin. He took great delight in ever so slowly removing her lacy panties. She moaned loudly in pleasure at the kisses she had only dreamed about. He was trembling as he rose to remove his clothes. He stood naked in front of his lover.

She whispered, "Please stand there and let me admire your toned, tan body." She reached out and touched him, and he sighed with pleasure. She pulled him on top of her. As they passionately kissed, their bodies moved together. She arched up and accepted her lover.

Finally the moment they'd dreamed about was here. He sighed. "I love you so much."

She whispered, "I love you, and I want you now."

Without hesitation, he gladly obeyed her request. Heavy breathing and rapid heartbeats carried the loving couple to the pinnacle of sexual bliss. Their physical love for each other sated, they collapsed in each other's arms, savoring the sweet satisfaction of sexual fulfillment. Robert gave Becca everything she wanted, just the way she wanted it. Her dream had come true.

The next morning Robert lay awake in bed, looking at his princess. He wondered if last night had really happened. Then he wondered if last night should have happened. *A commitment of love was made last night. From now on we will travel life's journey together.*

Becca stirred and rubbed her eyes. A big smile spread across her face. "Good morning, Mr. McAlister."

He grinned naughtily. "And a lovely morning it is, Ms. Carlsbad."

Becca realized that this was a new Robert. She didn't know if it was because of last night or if he had finally admitted what she had known for so long: that they were made for each other.

"Come here, lover, and kiss me," she demanded.

Smiling, he promptly obeyed. "It would be a pleasure, my beautiful one."

She pulled him down, wrapped her sexy legs around his thighs, and squeezed. She slid her hands over his buttocks and pulled him close. In a low, sensuous voice, she asked, "Are you ready to show me how much you love me?"

"How could I ever say no to you?"

Later that day, as they were chatting, she nonchalantly asked, "Robert, it was our age difference that worried you, wasn't it?"

"Yes, dear. I was concerned about the twenty-year difference—"

"Twenty-one years, to be exact, but who's counting?" She giggled. "Sorry. I didn't mean to interrupt."

"I thought you would be better off with a younger man, one with energy who was always on the go, never slowing down. One day I'll be old, and you'll still be young. Your whole life is ahead of you—your career, your talents, your dreams."

Becca laughed. "You are my dream, and as far as my talents, are you talking about my lovemaking talents or my biology talents?"

Robert blushed. "Well, having experienced each one, I would have to say that both are excellent."

"Always the diplomat, but thank you for the compliment." She kissed him and smiled. "Care to show me your love one more time?"

"If you continue to seduce me, we won't have to worry about our future; I'll be history."

Both enjoyed the humor.

As Deb left her chalet, she decided to check on her sister. She walked up and knocked. Becca answered the door with a sheet wrapped around her, her hair standing on end and a big smile on her face.

"Oh, I'm sorry. I didn't mean to wake you."

"We weren't sleeping...uh...I mean, I wasn't sleeping."

At that moment Robert walked out of the bedroom in a sheet of his own. He smiled sheepishly. "Good afternoon, Deb; I didn't know you were here."

Deb blushed. "I am so sorry. I didn't mean to interrupt you—I mean, disturb you."

Becca replied, "Don't apologize. We were just preparing for the toga party, right, Robert?"

"Uh...yes. Yes, of course. The toga party."

"Well, enjoy whatever you were doing...at three in the afternoon. I hope I didn't interrupt anything."

The next morning at the regular team briefing, Deb told the group that Becca and Robert had an announcement to make. The pair stood up, holding hands, and declared that they were officially a couple. Cheers and applause echoed through the lounge. Vic tapped on his water glass; more tapping followed. Finally, Robert got the hint and kissed Becca. The applause started again. Everyone was ecstatic about the proclamation. Most had known that it was just a matter of time.

———

Robert had a history of making awful choices concerning women. They would cheat on him and blame his frequent business trips, or they would push for marriage to get access to his bank accounts. Carlie was one of the few who had loved him and truly cared about him. Elaina didn't want to see her brother hurt or taken advantage of, so she had become very protective of him.

She had mixed feelings concerning Becca. She didn't know Becca that well and set out to uncover any hidden agendas. First she confronted Jerimiah, as he'd helped Robert hire her. "Jer, do you mind if I ask you some questions about Becca?"

"Not at all. She's a sweetheart, honest and true. I can tell you that she is a hard worker and that money does not motivate her. I have nothing but praise for her, both as a woman and as a biologist."

Elaina thanked him for his honesty. She made several more inquiries, and all had nothing but good things to say about her.

CHAPTER 34

Elaina didn't believe that Becca was as perfect as everyone said she was. In her opinion Becca was too good to be true. *She must have an ulterior motive*, Elaina thought. *Robert is too old for her.*

Elaina decided it was time she had a face-to-face with Becca. She called to set it up. "I was wondering if we could have lunch together…at your convenience, of course."

"I would love to have lunch with you. Would tomorrow be OK?"

"Tomorrow will be fine. The Crescent City Ale House at one o'clock?"

"That sounds good. See you then."

Becca looked forward to lunch with Elaina. She wanted to know Robert's sister better.

The next day Becca was waiting at the restaurant. Elaina was fashionably late on purpose. "I'm sorry I'm late. I was delayed with a business call. My, you look beautiful, and that glow…wherever did you get it?"

Becca blushed. "Oh, I guess I've been blessed." She really wanted to say, *Robert gave me that while we were making love for the third time*, but she didn't. "You look wonderful also. I guess we've both been blessed."

"Would you like to chat a bit before we order?"

"Yes, that would be nice."

"I understand that you and my brother are an item."

"Oh yes. Robert and I are in love. I guess we have been for a while now but didn't know it. Did he tell you?"

"Yes, he did, and so I would like to get to know you better. You don't mind, do you?"

"Not at all. I'd be happy to answer any questions."

"Good. Where do you expect this relationship to go?"

"Well, it's too early to predict where it will go, but I'm hoping that Robert and I will be together for a long time."

"Becca, do you plan to marry my brother?"

"I will marry him if he asks me. But if he doesn't, I'll be very happy just to be with him."

"Becca, you must protect yourself. You must get a legal document stating that you desire to be…compensated…for your…well, let's just say for your companionship and other favors."

Becca took offense to this advice. "Are you implying that I should be paid to fuck your brother?"

Embarrassed, Elaina quickly looked around. "Please, keep your voice down. But really, that's what you're doing, isn't it?"

Becca quickly controlled her anger. "Elaina, Robert doesn't have enough money to compensate me to lie with him. He loves me, and I love him. That's all that matters. I will forget that we ever had this conversation. And don't worry; I won't tell Robert that his sister is a bitch."

Elaina was shocked and visibly shaken. "I apologize sincerely for offending you, Becca. I was just looking out for Robert's best interests. I can see now that I have made a terrible mistake, and I humbly ask your forgiveness."

"I do love Robert, and I know that he loves me."

Ashamed by her actions, Elaina implored, "Becca, he does love you, and you're the most important person in his life. I now know that your love for each other is sincere. I pushed you, and that was wrong. Again, I apologize."

"I appreciate your concern regarding your brother, but your implications are out of line. I hope you have your answer so that we can move on. Do we understand each other?"

Elaina was dumbfounded by the admonishment; she had never been spoken to so harshly.

Becca acted like nothing had happened. In a passive tone, she asked, "Now, Elaina, would you like to order?"

She took a deep breath, regaining her composure. "Actually, my dear, I always seem to have an appetite after clearing the air."

"Good. Let's look at the menu."

This lively discussion earned Becca newfound respect from Elaina. As they left the restaurant, Elaina watched Becca walk to her car, thinking, *I now believe Becca is the woman my brother will share his life with*.

Becca was pleased with her performance. With her back to Elaina, she walked away with a big smile.

CHAPTER 35

The chatter between Iran and Colombia had increased. Although the words *mutant cell* were never repeated, Vic knew that increased chatter meant that something was going on, and he knew that it was because of the four drums. Sure enough, the satellite tracked the drums to Bogotá, Colombia.

Vic was concerned. Bogotá was riddled with corruption and illicit activities. Everyone knew that customs was a joke; for a few hundred dollars, anything could pass through. The only saving grace was that foreign agents abounded in the region, so there were no secrets.

Vic contacted an old friend and asked him to verify that the four drums were still at a certain warehouse. He got right back to Vic and confirmed that the drums were there and that they were marked with labels that read:

CROP GROWTH ENHANCER

DO NOT PUNCTURE

A greatly relieved Vic thanked his friend. "I owe you."

Knowing for sure that the drums were in the warehouse was comforting, to say the least. The labels identifying them as crop growth enhancers sealed the deal. When Vic told Robert, he immediately wanted to go to the NSA and give them a heads-up.

Vic balked. "I disagree. We don't have enough proof to give it to them. Diplomatic BS and red tape will interfere with the investigation, and right now that's all it is—an investigation."

Robert conceded, "You're probably right, Vic. You know better than anyone."

———

Just when Deb had the lab running like a well-oiled machine, Vic's mission threw a monkey wrench into the lab's tranquility.

Deb received a letter in the mail. Inside was a note that read, "Regarding a cell, go to a small locker at the bus terminal." A key was taped to the note.

Deb knew better than to go herself; she called Vic. "You need to come to my office now."

He was there in minutes. "What's up, honey?"

"Read this," she said and handed him the note.

He did so with a look of concern. "This could be a trap. There still might be someone out to hurt you. I'll go."

"OK, but please be careful."

Vic staked out the locker room for hours, but nothing looked suspicious. He put his rubber gloves on and walked over to the locker. He stuck a tiny camera in, the kind used for medical procedures, through the keyhole and looked around. Inside was a plastic container. He removed the camera, put the key in, and twisted. He opened the locker and removed the container. So far, so good. He placed it in a sealed box and drove straight to the lab. Deb had alerted the team, and they were prepared for the mysterious item. In a clean room, with everyone wearing protective suits, Ethan opened the container.

Inside was a microscope slide. He put it under the scope and looked through the lens. He quickly backed up, and everyone outside jumped. He looked in the lens again. "It's the mutant cell attached to a host."

Shock filled the room. Ethan quickly put the slide back in the container. There was clearly some sort of bacteria acting as a host to keep the cell alive. Vic didn't like gifts, as they always came with a hidden price tag. The pressure was on Deb. She didn't know what her next step would be, and she didn't know how much time she had. "Team, we'll have to work around the clock. We must find out everything we can, as we don't know how long the cell will survive. You know the routine. Let's go."

As the sun rose over the resort, the group was still running formulas. Finally, at 4:00 p.m., the scientists had cloned six more mutant cells. Now they could afford to do some serious testing. Two days later, using a human hormone as an activator, they had replicated a deadly human virus. This strain attacked the brain cells through the sinuses. Within days the victim would be in a vegetative state, clinically dead.

Deb told the team, "Great job. I'm proud of you. Now go home and get some rest. We still have a lot of research ahead of us."

———

Becca was walking to her chalet when she met Robert on the path. "Hello, Becca. You must be exhausted."

"Actually, I'm too excited to sleep, but when I do, I'll crash." She laughed, and so did Robert. "What about you? I heard you were right there with us."

"Yes, it was exciting to see the team at their best. I'm so proud of you all."

"Did you eat? I have some leftover lasagna. Care to help me finish it?"

Having not expected him to accept her offer, she was surprised by his response. "Thank you. I love lasagna."

"Follow me." Inside the chalet she said, "Make yourself comfortable. I'll change and be right out." She emerged wearing a pair of ripped jeans and a cropped top. "Can I get you a drink?"

"Water will be fine."

She handed him the beverage and indicated that they'd eat in about fifteen minutes. "Robert, kick off your shoes and relax."

Dinner was served a short time later. He complimented her on the delicious meal. "Let me know the next time you make lasagna."

"I'll do that."

The pair sat on the couch, and she turned on the TV. Robert seemed nervous.

"Robert, is there something wrong? Do you want to tell me something?"

"No, Becca. Everything is fine."

"You're acting strange. Don't you love me anymore?"

"Becca!" he exclaimed. "What would make you think that?"

"I'm just asking."

Both could feel the tension in the air. Becca joked, "Would you like to make love to me?"

He couldn't get the words out fast enough. "Could we? I mean…I'd really like to make love to you. That's all I've been thinking about. I love you so much, but I didn't want to seem anxious."

Becca laughed. "Don't hide your feelings. If you want to make love to me, just tell me. I sure as heck will tell you. I'll start to take your clothes off—or mine, for that matter." They both laughed heartily. Then he kissed her hungrily; their clothes slowly fell to the floor.

Robert was up early the next morning. As he left Becca's chalet, he was still smiling as he recalled the previous night. *Amazing the gifts that love brings.* As he turned, he saw Vic and Deb on their porch.

"Good morning, boss," Vic said. "Did you sleep well?"

"I didn't sleep a wink; Becca and I made love all night. To tell you the truth, I'm worn out, but you don't want to hear about that."

Vic barked, "The hell we don't." There was a loud slap, immediately followed by a yell. "*Ow!*"

"On second thought, we don't." Deb and Vic looked at each other and smiled.

Later in the day, Becca went into the nursery. The plants and trees quaked when she walked in. They greeted her jubilantly. She was in love, and they knew it. She went over to the kapok sapling that was doing very well. It reached out and wrapped around her hand. She squeezed it gently, and the whole tree quivered.

Becca walked up to the jacaranda tree from Argentina. "Well, what about you, mister? Nothing to say?"

The tree began to flutter its branches in a rhythmic wave.

"Thank you. I'm pleased too," Becca happily replied.

The nursery was growing, and they were almost out of space. Soon the boss would need to build a larger facility.

That evening Robert went to Becca's chalet to watch some TV. Becca had other plans. She knew Robert loved her cutoff jeans and cropped T-shirt. So naturally that would be her attire. When Robert saw her outfit, he smiled; she winked and nodded her head in the direction of the bedroom. His smile grew larger. The door closed, and the couple made passionate love.

CHAPTER 36

Becca finished her work early and decided to get some sun. She loved the sun and the warmth it brought to her.

After a while a figure blocked her sunlight. "Good afternoon, Becca."

"Hello, Carlos. Haven't seen you for a couple of weeks."

"I know; I had to go back to Brazil to take care of some personal business."

Carlos had a pleasant demeanor. He was polite and friendly. Everyone liked him. And he liked Deb and Becca. He would flirt with the ladies whenever he had the chance. But he kept his distance for obvious reasons: Becca was the boss's woman, and Deb had Vic. Enough said.

At first Carlos was quiet, but then he began to ask questions. Nothing personal—mostly about businesses and the local area. All and all, he seemed to be a decent guy.

While sunning at the pool, he received a call. The sisters overheard him say, "Yes, sir. I'll be back to the plantation in a few weeks."

There was nothing strange about that, although Deb did mention it to Vic. "Back to the plantation." He thought, *I know it is a long shot, but maybe Carlos knows Eduardo, plantations and all.*

Vic made it a point to accidentally bump into Carlos. "Hey, Carlos; how are you doing?"

"Vic, hey. I'm doing well. How about you?"

"Everything's good. Say, I was wondering if you knew a friend of mine in Brasília. He owns a plantation—his name is Eduardo Morales."

"Eduardo Morales." Carlos thought for a minute. "No, that name doesn't sound familiar. Sorry."

"It was a long shot; I just thought I'd ask."

Vic could spot a liar a mile away, and Carlos was lying.

When Vic saw Robert that evening, he asked, "Robert, is it possible someone living in Brasília may not know Eduardo Morales?"

"If they were living under a rock, maybe."

Then something very odd happened. Robert got a call from his good friend Eduardo. "A while back you asked me about Evergreen Farms. I asked around but was met with silence. Finally, I was told that I had no business with these people and that they were very bad hombres. They will kill you for no reason. I don't know why you were interested in this place, but please listen to me: never mention that name again. Please, my friend!"

Robert agreed. "I believe you. I'll never mention the name again. Thank you for the warning."

"That's what friends are for. Should you have any other inquiries, please call me first. I will tell you if they are good or bad people."

"Thanks and goodbye, Eduardo. Stay safe."

Vic heard the conversation and thought. *Two phone calls, one* to *Brasília and one* from *Brasília. Coincidence? Not a chance.* It would be impossible for Carlos not to know a wealthy public figure like Eduardo Morales.

———

Vic was taking his morning laps around the parking lot and bumped into Carlos. Until now they had only spoken a passing greeting.

Today was different. Out of the blue, Carlos asked about the abandoned chemical plant near town.

Vic played dumb. "I heard they folded—something about poor management."

"You don't know anything about the owners? Where they may have gone?"

"Not really. The father may still live around here, but the son disappeared."

Vic kept feeding Carlos bits of information, hoping to lure him into a specific question. But Carlos was smooth, and he asked nothing more. The game was up. Vic decided to do some checking on Carlos.

Later that day Becca and Carlos waited in a cabana for a sun shower to subside. Making small talk, Carlos quizzed Becca. "And just what assignment do you have? Something top secret, I bet."

"Actually, I'm working on the interactions between humans and trees."

He laughed. "Yeah, I bet you can write volumes on that subject—like zero," he said sarcastically.

The pair didn't say much for a while. Then Carlos asked, "Who is the top dog here at the lab?"

"My sister is the manager, but Jerimiah's knowledge of plants and trees surpasses us all."

"Who's Jerimiah?"

"Jerimiah Simpson." Later Becca said, "I think I had enough sun for today. I'm going home."

"I was wondering if you'd like to grab a bite in town. I'm tired of microwave dinners."

"Thanks, but I have other plans."

"Hey, I know you're the boss's woman. It's just dinner."

"No, Carlos," Becca said again and walked away.

Robert saw the exchange from the window of his suite. Becca was taking a shower when he arrived at her chalet. "I'm here, Becca. Just letting you know so that I don't startle you."

"Thanks, babe."

Becca came out of the bathroom and into her bedroom wearing her robe, her hair wrapped in a towel. They conversed between rooms.

Robert asked, "How was your day, my princess?"

"Just a regular day. Nothing exciting. How about yours?"

"Business as usual." Regretfully he replied, "But you know what time of year it is."

With a pout she sadly replied, "Yes, contract renewals. And you'll be gone for weeks."

"Becca, you know how time flies. I'll be back before you know it. By the way, did I see you talking to Carlos?"

"Yes." Jokingly she asked, "Were you spying on me?"

He laughed. "No, not at all. I just happened to glance out the window."

"He sure does ask a lot of questions. Nothing personal, just general questions. He's very curious."

"I wouldn't be surprised if he asks you out to dinner."

"You already know what my answer will be: *n-o*."

The bedroom door was open. He turned and saw Becca drop her robe as she slipped into a lacy pair of panties. He couldn't help himself and stopped to admire her sexy body. She looked up and caught him staring.

"Like what you see?"

Embarrassed, he replied softly, "Indeed."

She smiled and then finished dressing. She kissed him before brushing by him and into the kitchen. "I'd love to continue this, but I have dinner to make."

———

Carlos was in his room at the resort. He made a phone call to Brasília. "Hello, Pia. I'm almost finished here. The chemist's story checks out. I do have one more item on my list to complete. A pretty little thing needing some Latino love…I know, Pia: business before pleasure…yes, I'll be careful. See you soon."

———

The following week Robert was away on his yearly contract renewals. Carlos figured that this was the best time to pay a friendly visit to Becca.

When she opened the door, he said, "Hi, Becca; can we talk?"

"Just for a minute."

"I'm leaving soon, so I wanted to say goodbye."

"That's very sweet of you."

"Could we take a little walk down by the lake?" Carlos asked.

"Sure, but just for a few minutes."

They walked the path to the lake. There was a picnic table and a bench set off in a clearing far from the chalets. He said, "Let's stop here for a minute."

They walked over to the table, and Becca sat down. Unexpectedly he bent over and kissed her. Becca quickly pulled away. "Hey, what's going on here? Don't ever touch me again."

"Come on, Becca. Pops is gone. You need some Latino love, and I'm here to give it to you."

Becca looked at him and thought, *You picked the wrong woman, Romeo.*

Carlos laughed. "Do you really think you can resist me? Once I smack you around, you'll think twice about refusing me. Come on, be sensible. Lie back and enjoy it."

Becca calmly replied, "Walk away now and leave the resort. I'm warning you."

Carlos pushed her down on the bench and started to undo her jeans. Suddenly his eyes bulged, and his mouth gaped. With the speed of a viper strike, the vines began pulling him away from Becca. He frantically tried to hold on to the bench, but he couldn't and hit the ground with a thud. In the blink of an eye, he was wrapped up tight. His violent struggle was futile. He screamed like a sissy. Becca sat on the bench with a look of satisfaction on her face.

The vines began to tighten, gripping him like a huge boa constrictor.

He begged, "Please help me. I'm sorry. Please, Becca. Please help me!"

"No, Carlos. I won't. How many girls have you raped?" He didn't answer. "This time, Carlos, you're gonna pay—big time."

By now he could hardly breathe. In a whisper he cried, "I don't want to die. Please help me. I'll never hurt anyone again."

Becca said nothing; she just glared at him. His face was pale. As he took his last breath, there were tears in his eyes. He knew that he was a dead man.

Suddenly the vines loosened their grip. He gulped a breath of air to fill his empty lungs. He lay on the ground, too weak to move.

Becca stood over him. "I'd like to kick you in the balls, but that might delay your leaving. Get out of my sight before I change my mind and give you back to the vines."

Carlos ran as best as he could. Fifteen minutes later he left the resort in his car.

He was thankful he was alive but angry that Becca had disgraced him. He vowed revenge.

CHAPTER 37

The McAlister Foundation received a request from the local Tule River Indian tribe. They wanted permission to use the land on the far side of the lake for a sacred ceremony. Elaina and Jerimiah agreed to meet with an elder to discuss the request. A meeting was set for two days from then. The morning of the meeting, Jerimiah drove Elaina to the far side of the lake. The elder was waiting.

"Good morning. I'm William Ten Ponies." He reached out and shook their hands. He was a tall, thin man with long, black, braided hair. He was dressed in a suit and looked very professional.

"Hello, Mr. Ten Ponies. I'm Jerimiah Simpson, and this is Elaina McAlister."

He smiled. "Pleased to meet you both."

The pair had never been on this side of the lake. Its beauty was breathtaking.

"My grandfather, Chief Ten Ponies, will soon die. To help him make the journey to his ancestors, he needs to cleanse his soul. Where we are standing is sacred ground. In his youth the tribe would come here to prepare for war. It was usually an enemy tribe wishing to take their land. In times of peace, the tribe would come here to celebrate life and give thanks for the bounty this land provided. We wish to set up two sweat lodges for two days. This will give Grandfather time to prepare for his journey."

Elaina looked at Jerimiah. "I don't see any reason why we can't grant this request."

Jerimiah agreed. "This couldn't have come at a better time. The team could use a distraction."

With Elaina and Jerimiah in agreement, permission was granted.

William Ten Ponies thanked them. "There is one more thing, and it's going to sound very strange. In my grandfather's vision, a man—a very special man—took his hand and led him into a tree. I know that it's odd, but this was his vision. He also invited you and members of your team to join him. This is a great honor, but he will understand if you decline his offer."

Jerimiah said, "I'll ask the team and get back to you."

"That will be fine. In the meantime we will start to construct the lodges."

Chief Ten Ponies knew that the sweat lodges had to be built on sacred land between two large sequoia trees. That was the way of the TREEZZ.

McAlister's two emissaries did some research on the sweat lodge ceremony. It was considered an honor to attend the ceremony and an insult to turn it down. It was said that for some, it was a life-changing experience. Others saw visions of the past, some the future. No matter what, it was an experience.

Jerimiah informed Deb of the invitation. She in turn passed it on to the team. Bart and Carlton were in; Ethan was superstitious and opted to hold down the fort. Vic and Deb were hesitant but eventually agreed to attend. They had no wish to insult Chief Ten Ponies. Robert had reservations, but Becca convinced him to go. Jerimiah contacted William Ten Ponies and gave him the names of the attendees. Both William and his grandfather were pleased.

The morning of the ceremony, William gathered the guests at the sweat lodge, explaining the ritual. Two women assisting the tribe would place hot rocks inside the lodge. Each participant was given a small bucket of water to pour on the rocks. When it was their turn, they would put the water on the rocks to create humid, steamy vapor. At the end of that individual's session, they would walk to the lake, where the two women would attend to them.

He cautioned, "The temperature will be over one hundred degrees."

The women wore loose dresses, and the men donned shorts but no shirts. Both men and women were given towels for their comfort.

William said, "If you began to feel light-headed, step outside until you feel better. Now we will divide up the guests. In the first lodge with my grandfather and me will be Deborah, Becca, Vic, and Robert. Elaina, Jerimiah, Bart, and Carlton will be in the second lodge."

A person could stand up inside the lodge. It was made from animal skins. In the center was a pile of hot rocks. In the first lodge, with everyone seated in a circle, William's grandfather began chanting. He stopped and poured water on the stones. A cloud of steamy vapor rose from them. Ten Ponies reached down and picked up a peace pipe containing kinnikinnick, a mixture of tobacco, herbs, and bark. He inhaled and then said a prayer to the east, west, north, and south. He passed it on. Everyone followed the chief's lead.

The old man looked to the skies and prayed as he threw water on the stones. A ghostly image of a horse and rider flashed by as it ran through the lodge. The rider threw a lance, just missing the old chief. The horse and rider turned and charged again. The chief pulled the lance out of the ground and thrust into the chest of the empty spirit. The aggressive horse and rider vanished into the vapor. This time the steam didn't evaporate. The next vision was of Chief Ten Ponies standing in front of a giant sequoia. He waved and smiled; then he was gone.

Two women helped him to the lake, disrobed him, and bathed him in the pristine mountain waters. When they were finished, the women escorted him back to the lodge.

Now it was Robert's turn. He took the pipe, inhaled, made a prayer to the four corners, and passed it on. He poured water on the rocks, and a steam cloud appeared. He began to hallucinate, either from the heat or the kinnikinnick. The steam cloud circled him, and two figures materialized. Two blond women stood in front of him; both had their arms outstretched, as if welcoming him. He ascended and joined them. A sensuous voice beckoned, "Come join us. Come with us." The trio seemed to glide as they circled the rocks. Then they began to fade, and the three became one.

Becca looked over at Robert and smiled. He was about ready to pass out. Two Native American women helped him to the lake, undressed him, and submerged him in the crystal-clear water. Minutes later he walked out of the lake clearheaded, and the women dried him off and dressed him. He returned to the lodge.

Deb was nervous and wondered what her vision would be. She passed the pipe and poured water on the rocks. A cloud of steam turned into two ghostly figures. She watched the apparitions take shape. Then she and Becca recognized the figures as their parents. The two women jumped up and hugged them. "Mom and Dad, we've missed you so."

After hugs and kisses, their mom said, "We are so sorry we had to leave you. But we are so proud of you girls. We are always with you. We love you."

Becca sobbed as she held them tightly. Slowly the images began to fade, and she was left holding nothing. Deb took Becca's hand, and they both walked to the lake, where they removed their clothes and immersed themselves in the cool, healing waters. They walked out, and the women dried them off. After they'd dressed, they returned to the lodge.

Vic inhaled the peace pipe and poured the water over the stones. The lodge filled with steam. The vapor began to swirl as a cool breeze chilled the occupants. A dark cloud loomed in front of him. The ominous vapor took the shape of a huge warrior in full war dress. Vic looked up into the eyes of the war chief, whose name was Victorio. Many moons ago his name alone put fear into the hearts of his enemies.

A deep voice echoed through the lodge. "Victorio, I am proud of you. You have brought honor to our family. I lived as a warrior, and you, too, live as a warrior. You still have many battles to fight, many wrongs to right, and a beautiful lady to love." Chief Victorio's eyes shifted to Deb. "Go now, and absorb my strength from the sacred water of the lake."

As the vision faded, the cool breeze carried off the last of the vapor. Vic walked to the lake and removed his clothes. He plunged into the invigorating waters of the serene mountain lake.

He could feel Chief Victorio's power surge through him. Minutes later he emerged with a renewed force. Dried by the tribal women, he dressed and returned to the lodge. The night's darkness fell as the ceremony continued.

William Ten Ponies smoked the peace pipe and passed it on. He splashed water on the hot rocks. Steam began to take shape, creating a picture of a man looking into the future. The man stood tall among the children of the tribe.

He signaled the children to follow him. They walked out of their poverty-stricken village to a lush valley full of crops ready to be harvested. The children picked wild berries, apples, and oranges. Plenty of jerky hung from nearby trees. The man turned around, and behold, it was William Ten Ponies. This was his mission—to take his tribe out of poverty and into paradise.

He would battle modern-day prejudice, corruption, and jealousy from his own tribal members. Even the deities couldn't predict the outcome. He went to the lake to cleanse his spirit for the long battle. Dried and dressed, he returned to the lodge.

———

In the second sweat lodge, the same cleansing spirits were taking place. Supernatural occurrences emanated from the steam vapors and gave the occupants meaningful visions.

Elaina watched the men who had touched her private life flash by like playing cards being shuffled. She was intelligent and beautiful but extremely independent. She'd turned away many suitors. She poured more water on the glowing stones.

Jerimiah had the daunting responsibility to propagate and preserve the TREEZZ. He felt honored to have been chosen to serve the TREEZZ and mankind. Carrying out these duties left little time for a relationship. His vision gave him a fleeting glimpse of a lovely woman glancing over her shoulder, smiling, and inviting him to follow her. He couldn't see her face, but he was intrigued and followed her down the dark path. Suddenly the vapor dissipated. As she faded, she said in a whisper, "Wait for me. I'll be back." He jumped up to follow, but she was gone.

Carlton poured the water onto the hot glowing rocks. The water sizzled as a cloud of steam spread through the lodge. He anxiously waited for an image. He strained to see, but the steam cloud was empty. What was it that the spirits were trying to tell him?

Suddenly he realized this was his life: empty. It frightened him. He poured more water on the stones, creating a huge cloud of vapor. Carlton saw a boy in the field. He went to him. "What's wrong, boy?"

"I'm lonely; I have no one. Will you help me?"

Carlton answered, "Yes, boy, I will help. I don't have anyone either." He took the boy by the hand, and they walked to Carlton's chalet. The boy turned to see a small dog following them. The boy said, "He's lonely too." Carlton and the boy entered the chalet; the dog followed. Once they were inside, the loneliness faded and was replaced by joy and love.

Carlton had tears in his eyes as he watched himself, the boy, and the dog romp through the fields. They were lonely no more. A voice emanated from the cloud. "You will find a boy and a dog. And your life will no longer be empty." Carlton buried his face in his hands and sobbed. He now would have a boy and a dog to love.

Bart enjoyed the whole adventure. He watched in awe as the visions played out right in front of his eyes. He felt close to his partners, closer than he'd ever felt to anyone before.

From his wheelchair he cast the water onto the hot rocks. The steam erupted in billows of vapor. He looked into the vapor and saw nothing but white. Suddenly he realized that he was sailing through the air, his feet buckled into ski boots, his skies pointed upward. He heard a loud smack. His skis touched down on the steep slope. He followed the slalom course to the bottom. Sliding sideways, he ended an Olympic time trial as the leader. It was exhilarating—the rush of adrenaline, the thrill of being airborne, the biting cold, and the aroma of freshly fallen snow.

"Yes!" he shouted and pumped his fist. His lodge dwellers applauded him for his enthusiasm. Bashfully he smiled and thanked them. He wheeled himself down to the lake. The women helped him out of the chair and undressed him. He didn't mind. They submerged him in the magical waters of the sacred lake. What the women saw next shocked them to the core. Bart walked out of the lake. Was this a part of his vision, or was he really walking? The tribal women watched in amazement as he walked to the lodge. He was wearing nothing but a smile. The women quickly ran after him and covered him in a blanket. He pulled back the cover and walked in.

Gasps of astonishment resonated within the lodge. The participants also wondered if this was part of a vision or if it was real. They reached out and touched Bart; he was glowing, and he was real.

The word spread to the first lodge. They all ran out to see Bart walk. In the second lodge, the chief chanted for a time, giving thanks to the god of the TREEZZ. "Because of this ancient ritual of cleansing, and because of your faith, a gift was given to us. That gift was this man's ability to walk among us again." The chief's words were profound, and everyone felt blessed that they'd been invited to attend.

The ceremony continued with prayers, chants, and storytelling throughout the night.

———

The next morning, Chief Ten Ponies took a turn for the worse. His breathing was shallow, and his blood pressure was weak. The chief asked to see Jerimiah and Becca. The pair went to the sweat lodge. The chief called Becca over. He held her hand in his and lightly squeezed it. "You are the TREEZZ's princess. You are special and have been blessed by them. I am grateful to have met you. I must go soon, but we will meet again in the world of the TREEZZ."

He called Jerimiah over and whispered, "I have venerated the TREEZZ all my life. I wish to be with the TREEZZ in their world beyond. I know that you are the TREEZZ's man. My last wish is that I am taken into the TREEZZ to live there for eternity. Will you grant me my last wish?"

The old chief was an honorable man; Jerimiah and Becca couldn't deny his wish. He proudly shuffled up to the giant sequoia. Becca took one of Ten Ponies' arms, and Jerimiah took the other. The trio faced the tree and, with their last ounce of energy, waved goodbye. The chief smiled as he faded away.

William fell to his knees in reverence for his grandfather and the TREEZZ. Becca was also saddened and lowered her head in respect. It was a mystical, magical event that enlightened all the attendees. The memories that had been made over those two days would last a lifetime. The sacred experience was a godsend. The team came away enriched in both mind and body.

CHAPTER 38

They were anxious to find a neutralizer for the deadly virus. The lab developed several mutant clones on which to conduct experiments. Test after test produced negative results. They sometimes felt that they were so close to the answer, only to be thwarted by an unforeseen negative reaction. Undeterred, the scientists continued their quest. After weeks of dead ends, it was time to take a different direction.

Carlton suggested, "Since L&L Chemical was working with trees and plants, maybe we should try cells derived from plants?"

Deb was shocked that he would even consider that option. "Carlton, you know that it's forbidden to integrate human and plant cells. We shouldn't go there."

Bart pondered the idea. "Deb, if we adhere to the strictest policies, we may be able to manipulate the cells to our advantage."

Deb said she'd take it under consideration.

Days later Bart called Deb and asked her to come to the lab. Soon afterward she walked through the door.

"Hi, everyone. Do we have good news?" She held up her hand with her fingers crossed.

"Deb, we're out of options—except for one."

"And that would be?"

"Take a plant cell and combine it with a human cell."

Deb's mind again raced through the several scenarios; many were nightmares. Then she said, "I've given this some thought, and I realize that it just might be possible. Last month I read an article dealing with the exact same challenge. The university defined the procedure to follow for this type of research. I believe that if we adhere to their strict guidelines, we can do our analyses and testing safely."

———

Weeks later Bart inadvertently used a contaminated slide and created a virus. He broke out in a cold sweat and hit the emergency contamination button. Carlton and Bart immediately sealed off the room. Bart stripped and ran to the decontamination shower. Donning protective gear, Carlton collected his clothes and put them in a sealed container marked DANGER—BIOHAZARDOUS MATERIAL. Deb, Becca, and Ethan waited in another decontamination room.

Following the strict procedure, everyone went through two decontamination showers. Extensive testing was conducted, which revealed that the virus was contained in Bart's sealed lab. Because everyone had adhered to the rigid guidelines, they'd avoided a catastrophe. Deb was obligated to notify the Centers for Disease Control and Prevention about the discovery. The CDC thought it would be much safer for them to remain at their state-of-the-art facilities. They were sending a specialist out to gather all the information available.

The lab was put on a code-red alert. The compound was shut down, and no one came in or out without authorization. As a precaution, Deb suggested that Carlton and Bart confine themselves to the lab building. Cots were set up in the decontamination room. They all hoped that this would be a short-term inconvenience. Becca and Ethan had been in the nursery at the time and were not at risk of infection. Deb was beside herself. Precious time had been lost due to the accident.

CHAPTER 39

Deb and Vic were relishing their relationship, even though they had little time together. It was one both had only dreamed of. Vic learned to love again. Deb always came first, both in his thoughts and in his actions. He would do anything to make her happy.

She in turn gave him all her love. She enjoyed his he-man behavior and knew that most of it was just his bark, though she also knew that if necessary, he could bite. She knew what he liked, and she knew how to turn him on. Most of all they enjoyed being together and holding hands.

———

Deb received a disturbing call from the World Health Organization. A chemical weapons expert told her, "A small Iranian village was annihilated by some form of deadly chemical or virus. We are unable to identify the cause because all the cells that we found were dead. We understand that you have been researching something similar. We feel that your sophisticated laboratory may be able to identify the cause of this horrible incident."

Deb didn't really want to get involved with the WHO and their political BS. On the other hand, she felt they may have uncovered some new information. Reluctantly, Deb agreed to look at their findings and compare notes. Deb assigned Carlton and Bart to the WHO incident as they had the most experience dealing with the deadly cells.

Days later the Iranian samples arrived. Fortunately, the WHO scientists had done a great job of categorizing the samples.

Bart's eyes were tearing from the constant use of the microscope. Deb walked by and saw Bart's distress. "Bart, let me take over. Go rest your eyes."

He didn't hesitate to accept the offer. Deb put on her protective suit and moved the next slide under the microscope. She looked again and again. *This can't be*, she thought. *I'm looking at the mutant cell.*

"Bart, come look at this slide."

He quickly dried his eyes, put on his protective suit, and looked into the microscope. "Holy moly! It's the mutant."

The mutant cell was almost dead, but this was all the proof they needed. It was the deadly virus. By dissecting the cell, the researchers could separate and identify the host and the accelerator.

Just when the team thought they could take a deep breath and relax, they were thrown back into the fray. Vic informed them that the drums were on the move. The biologists were under the gun again.

Deb stated with regret, "You all know what's at stake here. We are entering uncharted waters in our research of a combination of human and plant cells. It will be very challenging to find an antivirus or any other way to neutralize this deadly virus. I have complete faith in our team. I know that we will succeed. We have to—millions of people are counting on us."

Robert walked into Vic's office. "Vic, I have to ask, do we know for sure that the virus is in those drums?"

"Would you feel better if I lied to you?"

"You know the answer to that."

"Robert, I've never lied to you, and I'm not going to start now."

"Thank you. I believe I have my answer. Fill me in. Where do we stand?"

"The drums left Bogotá and took a northerly course toward Mexico. I'm thinking the western section of the US."

"That's a mighty big area."

"Yes, it is. I could venture a guess and say LA, San Francisco, or maybe even Hawaii, but I doubt that. Here's what I base my theory on. The Chinese bought a mutant cell. They converted that cell into a deadly airborne virus. China contacted terrorists and sold the virus to Iran. Iran added an accelerant to make the virus act quicker. But in doing so, they weakened the cell. Now it has an abbreviated life span and will expire within a week, but that doesn't matter because it will have completed its deadly mission. It's imperative that we find an antidote for the virus. If the virus is successful, they will use it again and again."

Robert said, "Vic, you have an uncanny ability to see things that most of us don't. I'll back your instincts every time. That's why you're here."

"Thanks, Robert. Sometimes even I need someone to back me up."

CHAPTER 40

Deb looked at the stacks of paperwork—the result of following CDC guidelines for dealing with an unknown virus. With the preliminary tests and data recorded, the biologists Carlton and Ethan moved to the next testing phase. They began the labor-intensive task of combing the virus with thousands of varying quantiles. This procedure required continuous monitoring of the analysis and collection of the data. Two members of the team would be sufficient.

Becca and Bart were assigned to resume the research on an herbal blood pressure medicine. The pair retrieved all the information they had previously uncovered. According to the documents, several herbs looked promising. The list contained the following herbs: matricaria flower, nigella seed extract, ginseng, olive leaf tea, and blueberry juice. Other herbs written in Robert's book were amla, triphala, haritaki, arjuna, and black myrobalan. It was a daunting task, but if the results were positive, it would save countless lives. That was the incentive the team needed to do their best. Each morning the scientists were greeted by stacks of overnight test-result readouts generated by the computer. That data alone would take hours to sort through, most of the time with negative results.

Finally Bart called out, "I think we may have something, Becca. Look at these readouts."

Becca glanced at the results. "Yes, I think you're right; this looks good."

Becca called Deb with the news. "I'll be right there." Deb read the results and smiled. "This is positive; let's get a sample ready."

After Deb left, Bart said, "I have the perfect guinea pig." He took a deep breath and stuck out his chest. "Me!" he exclaimed.

"Oh no, you know that's against the rules; my sister would kill us."

"Becca, nobody would know. Look at how much time that would save."

"Bart, you can't do this. We're making progress. It's slow going, but that's how our business works: safety first at all times."

With a scowl, he relented. "OK, we'll do it your way."

Bart came in early the next morning and went straight to the lab. He quickly took a vial out of the refrigerator. He opened a new syringe and extracted a small amount of liquid from the vile.

Becca was awakened by the rustling of the TREEZZ. They told her to get to the lab. Alarmed, she quickly dressed and went to the lab. As Becca walked in, Bart was sitting on his stool with a Cheshire cat grin.

Becca remarked, "Bart, you look pleased with yourself. Do I dare ask why?"

He wrapped the blood pressure monitor around his arm and hit the start button.

Moments later he held up the reading: 121 over 80.

Becca was thrilled but asked, "Did you inject the experimental formula? Bart, tell me you didn't." He sat there with the same grin. "Damn you, Bart; that is so stupid, so dangerous. Check your blood pressure again."

He did—it read 118 over 70 and was dropping. Becca could tell something was amiss by his glassy eyes and pale skin tone. Becca had him lie on the floor and rechecked his pressure: 110 and dropping. She yelled, "Bart, stay with me!"

Bart's eyes rolled back, and he passed out.

Becca quickly raised his legs, loosened his clothes. She called Deb and began to wipe him down with a wet towel. Deb rushed in just as Bart was coming around. He tried to get up, but Becca held him down.

Deb looked at Becca. "What happened here?"

Carlton and Ethan came running in to assist. They carried him to a folding cot and set him down. Deb took his blood pressure several times; it was 118 and rising.

Deb asked, "Carlton, will you keep an eye on Bart?" Deb was furious with Becca and Bart. She looked at Becca. "I'd like to speak to you. Follow me." Deb took Becca into a room and closed the door. Becca knew she was in for it. "Becca, I am so mad, so disappointed in you. Was there anything you could have done to stop this?"

Becca was flushed and ashamed. "I am so sorry; I should have notified you as soon as I found out what he did."

"We could have lost Bart today because rules weren't followed. "

"OK. Let's get Bart stabilized, and we'll deal with the consequences later."

"OK." She hung her head down and walked away. She knew she had been wrong.

When Deb returned, Bart was feeling better, and his pressure was normal—well, normal for him—at 145.

Deb glared at him. "You know the risk you put everyone in. I know your reason, but that will not prevent a reprimanding." Deb was angry not because of what they had done but because a team member might have been lost. As manager of the lab, Deb would have had to live with that.

At the end of the day, Becca and Bart apologized to Deb. Bart, humbled, said remorsefully, "I'm sorry, Deb; I was a fool to attempt it. Becca had nothing to do with my actions. She probably saved my life with her quick response."

Becca also apologized again for her part.

Deb commented, "I have no choice but to officially reprimand both of you for not adhering to lab policy. I'm required to notify the FDA and the CDC of the violation. I have no choice."

They understood and held no hard feelings.

The next day Bart and Becca ran the tests following proper procedure. The results were promising. The formula that Bart used was the correct mixture and lowered blood pressure. Deb, Becca, and Bart knew he had saved weeks of testing by injecting himself. Yet the fact was never mentioned. It was a bittersweet victory.

The formula now had to be produced in volume. This was the next step in the FDA process. After that scare, the biologists were acutely aware of the regulations and carried them out to the letter. That pleased

Deb. Producing the formula at scale was where Becca would excel. Based on her expertise and the TREEZZ's instructions, the lab had no doubt she would succeed. Becca knew she couldn't just use the ratio principle of quantity. No, this was a complicated equation involving unknown dynamics. This was where the assistance of the TREEZZ would be invaluable.

Becca worked tirelessly to add ingredients to create a highly concentrated liquid referred to as Ruienetic concentrate. In less than a week, Becca had finalized the formula. With the testing procedure certified, the paperwork was the last item to complete.

CHAPTER 41

It had been a week since the crated drums had arrived at the warehouse in Bogotá. Now the surveillance techs observed some activity there. A box truck pulled up to the loading dock. A short time later, a forklift loaded the drums into the truck. The techs called Vic immediately.

He quickly dressed and kissed Deb goodbye. Half asleep, she said, "Bye, hon."

He looked down at her. He shook his head, thinking, *Lord, what did I ever do to deserve such an angel?* He gently kissed her cheek and left.

Arriving at his office, he brought up the video of the warehouse and the vehicle hauling the drums. He called surveillance. "Don't lose that truck, guys. It's all we have." The vehicle took a northerly direction, its destination unknown.

The National Oceanic and Atmospheric Administration had put out an alert for Central America. There was a possibility of heavy rains and low clouds over the region for the next forty-eight hours due to a low-pressure system in the Gulf of Mexico. This was not good news. Bad weather was a surveillance man's Achilles' heel.

Vic told the techs, "I'd like you to plot several routes to the north. Estimate their speed for the antici-pated road conditions. Be ready to survey that area when the weather breaks."

Vic sat back, ready to suffer through his least-favor-ite pastime—waiting. As he sat there drinking his coffee, he closed his eyes, and an image of Deb appeared. He couldn't get her out of his thoughts. *What a lucky man I am to have such a wonderful woman. She's all I ever dreamed of and more.*

He walked over to her office and poked his head in. "Hi, hon. Just wanted to tell you how much I love you."

"Aw, babe, that's so thoughtful. I love you too."

"See you tonight."

She smiled and blew him a kiss.

Back in his office, Vic left Robert a message. "Call me for an update on the drums. All is not well."

The techs called and reluctantly relayed an update. "We lost visual contact with the vehicle. The weather rained on our parade—literally."

Robert called Vic about an hour later. "Hello, my friend. How are you doing?"

"We were doing well, but now we're not. Mother Nature frowned on us, and we lost visual on the drums."

"How badly will this affect us?"

"We plotted various routes north and have an approximate time and location on each one. When the weather breaks, we'll be on it."

"Sounds like right now that's all we can do."

"That's it, boss."

A short time later, Robert walked into Vic's office and closed the door. "I'm wondering if we should tell the authorities what we have and let them handle it."

Vic said, "I'd like to turn this over to the NSA, but there is no solid evidence of a sinister plot. They'll ask what's in the drums, and when we say we don't know, they'll laugh us right out of the building—we don't have any hard evidence."

"Understandable. What do you suggest?"

"I'd like to keep the drums under surveillance. Someone is spending a lot of money sending four drums halfway around the world. I firmly believe that the drums contain a deadly virus and that its intended target is the United States. Until we're sure one way or the other, we need to follow the drums."

"You're right. There are too many lives at stake not to track every lead."

The biologists were having much more success than Vic and the surveillance techs. There was a friendly rivalry going on. Right now the biologists were winning. Deb grinned, and Vic frowned.

The weather broke after a couple of days, and the satellites began scanning every sector in the projected location. "We got a hit," called a tech. The satellite had pinpointed the location of the targeted vehicle. It was five miles north of the search area—not a bad projected position.

The listening techs picked up chatter referring to "the fruit" from Iran. Vic was notified. "We have a visual on the target vehicle, and we've picked up chatter in which the words *fruit from Iran* were heard being used several times. The transmission originated from the lab just outside Tehran."

Vic said, "More pieces to the puzzle. We still don't have a full picture, but we're getting closer."

———

Robert had just returned from a trip to Washington. He had been there for a closed-door session; the subject was a raid on the resort. His first stop was to see Deb. "Would you please call Vic and Becca and ask them to come to my office?"

Seeing the stress and anxiety in his demeanor, she immediately made the calls. When Vic and Becca walked into the room, they realized that something was seriously wrong.

"My friends," Robert said as his voice cracked, "I just returned from the Capitol and have distressing news. Some of the large pharmaceutical companies are questioning our research and herbal medications. With their power and money, they are asking Congress for an investigation into our research. As we all know, some of our discoveries can't be explained logically. We also know that this scrutiny is driven by greed. We have stepped on the toes of the drug companies. Some individuals want to destroy our team and shut down our lab. The drug companies have lost billions due to our free medications. It's so sad that some people would take a dollar over a human life." He hung his head in disillusionment and regret.

No one uttered a word. The silence was deafening.

After a few moments, Deb questioned, "Is there anything we can do, Robert?"

"I honestly don't know," he said with sadness in his voice. This awful turn of events couldn't have happened at a worse time, as the team was very close to isolating the virus and an antidote.

Vic inquired, "Robert, do we have a timetable for the investigation?"

"I spoke to my attorneys, and they can postpone any requests for information by claiming patent infringements and foreign government privacy laws. The problem with that is it brings unwanted publicity. Some of our customers may distance themselves from us."

Vic became visibly angered. "By God, I have always played by the rules, even when I was put at a disadvantage, but this time there will be no rules. I'm playing dirty. These evil men will not hurt the ones I love. I can promise you that."

Robert cautioned, "We will not lower ourselves to the level of these few greedy men. I know you're angry, and I know you've seen this happen to good people before, but we have our pride, honesty, and integrity. Those values must be upheld at any cost."

Vic calmed down. "You're right. We need to walk away with our heads held high. I have only one more thing to say: what they don't know won't hurt us."

Everyone laughed. Robert gave him the evil eye.

––––––

Ethan, Carlton, and Bart ran into Deb's office. "We've isolated the virus!"

Deb was ecstatic and ran to the lab. Sure enough, the team had it contained.

Deb called Robert and Vic. "The team did it. They identified the strain of the virus as human/plant. Now they can dedicate their time to finding an antivirus serum—if one exists."

———

Robert convinced Vic that it was time to go to the NSA and give them their information. It wasn't hard evidence, but they couldn't be held responsible for withholding national security information if things went south.

Vic relented. He had to admit that Robert had some good points, and he wanted to protect his people if things got nasty. Vic asked for a meeting with the director of the NSA.

At first the director refused but then reconsidered. *He may be on to something dealing with national security.*

When Vic walked into the NSA building, he was greeted by old friends who were now in charge of wooden desks. He felt sorry for them. *I'm glad I got out with my dignity.* It was a young man's game now. Vic wasn't impressed.

"Come right in, Vic Bowden." Director William Billings stood up and shook Vic's hand. A young man stood off to the side. "Let me introduce you to Special Agent Myron Weeks."

The two men shook hands. Weeks's grip was wimpy.

The director continued. "He's our top agent. Nothing gets by him. We've heard a lot about you—not all good." He laughed.

Vic mumbled under his breath, "You're a regular comedian."

"What can we do for you?"

Vic said, "I have some information that may be important, but I'll let the professionals decide."

Weeks said mockingly, "You're a smart man. Go ahead; tell us what you've got."

"I believe that the Iranians are planning a biologic attack on the US."

Billings and Weeks looked at each other. Weeks chuckled and then said, "We get a hundred threats a week. Which one are you referring to?"

"The one with the four drums."

That got their attention. He knew he'd struck a nerve.

The director said, "We ran that one down. It was a dead end; nothing to it. Is that all you have?"

Vic could see that he was getting nowhere and didn't want to waste any more of his time. "Glad you boys have it covered. I'll sleep better tonight."

Weeks escorted Vic to the door. "You retired guys are always trying to get back in the game. You're bored at home, and so you start imagining sinister plots to destroy the country. A vague report of four drums containing a bug or the flu—what a joke. I'd be laughed right out of the agency if I sent agents out on a wild-goose chase. Sorry, Vic, but I don't buy it. Goodbye."

Disappointed and upset, Vic shook his head at the incompetence of the agency. *I'm glad I'm out of that bureaucratic bullshit.*

He called Robert and told him what had happened.

Robert was just as angry. "They did what? Those pompous asses. We'll show them just what our team is capable of. We'll destroy the terrorists." Robert's sudden vehemence was unlike him. "Sorry. I'm a little upset right now."

Vic was surprised by Robert's outburst, but he knew it was justified. "I guess we all reach the end of our rope sometimes."

Vic began to assess his options and plan a defense. Disgusted with Washington's complacency, he looked forward to his return to the resort and Deb.

Back at the resort, the group was gathered, helping Elaina and Jerimiah. Elaina took off her reading glasses and rubbed her eyes; she was tired of going through the applications for grants. She said to Jerimiah, "Put down the paperwork, and find a place somewhere exotic where I can lie in the sun, sipping a piña colada. Oh, and don't forget to have handsome young men bringing me my drinks and tending to any other requests I may have." She winked at him.

He frowned. "What?"

She cried, "I can dream, can't I?"

"Are you serious?"

"Yes, I am—I want some action, some excitement, something…precarious if you know what I mean."

Robert looked over at Becca and said, "My dear, your days of risky escapades are over. You can lie by the pool, get your sun, and sip on a piña colada."

Becca was noticeably perturbed by his comment. "Robert, that's my job, and I have no intentions of giving it up. I appreciate your concern, but I'm not going to stop what I do. That's what I was hired to do, and that's what I will do."

Elaina looked a Jerimiah and nodded at him; it was time they left. Elaina said, "I think we have enough information. We can sort out the paperwork at another time."

There were no objections, and they quickly left the room.

Robert said, "Do you think I would risk your life by sending you into a dangerous jungle in search of some sap? I love you and will protect you from harm."

Becca protested. "I have been given a gift from the TREEZZ, and I must use that gift to save them. How could you deny the world the opportunity to save a rare or nearly extinct tree or discover a new herbal medication to aid mankind because I didn't use my gift? This is what we have all striven so hard to accomplish. I must continue to use the skills I was blessed with."

He looked at her, knowing she was right. "I'm sorry, my dear. If I ever lost you, I would never forgive myself. My world would collapse. But I understand we all have a purpose, a destiny, and you must pursue yours."

Elaina and Jerimiah went back to her suite. Elaina stretched and asked, "Jer, would you be a dear and massage my back?"

"Sure, Elaina. I'll do that for you."

"Good boy. I'll slip into something appropriate." She walked out of the bathroom in a short robe. "I'll just lie on the bed."

She went over to the bed, turned her back to Jer, and slipped off her robe. She kept her panties on, much to his relief. He rubbed lotion on his hands and began to massage her back.

She moaned as he rubbed her lower back. "A little lower, please." She moaned again. "Jer, you have such strong hands. Can you go a little lower?"

He now was massaging her buttocks.

Minutes later she said, "Oh, Jer, that's perfect; thank you." She put her robe back on.

He quickly turned his back to her for obvious reasons.

Suddenly she realized he was aroused. "Jerimiah, I am so sorry; I didn't mean to—I should have been more considerate of your feelings and needs. I just feel so comfortable around you. I didn't think. Jer, I wish I could do something. Can I get someone to—make you feel better?"

"Elaina, it's OK. I let my imagination run away."

"I'll never put you in that kind of situation again. You are my best friend, and sure, I have fantasized about us, but if we slept together, it would end our special friendship. I never want to lose your friendship."

He laughed. "I'm glad we cleared the air about that. I will admit I do enjoy your teasing—it adds a little spice to my life and makes for some interesting dreams."

She kissed his cheek, and he left her suite.

CHAPTER 42

The four crated drums were nearing the coastal city of Buenaventura, Mexico.

Vic scratched his head. "A small city on the coast? Why would the drums be heading there?"

He had the techs bring up all the information they had on the location. "Sir, we found nothing other than a good-size fishing fleet getting ready to head north to the huge fishing grounds this time of year."

"Where is the truck now?"

"It's parked near the docks."

"Zoom in the best you can, and look for any suspicious activity. If you find something, call me."

"Will do, sir."

Vic called Deb and told her that he was on his way home.

She was bubbling with curiosity. "What happened in Washington?"

"You don't want to know. I'll tell you when I get home."

It was late when the G700 landed at the resort. Vic went straight to the chalet. Deb met him at the door and gave him a big hug and kiss.

He smiled. "Why would I ever leave this place? It has everything I need and want...which is you."

"Thanks, babe. A girl likes to hear that. Can I get you something?"

He pulled her close and whispered, "I want you."

The next morning Deb and Vic were sitting on the porch with their coffee. "Hon, I just can't figure out why the drums went to some little city on the coast. Maybe I'm barking up the wrong tree. Maybe I am too old for this game."

"Don't you dare think that. You're on the right track, and you'll figure it out."

"Thanks for the vote of confidence. I needed that." They finished their coffee and prepared for work.

He checked in with the techs. "Any changes?"

"No, sir." He knew they would have called if there was new information; it was wishful thinking. "By the way, where is this huge fishing ground the fleet is headed to?"

"It runs almost the whole length of California."

———

"Sir, the crates are moving." Vic looked at his screen. A forklift was unloading the drums and setting them on the dock. *These guys have got some balls, unloading the truck in broad daylight. But again, it may only be fruit from Iran.*

The men pried open the wooden crates and set the plastic drums on separate wooden pallets. A short time later, a crane on wheels set one of the drums on the deck of a fishing vessel. The workers completed this task for three more vessels. One of the techs also noticed that a pallet had an oddly shaped large canvas bag on it.

He told Vic, "I didn't think much of it until I noticed that all four vessels had the same bag."

Vic thought, *Just a piece to the puzzle. Every piece counts.*

Within an hour sixty fishing vessels departed the harbor, taking a northern route. The techs settled back for a long day of visually tracking the trip. The listening techs weren't that lucky. Chatter began to increase; the phrase *fruit from Iran* was used in several conversations, as was the phrase *Allahu Akbar*.

Vic received a call from an old friend at the NSA. "Hello, ex-agent Bowden."

Vic recognized the man's voice. "Well, if it isn't Walter Bando. Good to hear from you."

"I heard you had a conversation with the director. That must have been a thrill." He chuckled.

"Yeah, it was a joke."

"Well, they shit when you mentioned the drums. They've had surveillance on them since they left Iran."

"So the NSA believes there is a deadly chemical in the drums?"

"They do. They got the information from a double agent working in Iran. Unfortunately, they lost the drums in a storm. Special Agent Myron Weeks has the director convinced that his men will soon uncover the terrorist plot and arrest the perps involved."

"Walter, does he have any idea how the terrorists intend to carry out this attack?"

"He's leaning toward an attack from the air. Maybe an air tanker or crop dusters."

"I'll give him credit for that much. I agree with him; it'll probably be from the air. Walter, you must be ready to retire."

"I can't wait. It's not like the old days, Vic. You were smart to get out; this job sucks. Some of the guys wanted me to tell you that if you need anything, just let us know."

"Thanks, Walter. I'll keep that in mind."

The techs were picking up lots of chatter. Vic thought, *This is too much chatter. They're doing this intentionally to overload the NSA with too much information—or too much misinformation—and many false leads. This is where years of playing the game, combined with instinct, help you make the right decisions.*

———

The biologists had isolated the deadly virus but were not making much progress finding an antivirus. This delay was because it was a human-and-plant hybrid. Time was now becoming a factor. The consensus among the experts was two to three weeks. That added pressure didn't help the team.

Bart was straining his eyes, looking through the microscope, when a tear fell on the slide. He set it aside; it was contaminated and would be put in the hazardous waste container.

An hour later he returned to collect the bio-waste. He was just about to discard the slide when something told him to check it first. He placed it under the microscope and was astonished to find that the virus cell was dead.

He thought for a minute. *What did I do differently?* Then he remembered that a tear had fallen on the slide.

In his mind he quickly dissected a tear. *Tears contain water, salt, and fatty oils.* He took a saline solution and repeated the procedure. An hour later the virus was dead.

He paused and thought out loud, "There is no way a simple drop of salt water could destroy the virus—or could it?" Ecstatic, he called, "Deb, everyone, the virus is dead! I found the antivirus."

Carlton and Ethan ran over to see. They both looked at the slide and confirmed the statement. Deb donned her protective suit and went into the isolation room. She excitedly confirmed the finding. She didn't know whether to laugh or cry. The team was euphoric. Deb called Robert and Vic with the good news. Vic was so happy that he did a little two-step. Of course, his door was closed.

Vic called a meeting to go over where they stood now and what would be the next step. With the team present, he began. "Thanks to all your hard work, we have an antivirus. We can go over the details after the meeting. Right now we have four fishing vessels off the coast of California—San Diego, to be exact. They have aboard them one drum each of an unknown chemical. Inside the plastic drums is a sealed five-gallon can of an unknown liquid chemical. We believe that these drums will be used in a chemical attack somewhere on the West Coast. That's an educated guess for now. We hope to be able to narrow down the location. But for now, let's go with the scenario that it's an airborne virus and that it will be inhaled through the nasal passages or sinuses and carried to the brain. In days the victims will be rendered brain dead.

"We figure there are several ways to disperse the chemical. A rocket launch exploded high above a city would allow the chemical to rain down on the population. Another would be to spread it from an air tanker, similar to the forest service's wildfire planes. Another way would be to launch hundreds of weather balloons and have them explode at a certain altitude, thus saturating the atmosphere above the city. We welcome any other suggestions on how this deadly virus could be spread. I don't care how outlandish they may seem; I want to know your thoughts. Needless to say, we are desperate for ideas. This all is speculation, but I believe something close to these scenarios will be used." Vic looked at the team and smiled. "I can hear the wheels turning in your minds. I'm pleased."

The next day Vic's email inbox was full of ideas. He began sorting through the feasible possibilities.

At NSA headquarters similar scenarios were being played out by Special Agent Myron Weeks and his team. Not surprisingly, many were of the same mindset as the biologists. Everyone was in agreement on an aerial assault. The question was: What would be the deadliest weapon? That would be the terrorists' goal. Myron decided that some type of aircraft would be used. After all the facts were in, and by process of elimination, he was left with an air tanker, the type used in forest fire suppression, or a crop duster.

His team would now concentrate their resources on that scenario. He backed up his decision with the chatter the agents were hearing and the launch of several surplus weather balloons. He believed that had been a diversionary tactic.

Walter Bando called Vic again. "Hey, buddy, I have some news. Myron thinks the virus will be spread by an air tanker or crop dusters, so he's concentrating all his resources on that plot."

Vic was shocked. "He can't be serious. You never put all your eggs in one basket."

"We tried to tell him, but the kid thinks he's got it all figured out. Some of the older agents are not pleased with his decision. We didn't want you wasting your time on something the agency has covered."

Truly grateful, Vic replied, "Walter, thanks for the heads-up, old friend. Be careful out there. You're too close to retirement."

CHAPTER 43

Robert's team could now discard the airplane theory, as the NSA had that one covered.

Ethan suggested, "Since the chemical was on a fishing vessel, what about a missile? The weapon could be programmed to explode at a certain altitude, spreading the virus with the prevailing winds."

"I like that one," Vic said, a serious expression on his face. "Let's do some in-depth research on that and see if it's feasible."

Jerimiah advised, "Weather will play a huge part in this operation. We should bring aboard an expert meteorologist who is an expert on wind currents, temperature, and humidity. These elements would most certainly factor into this method."

"Brilliant, Jer. That's something we overlooked. Would you make the arrangements and hire a meteorologist?"

"I'll get right on it."

Deb brought up the five-gallon can and the small box attached to a submerged five-gallon drum. "I believe that the five-gallon can is designed to explode within the larger drum and that the box may be the explosive device."

Everyone, including Vic, was dumbfounded by her assertion. Not a word was spoken as the team digested her hypothesis.

Finally Vic muttered, "My God, I believe that you're absolutely correct. That's ingenious. How you came up with that is beyond me, but we all thank you for it."

The team was in awe. Vic thought, *so beautiful, so intelligent.* Deb smiled proudly.

Bart jumped into the conversation, continuing Deb's line of thought. "The content of the five-gallon can is the activator. When it explodes, millions of tiny droplets will be spread through the air. If they added a detergent, the infected bubbles would drift slowly to earth, spreading inland for miles."

The meeting concluded, and the team went about their research.

Jerimiah called his stepfather, Todd, knowing that he'd worked closely with a forest meteorologist on several wildfires some time ago. "Hi, Dad. How are you and Mom doing?"

"We're good. How are you?"

"I hate to be so abrupt, but we have an emergency, and I was wondering if that meteorologist you worked with was still around and if he'd be available to help us."

"Yes, he's around. He was the best weather forecaster I ever met. I'll call him and see."

Hours later Todd got back to Jerimiah. "I contacted Peter Russell and asked if he would be interested in a part-time job. Seems he ran into hard times. His wife passed right after he retired, and he took to the bottle. He said he's been dry for over a year. I set up a meeting with you for tomorrow at ten o'clock. It's kind of sudden, but I know you're pressed for time."

"That will be fine, Dad. Thanks a lot. See you soon."

The next day Peter Russell, meteorologist extraordinaire, was at the gate. The guard let him in and gave him directions to the lounge. Vic, Deb, and Jerimiah greeted him.

Vic said, "Here's the deal, Peter, and I tell you this in the strictest of confidence. We believe that a terrorist attack is imminent. The assault may be chemical, or it may be an airborne attack. We'd like to know the best date, time, and location for this strike. Naturally, we need to know where it would do the most damage to our population."

Peter was shocked as he listened to Vic describe the scenario. The meteorologist took a deep breath and said, "That is a daunting task, and the consequences will be staggering, should my forecast be in error."

Vic asked, "Are you saying you'll take the job?"

Peter answered apprehensively, "Yes, I'll take the job."

"Welcome aboard, Peter."

Robert had a room set up with direct links to McAlister's weather satellites. Peter would have real-time weather conditions for anywhere in the world. Right then he was to concentrate on California. Peter looked around in awe. It was a meteorologist's dream. Every piece of weather information was at his fingertips.

Vic noticed that Peter had a notebook with him. "Is that notebook important?" he asked.

Peter said, "You're looking at twenty years of meteorological weather phenomena relating to atmospheric conditions for the West Coast of the United States. In other words, this is a history of the winds, tides, sea breezes, and rainfall. It's also a record of when all these weather events took place. If a fly pisses in the wind, I can tell you when and where it will land."

Vic was duly impressed. He smiled and patted Peter on the back. "I knew you were the best man for the job as soon as you walked in." They both had a good laugh, knowing he was full of shit.

Vic passed around some pictures of the fishing vessels, thinking that ten sets of eyes were better than a few. Someone might notice something.

Ethan said, "I know I've seen a large bag like that somewhere, but I can't place it."

"Take your time, Ethan," Vic said. "I'm sure it will come back to you."

Suddenly Ethan remembered. "It was at a balloon festival. It's what they store the hot-air balloon in."

The scientists looked at one another. That was how the terrorists were going to deliver the deadly virus: with a hot-air balloon.

Deb said excitedly, "This is all starting to make sense. The hot-air balloons will be launched from the deck of the fishing vessels with one man on board. He'll navigate the balloon to the desired altitude and location. At that time he'll detonate the explosive device, and there will be no way to contain the spread of the fatal virus."

"There must be some way to stop this horrendous attack," said Becca.

The team began to face a grim reality: there might not be a way to prevent it in time.

Robert had just returned and was briefed by Vic on the events of the last few hours. He looked at Vic. "Is there anything we can do?"

"We can turn it over to the NSA and hope that they try to intercept the fishing vessels. The terrorists will probably detonate the drums, and many lives will be lost either way."

Robert nodded to Vic. "Make the phone call."

He called agent Myron Weeks and explained the terrorists' plan in detail. Weeks answered, "We have everything under control. I can shut down the airports at a moment's notice. I have military fighters in the sky as we speak. I believe that this is a hoax perpetrated by Iran to alarm us and that it's bullshit."

Vic was shocked by what he'd just heard. "Agent Weeks, are you willing to take that risk?"

"Bowden, your scenario is too far-fetched to believe. Try peddling it to some other agency, maybe the CIA or the FBI."

Robert had heard the whole conversation, and he tried to console Vic. "You did the best you could, my friend."

Vic wasn't about to give up and began to hatch a plan B.

The team was disillusioned and disappointed with the NSA's response. As they sat around the lounge, Peter commented, "I wish I had a giant vacuum cleaner. I'd suck up all the droplets of the virus and take them far out to sea."

Becca added, "We know that the salt water will neutralize the virus, so it would be a win-win."

Jerimiah said, "I'll be right back. Don't anyone move." He ran as fast as he could, right into the sequoia. Minutes later he exited with a familiar sly smile and returned to the lounge. "Peter, I think we may be able to grant your wish."

Carlton said, "Is this a joke? A giant vacuum?"

Peter stood there like a deer in the headlights, he was baffled by the banter

Jerimiah continued. "Fellow team members, I give you nature's own vacuum—a weather event referred to as a tornado. The TREEZZ can create conditions conducive to creating a tornado—or a waterspout, in this case."

Peter wasn't quite sure what was going on but the idea creating a vortex fascinated him. He followed the teams lead.

Jerimiah continued, "I believe that with the help of the TREEZZ, we can create a vortex."

Peter was thrilled by this opportunity to create weather. He dismissed the idea of something super-natural might be involved. He rushed to his office and researched vortices. He discovered that it was possible and set up a test for early the next morning.

No one could sleep. Instead, the scientists filtered into Peter's office. Bart had made a fresh pot of coffee, and everyone indulged. The night turned into day, and it was a bright one for many reasons. The first was the orange orb in the eastern sky chasing away the night.

Peter announced, "Let's go generate a vortex." They went into the forest. The morning ground fog created an eerie and surreal picture in a large clearing, like a grave-yard in a spooky movie. Jerimiah and Peter knew that this would be the perfect place to make magic happen.

No one noticed a slight movement in the tree limbs. Then a light breeze, blowing in from the west, was detected by the team. Tree limbs undulated, and then a gust came in from the east. The tree limbs moved more rapidly, and the breeze developed into a steady wind.

The team watched as the fog was pulled one way and then the other, creating a low-pressure zone. The wind grew stronger. The fog began to swirl. As the winds increased, the swirl became a funnel and rose high into the morning sky. Leaves and twigs were hastily sucked up in the vortex, as if it were a vacuum.

Peter looked at Jerimiah in disbelief. The trees were actually helping to create this tornado. He hesitated for a minute then thought, *Who am I to question Mother Nature*. Peter smiled broadly, giving Jerimiah the thumbs-up. The team could hardly believe their eyes, but there it was: the tornado Jerimiah had promised. Everyone smiled widely. Robert and Vic congratulated Jerimiah and Peter for creating this magical, life-saving event. With the team invigorated, they planned the next step.

Peter remarked, "I'll get right on the prevailing winds and a timetable that will afford them the best conditions." Peter stayed up all night going over the meteorological charts and forecasts. His prediction for the best weather was three days from now.

When Peter called Vic later, his tone was sullen. "I have some bad news. There's a temperature incursion occurring off the coast that may cause a problem."

Vic barked, "In English, man, in English."

"In layman's terms, a dense fog bank is moving in. We'll lose a visual on the fishing vessels."

No sooner had he said that than the surveillance techs called with the bad news that they'd lost the visual. Vic was in a nasty mood and exhausted from this roller-coaster ride. The compound was dark as he walked the grounds. He noticed that Peter's office lights were on and decided to pay him a visit. The office door was open, but when Vic walked inside, the man wasn't there. *Maybe he stepped outside for some air*.

He walked out back and found Peter sitting up against a tree with a bottle of whiskey.

Vic's heart sank, and he whispered, "Oh no, the pressure got to him, and he started drinking again."

Peter looked up with a smile. "Don't worry; I didn't fall off the wagon. I keep a full one to serve as my temptation. As long as I can push it away, I'm good."

"I thought I'd keep you company for a while. Do you mind?"

"Not at all." The astute weatherman stated, "This is where we stand. A small low-pressure system will make the onshore breeze optimal for spreading the virus-infected bubbles. The optimum altitude will be fifteen hundred to two thousand feet. That will happen near the San Francisco shoreline. That gives us a little over two days to plan."

Vic looked at Peter. "I hope the terrorists' weatherman is as good as you. Timing and coordination will be the keys to the success or failure of this mission."

An exhausted Robert walked over to the two men. "Let's see if we can all get some sleep. We'll need to be at the top of our game."

———

Tuesday morning at eight o'clock, the smell of strong coffee brewing permeated the lounge. Tension, stress, and sleepless nights had been experienced by all. Vic was getting his second cup of coffee when Deb began the meeting.

Vic nodded to Pete. "You're up."

"The attack will likely commence Thursday morning at approximately eight thirty. That is when the wind direction and the atmospheric conditions will be optimal for spreading the virus droplets. The prevailing winds will carry the minuscule droplets over land, and gravity will bring them down to earth. The ideal location for the release of the virus will be at the shoreline before the droplets drift over the highly populated city. To prevent this atrocity, we will release a tornado. As it crosses the shoreline and moves into open water, it will become a waterspout. The vortex, or waterspout, will draw up the salt water and mix it with the virus, thus neutralizing the deadly cells. The droplets will fall harmlessly into the ocean."

The simplicity of the plan stunned the room into silence.

Vic questioned, "Jer, how will you communicate your instructions to the TREEZZ?"

"I'll go into a mystical trance and telepathically transmit your directive to the TREEZZ. It's simple."

"Whatever you say, Jer. I'd feel better if we did a few dry runs."

Peter agreed. "We have only one shot at neutralizing the attack."

Jerimiah knew a desolate section of shoreline just north of Crescent City. Vic, Deb, and Ethan went out to survey the site. Jerimiah, Peter, and Carlton stayed at the resort to cover the communications.

Becca kept track of the time, from the first command to the lapsed time to create the vortex, to the time it took to drift offshore and then convert to a waterspout to the time it took to intercept the virus.

Vic asked the surveillance techs to make sure that the area was deserted and clear of any people.

Vic began the mock exercise with communication with Jerimiah by radio. "The balloon was spotted four miles off the coast at coordinates 41-49-16.5 North, 124-13.37.16 West. Start the vortex."

The TREEZZ began to create the breeze and then the wind. A swirl began to form. The wind picked up, and the vortex was generated.

Vic breathed a sigh of relief. "Now we need to give the TREEZZ directions to intercept the balloon. Turn the vortex to the south about fifteen degrees."

Jerimiah received the transmission and walked into the tree. Once inside, he gave the location to the TREEZZ. Nothing happened.

Vic asked Jerimiah, "Did you hear my command?"

"Yes. I gave it to the TREEZZ."

Slowly, the vortex began to make the adjustment to the course.

Vic said, "Let's try that again. We need the vortex to respond more quickly. Jer, use the same coordinates but to the north."

Jerimiah walked into the tree and relayed the message. "OK, Vic. Message delivered."

"I still don't have movement."

Then, slowly, the vortex turned north.

Vic looked at the group and shook his head. "That's not going to work. We need the TREEZZ to respond more quickly."

It was back to the drawing board, and the team returned to the resort. Without the vortex, the plan was junk.

The scientists gathered in the hall, and Robert joined them. "This is just a minor setback. We're in uncharted territory, and it's normal to have a glitch. Let's brainstorm and see what we come up with. I asked the techs to join us via satellite."

Vic said, "The problem is with communications. We need to be more efficient. And no offense to the TREEZZ, but we need them to speed up the movement of the vortex, if that's possible."

Vic looked at Jerimiah. So did everyone else.

Jerimiah said, "I'll go to the TREEZZ and see if we can rectify the situation."

A tech spoke up. "The lab has come up with a super sophisticated listening and transmitting device that may be the answer. It will be a delicate procedure requiring Becca's expertise. The device needs to be located in the sapwood, near the heart of the tree. There it will detect subtle vibrations and electrical impulses. We can program the computer to locate and identify the balloon and then send the signal to the tree." The tech chuckled. "I apologize; I just never thought I'd be communicating with a tree. If we can implant the device in the tree, and if the signal can be received, I think that will save us precious time."

Vic said, "That's the first thing we should do. Let's get on that ASAP."

Jerimiah spoke next. "I'll go to the TREEZZ and see if the speed and direction of the vortex can be accelerated. I'm sure the TREEZZ will come through; they always do."

Becca said, "I'll second that. I know that the TREEZZ won't let us down."

Vic asked the group, "Do you think you'll be ready by tomorrow morning?"

Everyone answered as one: "Yes!"

The team worked all night on their projects. By the time morning rolled around, they were ready.

Vic went back to the practice site on the coastline. Peter, Jerimiah, and Deb were stationed at the resort. With his phone in hand, Vic gave the order to begin the exercise. The techs turned the mission over to the computer. Vic gave the simulated coordinates and watched for the vortex. In seconds a vortex was spotted. It took a track over land and then over the water, where it turned into a waterspout. Vic gave another coordinate, and the vortex instantly picked up speed. Vic and the team cheered. The exercise had been flawless.

Robert said, "Kudos to all. Tonight dinner is on me."

Vic cornered Jerimiah at the restaurant. "How did the world of the TREEZZ get along with the world of high tech?"

"Vic, it was scary. The TREEZZ and the computer began a dialogue. They were discussing how much better the planet would be if they ruled it."

Vic stood there in awe. "Wow" was all he said.

CHAPTER 44

Vic's phone rang; it was Walter. "I have some news. We just received reports of hundreds of weather balloons being released over the larger coastal cities. Week's is in a panic; he wanted to shoot them down. The balloons are wreaking havoc with air traffic. They closed the airports. He's got men running all over the place chasing the weather balloons. What do you think? Another diversion?"

"I believe it is."

"I can't help someone who doesn't listen. Can you use me and my partner, Willis Reed?"

"I could use both of you. Let me fill you in on our plan."

Walter and Willis couldn't believe what Vic had told them. It sounded like a sci-fi movie. But Walter assured the young Willis, "He is the man; trust him with your life. I have."

Walter and Willis drove to the San Francisco location that Vic had given them and waited for Vic's call. Vic still had the surveillance techs check in every thirty minutes.

"Sir, we still don't have a visual."

"Stay with it," he growled.

ZERO HOUR MINUS FOUR

Vic received the call he'd hoped for. "Sir, we have a visual of the fishing fleet, but our four vessels could not be located among them; they all look the same."

"How the hell do four fishing boats disappear?"

The tech zoomed out of the area. There, two miles offshore, were two of the vessels. The tech notified the coast guard, but they were chasing errant weather balloons across California. Their ETA was four hours, which would be too late for an intercept.

None of the team had gotten any sleep. The members were torn between wanting zero hour to never come and wishing it were over. Vic sat on the couch with Deb; they held hands. Both were in quiet contemplation. If time permitted, they would watch the sunrise together. They hoped that, like the sun, the day would be bright and cheerful. Becca and Robert were on the deck, embracing. They, too, planned to watch the start of a new day if the opportunity presented itself. Ethan, Bart, and Carlton were in the lab in case an emergency arose. In the weather room, Peter had just made a fresh pot of coffee. This could be a long day.

ZERO HOUR MINUS TWO

After watching the sunrise, the two couples walked into the lounge. Becca had an errant thought that the coffee machine would work overtime today.

As if reading her mind, Peter said, "I'll keep an eye on the coffeepot." The coffee station was just outside his room.

Vic thought, *are the bad guys getting the same weather information as we are? I hope so. Everything we do is geared to the weather.*

ZERO HOUR MINUS ONE

Vic paced the hallway in front of Peter's weather room. Another tech called. "Sir, we have a visual on two target fishing vessels."

"Good work, guys, and thanks." No other news would have been good news. That was just what he had wanted.

The weather room was crowded. This was ground zero for the mission. The weather was the key to the whole operation, and Peter held that key. The team looked on as Peter adjusted meters, tapped gauges, and looked at the weather station data in real time. Everything was exactly as Peter had predicted two days before. Robert looked at Peter and gave him a thumbs-up. "Your predictions were spot on, my friend."

ZERO HOUR MINUS TEN MINUTES

Surveillance focused in real time on an area just south of San Francisco. NSA Agent Bando had his partner, Willis, stationed at the projected intercept location. The surveillance techs focused on a hot-air balloon being launched from the fishing vessel.

"Sir, we have a launch. It's a balloon." It was music to his ears.

Walter quickly passed on the coordinates to young Willis Reed. He was about a mile away and hastily drove to the location. Willis immediately began searching the morning skies for one lone balloon. Several times he jumped up excitedly, only to have a gull or pelican glide by. He knew that it was vital that he positively identify the balloon. Thousands of innocent lives depended on his actions. He began to sweat profusely as he anxiously looked through the binoculars. He squinted and looked again. There seemed to be a dot drifting toward shore. Was this another seagull, or maybe a pelican? He wiped the sweat from his brow and looked again. He whispered to himself, "Please, God, help me get this right."

This time he was sure he saw the balloon. He quickly called Vic. "I see a balloon drifting my way."

Vic said emphatically, "You need to be sure. We get only one chance to do this."

Willis got really nervous and wiped the perspiration from his eyes. "Hold on, my vision is getting blurry."

"Take your time and be sure, son."

ZERO HOUR

"Yes, I see the balloon. It's about two miles out and drifting my way."

"Good work, Willis. Now watch for the tornado."

Excitedly Willis said, "I see the trees blowing, and the wind is getting stronger. I don't believe it! A funnel cloud just formed and is heading toward the balloon."

The roar, similar to that of a jet engine, was deafening. The agent took cover as the tornado crossed the highway to the shoreline.

Vic reminded Willis, "Make sure that your protective gear is in order."

Willis gasped. "I forgot all about that. Thanks for reminding me."

Vic glanced around the room. Fear and uncertainty could be seen on the team members faces. The next few minutes would be critical and would determine their success or failure.

The balloon was about a quarter mile from the beach. Willis gave Vic a small directional correction, which he passed on to Jerimiah. Seconds later the waterspout took on a new intercept, heading toward the balloon.

Suddenly a flash of blinding light and a loud explosion erupted. Willis looked up. The balloon had disappeared into a gray cloud of the deadly toxin. It was quickly drawn into the funnel cloud. Any errant droplets fell into the sea and were neutralized by the salt water.

Willis took out his aero-biosensor, which was used to detect pathogens in the atmosphere. After five minutes the meter gave a negative reading. Cheers resonated through the hallways of the resort. High fives and thumbs-up could be seen everywhere.

Vic quickly reminded the team, "One down, three to go. Let's not celebrate too early." Then he smiled. "But it's a great start!"

One lone cheer went up, and everyone turned to look at Robert as this was out of character for him. "Sorry. I got carried away."

The group laughed cheerfully. That little outburst of joy broke the tension and stress, and it was a welcome relief felt by all.

Once again the team waited for a vessel to launch a balloon. Just north of Los Angeles, a second NSA agent, Neil Abrams, had volunteered to assist Walter, Vic, and his team.

Vic thanked him. "I know you're taking a risk helping us. You may lose your job."

"I know, but I'd rather be on the winning team and
know that I did my part than on the losing team and
regret it for the rest of my life."

Neil watched diligently from his perch, waiting for
the balloon to appear. He had the same responsibilities
as Agent Reed: get a visual on the balloon, guide the
waterspout to the intercept point, and check the air for
any remains of the deadly virus. Neil didn't have to wait
long; a dot appeared on the horizon. He zoomed in and
now had a visual.

"Vic, this is Neil. I have a visual, sir."

He had barely gotten the words out of his mouth
when a stiff breeze blew his way. The wind became
intense. He looked over his shoulder and saw that a funnel cloud was taking shape. It began to move and crossed
the shoreline. Now it was a waterspout.

Vic asked, "How does it look for an intercept?"

"It's on the money, sir. Looking good."

"You're suited up, right?"

"Yes, sir."

Suddenly a gust of wind blew the balloon to the
south. Neil said urgently, "The balloon is headed south."

The waterspout gave chase. A flash of light was followed by a loud explosion. The waterspout began encir-
cling the toxic cloud of the deadly virus. The waterspout
slowly drifted out to sea and dissipated, the virus neutralized by the ocean's salinity.

Walter stationed himself at the third location,
Huntington Beach. This was a populous area and difficult to control. If the balloon were to come ashore anywhere near the center of town, havoc would ensue. Vic

was relieved to have Walter's presence at that precarious spot. Walter had enlisted local law enforcement to close off the highway for a half mile in both directions from his position.

Just after 9:30 a.m., the satellite imagery indicated a balloon launch two miles offshore. The techs called it in to Vic, and Walter was on standby in case the intercept went afoul. Thankfully, it was only a quarter mile south of his location. Looking through his binoculars, he thought he saw a balloon. He rubbed his eyes; he couldn't see as well as he had been able to. He readjusted the binoculars and looked again. The balloon was heading his way.

He called Vic. "I got the balloon; it's coming right for me."

"Good news, Walter. You should be seeing the vortex."

"It's getting breezy—no, it's getting windy."

It was still three to five minutes to intercept.

Unexpectedly, the balloon began to descend. Walter said to Vic, "Hold up on the tornado. The balloon is descending, but I have no idea why."

The tornado stopped moving and became stationary.

"Walter, talk to me."

"I can see a man banging on something. It might be the explosive device. Yes, I think it malfunctioned."

Vic heard Walter call to the man, "NSA agent. Stop what you're doing and raise your hands now, or I'll shoot."

The man continued to pound on the box while chanting, "Allahu Akbar. Allahu Akbar."

Walter fired two rounds. The man struggled to stand. He then collapsed and became still. Walter ran over to the man. He was dead.

"Walter, what happened?" Vic asked.

Walter replied regretfully, "I killed him."

"You did what you had to do. You did the right thing."

Suddenly a small cloud of white smoke appeared. Walter traced it to a hole in the drum. One of Walter's shots must have pierced it. This was bad, and Walter knew it. "I have to get this drum submerged somehow."

He cut the two straps holding the drum and began pushing it out into deeper water.

Vic asked, "Walter, do you have a plan? What are you doing?"

"This could explode at any minute. I need to get into deeper water and try to submerge it."

"Do what you think is best."

Walter accidentally dropped his phone, and communication was lost. Vic desperately called for Walter, but he didn't answer. The NSA agent continued to push the drum into deeper water. It was still buoyant, and smoke continued to pour out. Now exhausted and gasping for breath, he emptied his weapon into the drum. It was just barely floating. Walter took a deep breath, jumped on the drum, and went down with the toxic container. Seconds later the drum exploded with a burst of air and bubbles. The remains of NSA agent Walter Bando slowly floated to the surface.

Vic hung his head in regret. Another gallant agent had given his life for his country. Now wasn't the time to mourn the tragic loss of his friend and colleague. Walter would have understood that. The team refocused on the last balloon coming ashore near San Diego. Another volunteer of Walter's was at the location and in position.

"This is Agent Rodrigues standing by at Torrey Pines State Natural Reserve, awaiting further instructions."

At 10:15 a.m. the techs observed a balloon released from a vessel three miles offshore. Vic received a call from Peter, their trusty weatherman. "We may have a problem. I noticed a very small pressure system off the coast of San Diego. The anomaly affects air movement—in other words, it's a dead spot where there is no wind. Sailboats—or, in this case, a balloon—stay stationary."

Vic asked, "How long will it stay that way?"

"There's no way to determine that."

Robert was in the lounge listening to the conversation. He leaned back in the chair and closed his eyes. For some reason he drifted back to his childhood and pictured a toy sailboat floating in a pond. He would swim up behind the boat and blow as hard as possible on the sail, causing the little toy boat to move. He thought, *if I were a giant, I would blow that balloon toward shore.*

Then it hit him, and he made a call. "Hello, my friend."

The voice on the other end said, "I only know one man who greets me that way, the one and only Robert McAlister. Hello, you old dog. How the heck are you?"

"I'm very well, Beau. How have you been? Still flying the whirlybirds?"

"Actually, I'm just getting ready to do my traffic report for KFMB. What can I do for you?"

"Beau, this request is urgent. I need you to fly to a set of coordinates and push a balloon toward shore with your prop wash, preferably toward the state park."

"That is a very strange request, even for you, Robert. I'll be at that location in ten minutes and will give that balloon some air. You can consider it done."

"Thanks, Beau. I appreciate the favor."

"Anytime. Anytime at all."

Robert quickly called Vic and explained the plan to move the balloon.

"That's brilliant! That's why you're the boss." Vic notified the team that the balloon would soon be on the move.

Agent Rodrigues looked through the binoculars and saw the balloon heading right for him. Excitedly he notified Vic. The NSA agent donned his protective suit and waited for the balloon to close the distance. Minutes later Rodrigues told Vic that the balloon was in position. Rodrigues felt the breeze and watched in bewilderment as the tree limbs rippled and swayed. The faster the branches moved, the harder the wind blew. In disbelief, he watched a tornado form right before his eyes.

He called Vic. "I have a tornado." Rodrigues froze as the whirlwind came his way. Suddenly he was lifted into the funnel. He was spun violently and thrown to the ground. Shaken but unhurt, he caught his breath as the vortex moved offshore. A bright flash of light was followed by a loud explosion that destroyed the drum. The balloon fell into the sea. A deadly mist developed below the explosion and began to drift toward the mainland. The vortex turned into a waterspout and circled the mist. In no time the funnel enveloped the toxic mist and neutralized the lethal virus.

Agent Rodrigues quickly switched on his bio tester. The red light blinked for a moment and then turned green; the air tested negative for the virus. The NSA agent sighed with relief. He called in and reported, "All clear."

Rodrigues had never witnessed anything like this event, and he would never forget it. He walked away, proud to have been part of the team that foiled the deadly terrorist plot.

———

KFMB News at Noon reported that several tornadoes and waterspouts had been spotted along the California coast in a very rare occurrence. A retired meteorologist said, "The onshore and offshore winds collided, creating the perfect vortex. The twisters moved offshore and dissipated. Light debris was all that was left of this strange weather phenomenon."

The next day the morning news on Channel Eight reported: "Early this morning, the coast guard apprehended twelve men aboard four fishing vessels. They are believed to be smugglers of illegal narcotics. They were taken to federal prison and are awaiting arraignment. No other information is available at this time."

Walter Bando was awarded the highest honor from the NSA. NSA director Billings and Special Agent Weeks were put on paid leave pending an internal investigation.

EPILOGUE

As Becca and Jerimiah have learned to understand more about the TREEZZ, the TREEZZ have evolved to communicate with a supercomputer via an implanted device in a majestic sequoia. The group as a whole continues to endeavor to bring free herbal medicine to the needy.

Robert and Becca's relationship moved to the next level: a proposal of marriage.

Vic proposed to Deb; naturally she accepted.

Elaina and Jer have continued their partnership, focusing on her grants and his quest for forest land preservation. The two have taken the game of teasing to another level.

Ethan found a girl just like him. Their only disagreement is whose pocket protector can hold more pens.

Carlton found a young homeless boy; he adopted the boy and his dog. Life is good.

Bartley has continued to ski every chance he gets. No surprise—he married a ski instructor.

All still work for McAlister Industries.

Sinister plots by evil men will continue to threaten our democracy and our way of life. They will not succeed due to the efforts of gifted scientists, honorable men, and generous benefactors.